D0248917

WITHDRAWN

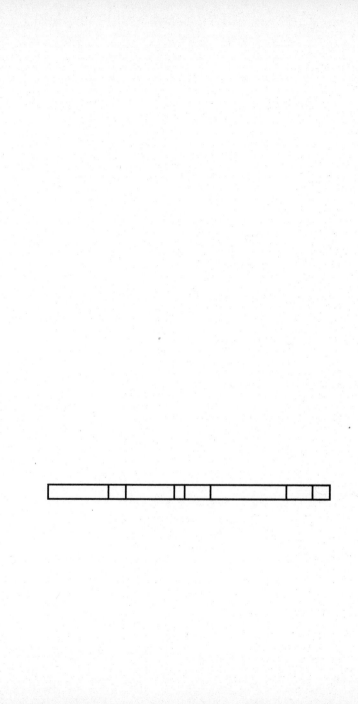

THE
MOSTLY TRUE
STORY
OF
JACK

BY
KELLY
BARNHILL

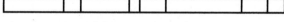

LITTLE, BROWN AND COMPANY
NEW YORK BOSTON

52172046

Copyright © 2011 by Kelly Barnhill

All rights reserved. Except as permitted under the U.S. Copyright Act of 1976,
no part of this publication may be reproduced, distributed, or transmitted in any
form or by any means, or stored in a database or retrieval system, without the prior
written permission of the publisher.

Little, Brown and Company

Hachette Book Group
237 Park Avenue, New York, NY 10017
Visit our website at www.lb-kids.com

Little, Brown and Company is a division of Hachette Book Group, Inc.
The Little, Brown name and logo are trademarks of Hachette Book Group, Inc.

The publisher is not responsible for websites (or their content) that are not
owned by the publisher.

First Edition: August 2011

The characters and events portrayed in this book are fictitious. Any similarity to
real persons, living or dead, is coincidental and not intended by the author.

Library of Congress Cataloging-in-Publication Data

Barnhill, Kelly Regan.
    The mostly true story of Jack / by Kelly Barnhill. — 1st ed.
        p. cm.
    Summary: Jack is practically invisible at home, but when his parents send
him to Hazelwood, Iowa, to spend a summer with his odd aunt and uncle, he
suddenly makes friends, is beaten up by the town bully, and is plotted against
by the richest man in town.
    ISBN 978-0-316-05670-0
    [1. Magic — Fiction. 2. Interpersonal relations — Fiction. 3. Friendship —
Fiction. 4. Family life — Iowa — Fiction. 5. Iowa — Fiction.] I. Title.
    PZ7.B26663Mos 2011
    [Fic] — dc22

                                                                    2010044934

                         10 9 8 7 6 5 4 3 2 1

                                    RRD-C

                     Printed in the United States of America

For Ella,
who read these pages and
pronounced them "not so bad";

and for Cordelia,
who has strong opinions about mothers:
good, bad, and otherwise;

and for Leo,
who wished that I had written a
book with a dragon in it
(perhaps next time, love);

this book is lovingly and gratefully dedicated.

There is
no utter truth or
utter falsehood in this
world. There is only *mostly.*
Which part of the *mostly*
you choose to accept,
well, that much is
up to you.

— *Tales from Nowhere (or Everywhere)*
by Clive Fitzpatrick

Chapter One
They Notice

FRANKIE WAS THE FIRST TO KNOW. FRANKIE WAS THE FIRST to know most things—but since he hadn't spoken since he was eight years old, it didn't matter *what* he knew. He couldn't tell anyone. Not so they could hear anyway. He sat at the dinner table, picking at his potatoes and pot roast, when a sound blew in from the wide expanse of the prairie.

A single high note, like a bell.

The rest of his family ate, wiped their faces, and excused themselves from the table. They didn't notice the sound.

Frankie laid his left hand over the knot of scars that curled over half his face. No one knew who or what had given him those scars, or what happened to him when he was taken away at the age of eight and returned, marked and silent, two months later. Frankie would not, *could not*, tell. After all these years, the scars were still puffed and angry and very, very red. The kids in town called him Slasher Face or Freak Show. His mother said his face looked like a field of roses. What his mother did *not* know was that the scars had memories. They *knew* things.

It's coming, the scars said. *It's back*, they whispered.

No, Frankie thought, shaking his head. *Not* it. He. He's coming.

We knew he'd come back.

That night, Frankie's twin sister, Wendy, woke to a dream of bells. She sat up in bed, wide-eyed and panting. The night was silent except for the early notes of crickets warming up for their summer-long choruses in the backyard.

But she smelled something. Something sweet and strange that she had not smelled since both she and her brother were eight years old — the year that Frankie disappeared and came back again.

"What is that smell?" she asked her mother at breakfast.

"Bacon," her mother said, handing her a plate.

"No, not that smell. The other one. The sweet smell."

"Bacon is sweet," her mother said in a tired voice as she poured her coffee into a chipped blue mug and drank it, black and steaming, in two quick gulps. She winced. "Eat your bacon," she said. "On your last day of school, I'd like you to be on time for once. Maybe we can trick your teachers into raising their expectations for you for *next* year."

Fat chance, Wendy wanted to say, but didn't.

Her mother lifted a heavy bag of dog food and brought it to the backyard, much to the slobbering joy of their three very large, very loud, and very stupid dogs.

"And anyway," Wendy said with her mouth full. "Bacon isn't sweet." But her mother had already walked out of the room and didn't hear her.

Frankie padded down the stairs, already dressed, washed, combed, and set to go. *Typical*, Wendy thought, gulping down her orange juice. He sat down next to her and took her hand.

"Frankie," she began, though she knew he wouldn't answer her. "Do you smell that—?" Frankie lifted her hand to his face, laying her fingers on his ruined cheek. "Frankie, seriously, I don't want to touch your scars, I—" She gasped. The scars burned and buzzed under her fingers.

Frankie looked at his sister, his eyes calm and unblinking. He kept her palm on the side of his face.

"Oh," she said, her stomach sinking. She turned toward

the window that faced west and felt her knees start to shake. *"Oh no."*

Outside of town, Wendy's best friend, Anders, felt something that he couldn't immediately explain. He had been standing for most of the early morning with four of his older brothers, leaning against the sunny side of the gray barn while his dad and his oldest brother, Lars, loaded up the tractor and the truck. The Nilsson boys had given notes to their teachers that they were needed in the fields and would not be present in the last week of school. Farming, thankfully, has never operated on a school schedule, and the boys were relieved of their books and put to work.

But not Anders.

Since he was only thirteen, he was one year too young.

Next year, his father said.

"Be good, little bro," his brothers taunted from the truck. "Study hard," they snickered as they drove off. Anders watched them as they drove down the well-grooved track, the wheels spitting a plume of dust behind. For a moment, their brilliant blond heads glinted through a brown cloud of dirt, but then there was only the cloud, and Anders was alone.

What his brothers and father did not know was that Anders had absolutely no intention of going to school. When the truck disappeared, he turned toward the broad stretch of field and the wooded bluff beyond and removed his shoes.

The ground was cool, still, and damp, though the day was already warm and would likely get hot. He began to walk, though he did not know where he would go. His feet, he knew, would lead him somewhere interesting. They always did.

But on the sixth step, he felt something different. A humming sensation in the grass. On the seventh step it was stronger. By the time he had gone thirty paces, the ground pricked at his toes as though with electric shocks.

He'd felt it before. A long time ago.

"So," he said out loud. The bees hummed, the ground hummed, even his bones and skin hummed and hummed. "So it's coming back. Now. Right?" He waited, as though someone might bother to answer: the growing corn, the tangled wood, the clear wide sky. Nothing did. Anyway, he was pretty sure the answer was yes.

Removing the green seed cap from his shock of blond hair, he rubbed the ragged border between his neck and scalp. The wind blew across the patchworked fields, ringing across the broad, flat farms to the edge of the sky. The breeze smelled of turned earth and dry seed and fertilizer.

It smelled like something else too. Something sweet and sick all at once, like rat poison dipped in candy. He ran back and grabbed his shoes.

School, then, he decided. It was only one more day.

Besides. He had to talk to Wendy.

Chapter Two
Someone Else Notices

CLAYTON AVERY, A TALL, BEEFY BOY OF THIRTEEN, LIVED IN the nicest house in town. Everyone knew it. It sat on a small rise in the center of town, with the gracious college campus on its left, and the long, narrow park leading up to the town hall on its right. It had stained-glass windows, a wide oak door, and gold-painted trim that lined the rim of the roof. The house, the town hall, the college, and every other building in town that mattered had all been built a long time ago by Clayton's great-great-grandfather. Since then, each subsequent Mr. Avery had been rich, powerful, and absolutely in charge. Being the son of Mr. Avery, the most important man in town, meant a great deal to Clayton. And he liked to make sure people knew it.

There was a room in the Avery house called the Retiring Room. No one except his father was ever allowed inside: not Clayton, not his mother, not visiting relatives. No one.

And yet, sometimes, when Clayton walked through the hallway, he thought he could hear a voice on the other side of the old oak door. A quiet, whispery sort of voice, as light as dandelion seed. And sometimes, even more quietly, his father whispered back.

Clayton spent most of this morning and the first half of the afternoon screwing up his courage to approach the door. He had never disturbed his father before.

He knocked.

Mr. Avery came to the door and opened it wide. He took a deep breath from his nose, and the sagging skin around his thin mouth and sharp chin pulled inward, as though he were trying to suck his face right into his nostrils.

"What is it." He did not ask this. He *said* it. Mr. Avery never asked questions. Clayton knew it was part of being *in charge.*

"Dad, there's something wrong with my ear." Clayton's ear was bright red from the grind and scrape of his knuckles.

"You interrupt me for ears," his father barked. "Tell your mother."

"I *did*. She says there's nothing wrong with my ear and I'm making it up."

"Well. Go to your room, then."

"But I'm *not* making it up. I think there's a bug in my ear or something. It's itchy and squirmy and I can't get it out. I can *feel* it. It keeps making a weird sound over and over. Like…bells or something." His father raised his eyebrows. If Clayton had been paying closer attention, he might have seen the pale folds of his father's skin grow a few shades paler. "It's driving me *nuts*, Dad." Looking desperately at his father, Clayton grabbed his right ear and pulled hard.

"This began today," Mr. Avery said in a flat voice, as though it was a statement of obvious fact.

"This morning," Clayton said, relieved that his father wasn't mad at him. "But it's been getting worse all day."

"Interesting," Mr. Avery said, bringing his fingers to his mouth. If Clayton noticed the slight tremble in his father's large, gnarled hands or the quivering in his lips, he didn't mention it. "Go to your room."

"But—" the boy began.

"*Now!*" his father roared. Clayton scampered away as though burned.

Mr. Avery waited for his son to disappear down the hall. Once it was quiet, he closed the door to the Retiring Room and leaned against it. Normally, the very sight of the room, with its aura of opulence—its velvet chairs, mahogany desk, and crystal goblets imported from Siberia — would have comforted Mr. Avery. But not now.

He would need information, research, reports. A few spies, too, most likely. He would not allow himself to make a mistake. Not again.

He would also need magic. And a lot of it.

Chapter Three
Iowa

JACK SAT IN THE BACKSEAT OF A RENTAL CAR, HIS SKETCH-book open on his knees, drawing pictures of bells. His mother hadn't spoken to him in the last four hours, not that it mattered. What was there to say, really? He'd already argued and cried and reasoned, but the result was the same: His parents, after years of fighting, were finally calling it quits. Jack was to spend an entire summer in Iowa with relatives he did not know. He couldn't *believe* it.

Jack watched the passing farmland as it rippled and

swelled like a green ocean stretching from the pavement to the sky. A darkened smudge appeared at the very end of the long, straight road. Jack squinted, trying to get a better look. There was something *familiar* about that, he thought, as the smudge slowly grew into the shape of a hill, though for the life of him he couldn't remember where — or *whether* — he'd ever seen it.

Jack closed his sketchbook with a firm slap and bound it tightly with a rubber band before slipping it into his duffel bag. He let his hand linger in the bag for a moment to run his fingers along the sandpapery surface of the skateboard hiding at the bottom. If his mother knew, he'd never be allowed to keep it. Still, as it was a gift from his older brother — and an unexpected one at that — it was the only thing that had even a remote possibility of making his time in Iowa bearable, and Jack wasn't going to give it up. Not without a fight anyway. He zipped up the bag and looked outside.

"Is that where we're going?" he asked, pointing to the hill ahead, but his mother was on her cell phone with her boss, and didn't hear him. Jack decided not to mind. *Nothing new there*, he thought. His mother often didn't notice him. Or hear him. Or even *see* him half the time. Same with his father. Not that he blamed either of them. They were, after all, very busy. His mother ran the communications department for the mayor of San Francisco, and his father was an architect — a *famous* architect, Jack liked to tell people, though no one ever listened or cared. Most of the time, Jack was very proud of his parents.

It wasn't so bad being invisible. Sometimes invisibility had its uses, though Jack couldn't help but feel that since the announcement of the divorce, he was growing *more* invisible than usual. Or that the world around him had shifted just enough that he didn't quite belong to it anymore. He worried he might disappear from their thoughts altogether. And though these worries troubled him, he tried to shrug them off. Why worry about what you can't fix? Besides, the car was slowing down, and he didn't really need an answer anyway.

The town rose up behind a tangle of gnarled trees on a gentle hump of land—the only hill for miles, as far as Jack could tell. A wooden sign stood at the side of the road, leaning slightly to the left. WELCOME TO HAZELWOOD, it said in large black letters, though the paint was faded and chipped in places, exposing the graying wood underneath like tiny bites.

"Hello?" Jack's mother raised her voice at the phone. "Hello? You've gone out on me, sir."

"No service around here, Mom?" Jack said.

"There's no service around here," his mother repeated, waving her phone as if she could catch signals like butterflies. She acted as though Jack hadn't spoken.

"Isn't that what I just—"

"And always in the middle of something *important*." She clicked off the phone and sighed. "Typical."

It was clear that his mother wasn't in the mood to chat, so Jack turned toward the window, examining the signal-free town.

The town was clean and quiet. Completely quiet. No cars moved, no buses groaned, no people jostled one another on the street. There weren't even any barking dogs. Instead, a quiet block of perfectly mowed yards, where each green square of lawn fitted snugly against the one next to it, with a thin border of geraniums or gravel in between. Neat white house followed neat white house with porches and weeded gardens and sometimes a swing set. Although Jack usually liked things neat and orderly and *predictable*, the sameness in the town unnerved him. It was as if each house wanted desperately to be pink or orange or electric green but couldn't.

Don't be stupid, Jack told himself firmly. *Houses can't want things.*

The only people he saw were three kids—a girl and two boys—standing at the weedy corner of an empty lot, halfway through town. Three bicycles leaned on their sides at random angles, as though they had only just been cast aside, the front wheels still slowly spinning around and around. The kids watched the road, their shoulders pressed together and their heads moving in unison as they tracked the rental car. Jack pressed his forehead to the glass and cupped his hands around his eyes, trying to get a good look at their faces, but they were shadowed and too far away. It didn't matter, he told himself, what they looked like—or even *whether* there were kids in town at all. He didn't have friends at home anyway, so he certainly wasn't expecting to make any friends in Iowa.

But the house at the end of the road...well, it was different. More than different. It *announced* itself. Big, bright flowers and tall, tangled grasses grew wildly in the front yard, with the house rising boldly behind, its edges shimmering in the heat.

Please tell me we're not going to that *house,* Jack thought desperately. Sharp pinpricks of worry erupted at the back of his neck, and the hairs on his arms stood on end. He thought he was going to be sick, though he didn't know why.

The car slowed down and they pulled up in front. Jack's mother opened the door with a rusty sigh. She pressed her lips tightly together and crossed her arms. "It's not supposed to look like this," she said, shaking her head. "This house is all wrong."

Chapter Four
The Wrong House

IT WAS AN OLD WOODEN FARMHOUSE WITH A LARGE PORCH, wide windows, and a small round porthole at the roof's peak. And it was purple. A deep, rich purple so intense it almost seemed to vibrate. Jack squinted. The front door was bright green, and the trim of each window was painted a different color: red, yellow, orange, and blue.

"It's *supposed* to be white," Jack's mother said, shading her eyes with her hand. "Perfectly white."

Jack looked at the house. He tried to imagine it

white, but the bright colors asserted themselves, even in his imagination. "Maybe," he said, "it just *wants*—"

His mother interrupted him. "My dad would turn over in his grave if he saw this."

"Are you even listening—" Jack started, but his mother interrupted him again.

"And here they come," she said, not looking at Jack.

The screen door opened and two figures stepped out.

"Well, bless my soul," the man-shaped figure said. He pressed his hand to his chest and leaned against the railing for balance.

"Clive," Jack's mother said to her brother-in-law with a curt, firm nod. "Mabel. How nice to—"

"*Clairy!*" the woman-shaped figure said, and ran down the steps toward Jack's mother, enveloping her in a hug. Clair stiffened. Jack's mother was not a hugger as a general rule, but his aunt didn't seem to know this. Jack wondered what *else* his aunt didn't know about his mother. *Probably a lot*, he thought.

Aunt Mabel kissed Clair on both cheeks. Like Jack's mother, she was tall and slim, with the same gray eyes with a shimmer of blue. But instead of a pressed suit, Mabel wore slightly frayed jeans. Instead of fancy shoes, Mabel wore sandals, her toenails painted a vivid shade of green. And even though Jack knew his aunt was fifteen years older than his mom, he was still surprised to see all that gray hair—or not gray *exactly*, but silver. It rippled and shone in slanting light.

"But what are you doing here?" she asked, looking from Jack's mother to Jack and back again.

Jack's mouth fell open. *What does she mean, what are we doing here?*

Mabel turned to her husband. "Clive," she said. Her voice shook and she looked back at the house. "We're not ready," she whispered.

"I..." his mother began, and then paused. She looked down at her hands and knitted her brow as though suddenly confused. Jack's mother was a sharp, driven woman. She was never confused. Jack bit his lower lip. "Surely I called," she said.

"No, dear, you didn't."

"We've separated. David and I. The proceedings should be final by the end of the month. I thought... well, *he*..." Jack's mother pointed at Jack, her face slack and dreamy. She narrowed her eyes and snapped her fingers a couple of times as though trying to remember something.

Jack pressed his hand to his chest. "*Jack?*" he said, prompting her.

"Right," she said, bringing her hands to her face and furrowing her brow. "Jack. Honestly, I don't know where my head is these days." She smiled and turned back to her sister, her face all business and control, like always. Jack relaxed. "He needed a place to be. For now."

His aunt and uncle exchanged a look that Jack couldn't quite understand. "Right," Clive said, running his hand along his wrinkled cheek and cupping his chin. "Things have unraveled. The poor boy's been unstitched. It happens." He winked at Jack with a smile that was somewhere between kindness and sadness. Jack attempted to smile back, though it felt more like a grimace. "He's got to belong somewhere, right?"

"Of course he can live with us," Mabel said. Was Jack imagining things, or was her lower lip trembling slightly?

"For now," Jack's mother clarified, looking at the ground and not at Jack.

Finally, Mabel cleared her throat, walked over to Jack, and gave him a hug.

"Honey, it's so wonderful to have you back." She squeezed him tightly and pressed her cheek against his. He couldn't remember anyone hugging him like that before.

"But I've never—" Jack began, but his aunt ignored him. Surely she knew this was his first time in Iowa.

Mabel gave Jack's shoulder a squeeze and, taking his mother's arm, led her into the house. Jack was left with his uncle Clive, a short, scrawny man with a wizened face and a slightly forced smile.

"Well," Clive said. "This is a surprise."

"But..." Jack said, feeling slightly sick. "My dad said they talked to you."

"Of course, of course. Parents say all kinds of things." Clive leaned back on his heels, as though thinking. "I suppose," he said slowly, changing the subject, "the ladies are expecting the men to bring in the bags." He fanned his fingers next to his face, flicked his wrists, and produced the keys. They jangled and rang like bells. "Shall we?"

"How did you—" Jack began.

"I have a way with shiny things," Clive explained. "It runs in the family."

Clive, despite his small stature, reedy arms, and narrow back, easily hoisted the large, heavy duffel bag onto his shoulder and practically bounded past Jack and up the stairs. It was as though he had springs in his legs instead of bones. That, plus the slight accent in his speech—English maybe, though Jack couldn't quite tell—made Jack think of an elf.

Jack grabbed his backpack and followed his uncle toward the front porch, laying his hand on the railing. It was warm, then overly warm, then hot.

"What th—" Jack began, but before he could say anything more, a deep, painful shock ran through his body, as though the thing he touched was not a wooden railing at all, but a live electrical wire.

"Ouch!" he yelled.

"A bit of trouble?" Clive stood in the doorway, holding the screen door open with his foot. For a moment, the door, the wall, and the entire house seemed to ripple the way a flag flutters in the wind. But before Jack could mention it, or even wonder at it at all, the house grew still, solid and immobile. Surely he'd imagined it. *Definitely*, he thought.

"No. I mean, it's nothing," Jack said quickly, rubbing his palm against his hip and walking carefully up the stairs. "It's just that I—ah!" He touched the screen door and again pulled his hand away as though something burned him. Or not burned *exactly*. It was another shock; he couldn't explain it. "It's nothing," he muttered, and pushed past Clive into the house, ears ringing, trying not to touch anything else.

"I'll just put these in the guest room, then," Clive said, his voice muffled by the duffel bag. He turned, walked up the polished staircase, and disappeared.

Mabel's voice poured out of the kitchen, a constant stream of words, broken only by the occasional *hmm* or *oh* or *really* from his mother. They were talking, Jack knew, about the divorce, and he did his best to shut his ears to the whole business. Even the word bothered him. It sounded like breaking glass, or a piece of cloth pulled tight and ripping in two.

Jack stood in the middle of the room, his hands shoved deep into his pockets. The house surrounding him was a jumble of books. Pretty polished bookshelves with curved trim and carved flowers twisting up the sides had been built into every possible wall. They wrapped around windows, ran along the back edge of the living room, and stretched nearly to the ceiling. And still the books hardly fit: They teetered in stacks all over the room.

Three animals crouched on top of the bookshelves—

one brightly colored parrot and two identical and astonishingly large cats. The cats flexed their shoulders, extended their hind legs, and lashed their tails, as though strongly considering leaping across the room and pouncing on Jack. Jack took a step backward. The cats winked their eyes in unison, first the left eye and then the right, before settling down into two matching lumps of shining silver fur, their faces turned attentively toward Jack. The bird, on the other hand, streaked across the room and hit Jack's chest like a bright, sharp missile. Jack screamed.

"*No, Lancelot!*" both Clive and Mabel shouted from different parts of the house. The bird seemed to deflate a little and swooped down, fluttering toward the stairs. He shot a backward *watch-it-bub* glance at Jack before vanishing around the corner.

Jack rubbed his arms and stood in the center of the room, not wanting to touch anything. The cats kept their gaze fixed on him, the unsettling glow of their golden eyes flickering with each blink. He shuddered. *Stop staring at me*, he would have said if he was the sort of person to talk to cats. Since he wasn't, he willed himself to look away.

Clive came down the stairs, nearly bounded into the room, and perched himself on the blue velveteen couch. He looked expectantly at Jack.

"What?" Jack asked.

"Nothing, dear boy, nothing. We're just so glad that you're here." He clasped his left hand on his chin the way Jack had seen other professors do on public television. Jack nodded vaguely and turned away to study the books, not because he was *interested* but because he did not want to talk to Clive. Clive, on the other hand, didn't seem to notice the snub and continued to stare at Jack pleasantly.

It was the staring, Jack decided, that unnerved him. It was *new*. No one stared at him at home. No one noticed him—even when they were supposed to. Even the hall monitors at school never saw him—and they caught *everybody*. It was as though their eyes just slicked past Jack. He hardly noticed it anymore.

Finally, Clive stood up, stood next to Jack, and examined the books alongside him. Jack took a step away, but his uncle didn't seem to notice. Instead he raised his fingers to the spines of the books.

"It's an occupational hazard. When one studies books for a living, the result is a house with more books than should be allowed. We don't have many for children, I'm afraid," Clive said, "except for the fairy tales. And I daresay you aren't a fan of fairy tales."

How does he know? Jack wondered. But it was true. Something about fairy tales set Jack's teeth on edge. He'd never liked them.

"I prefer nonfiction," Jack said without looking at his uncle. "I like it when things are *true*."

"Or mostly true anyway," Clive said, and though Jack

didn't really understand what his uncle meant, he decided not to push the issue.

Clive reached into one of the upper shelves and pulled out a book. "Here," he said. "You might enjoy reading this."

The title, *The Secret History of Hazelwood*, curved across the top edge of the book, and was written in a thin, spidery script that looked familiar to Jack somehow, though familiar *how*, he wasn't sure. It had a picture of a small, gnarled tree. Except if you looked at the tree a certain way, it did not look like a tree at all. It looked like a woman. And if you looked at it another way, it didn't look like one woman but two, their faces superimposed on each other like a double-exposed photograph.

"Thanks for the book," Jack said, noticing too late that his voice had a hard, sarcastic edge to it. He decided not to care. Jack set the book down on the end table and didn't think about it again for the rest of the afternoon.

When his mother and Mabel bustled in with cookies and lemonade, Clive lobbed questions about politics and the mayor's aspirations and social theory. Jack watched his mother light up with the questions, giving long, complicated answers. Jack wished he were holding a camera. His mother always looked better under the glare of flashing lights and the crush of insistent news reporters.

He sipped his lemonade.

He slurped it.

She didn't notice and didn't admonish him. His

mother's eyes slid from one side of Jack to the other, never quite resting on him. He tried to raise his eyebrows and grin at her, just to get a little eye contact. She did not grin back. Her eyes slicked past again and again without focusing once.

Two hours later, Jack's mother was back in the car and driving away. She hadn't hugged him or told him that she'd call him every day. She hadn't embarrassed him with tears or sobs or even the sniffles. Instead, in the moment before she got into the car, she took Jack's hand, held it upward by the knuckles, and uncurled each finger. She ran her hand against his palm.

"You can't turn something into what it isn't," she said, looking at the hand, then at the ground, then at the cornfield down the road. "Everyone's on a path that leads them to where they belong."

"I don't know what you mean. Can't I just—" Jack began, but his mother interrupted him.

"Sometimes all you can do is your best, and sometimes your best isn't good enough." She looked up, though not *at* him. Her eyes were slightly bloodshot and slicked with tears, and the muscles of her face twisted slightly, as though she was trying to remember something but it slipped just out of reach.

Look at me! Jack wanted to yell. *Say my name.* But instead, he said, "Good-bye, Mom," his voice thick and heavy.

Clair turned toward the car, her steps unsteady. She

shut herself inside and turned the key. It roared to a start and slid out onto the road. She didn't honk or grin. She never even turned to wave good-bye.

Jack told himself that was normal.

After a silent dinner, or at least he was silent, Jack headed toward his new room. *No*, he told himself. Not his new room. His room for *now*. He didn't belong here, he decided. He belonged in his mom's new house. Or his dad's new apartment. Either one. He had to belong *somewhere*.

Clive and Mabel let Jack find his own way up. *Up the stairs and the first door on the left*, Clive had said. Jack appreciated the privacy. He ran his fingers along the wall as he went up and felt that odd, warm, shivery sensation of the plaster under his fingertips. It didn't hurt like before. It just...trembled. He wondered whether the house was on a fault line. *Are there fault lines in Iowa?*

The cats—named Gog and Magog, which were, in Jack's opinion, the most ridiculous names for cats he had ever heard—followed at his heels. "Shoo!" Jack said. The cats just flexed their shoulders and blinked, their eyes glowing strangely in the half-light on the stairs.

Even on the upper floor, he could hear his aunt and uncle talking about him. Typical of adults, they talked around the subject instead of saying the things they were actually talking about. Instead of *divorce*, they said, *catastrophe*. They called it *a premature unraveling* and said that *sometimes a sapling graft won't take if the new tree isn't sound* and that *in the end, it wasn't as strong as we'd hoped*.

"In any case," he heard Clive say, "it doesn't do us any good to complain. I should have anticipated what would happen if that family unraveled, but it's too late to fix that now. The boy is here. And now everything starts. I just pray that we'll be ready."

There was silence for a moment, as though both Clive and Mabel were holding their breath.

"I just pray that Jack won't hate us for what we'll need him to do," Mabel said.

Too late, Jack thought. He hated them already.

Chapter Five
The Break-in

As she crouched in the shadows at the side of the Fitzpatricks' yard, Wendy Schumacher ignored the swarms of mosquitoes landing on her neck and arms and the backs of her legs. She had work to do. Once the last of the lights went out, she crept across the damp grass to the trellis on the eastern side of the house. She gripped the wood and vines, testing the trellis for stability, and with a grunt, she started climbing toward the open window.

It wasn't the first time. Wendy had climbed up that

trellis so many times she could have done it with her eyes shut. Four summers earlier, when Frankie disappeared, Wendy's house was overrun with pacing police officers and weeping relatives, and she found herself needing to be somewhere *else*. Someplace small and tight and *quiet*. One night, she slipped out of her house, and after wandering for a bit, she climbed into the first open window she could find—the second-floor guest bedroom in the brightly painted house at the edge of town. After that, she returned, night after night, whenever she got the chance.

Wendy liked the Fitzpatrick house—its shelves crammed tightly with books, its strange pictures on the wall. Most of all, though, she liked learning things that the other kids in town didn't know. She learned, for example, that her brother wasn't the first kid in town to go missing. She learned that people once relied on rawhide—wrapped around wrists or tied around necks or slipped into the sole of a shoe—as protection from... *someone*. A Lady, the book said. She learned that both souls and memories are slippery, fragile things, and easily snatched if a person isn't careful. Though she knew it couldn't be true—not *really*—she wore a thin rawhide bracelet on her left wrist every day, and encouraged her brother to do the same. Just a superstition, but still. It's not like a person can grow a new soul.

There was one book that was particularly useful: *The Secret History of Hazelwood*. On her second visit, she found it sitting on the bed in the corner. The bed was newly made and had been lined with pillows and teddy bears. The book lay in the middle with a plate of cookies right next to it. A glass of milk waited for her on the side table. She never mentioned this hospitality to the Fitz-patricks, and they never pried. Sometimes, Wendy thought, a silent thank-you is enough.

Later, when her parents and the police and neighbors had started to forget about Frankie, when he had slowly faded out of photographs and disappeared from conver-sations, the book told Wendy what to do. *Keep the memory alive*, it said on page seventy-nine. *A person's soul is bigger than his body. It takes root and lives in all who love him*, page forty-seven cautioned. *Hang on for dear life.*

Wendy hung on. And when Frankie was miraculously found, Wendy had a hard time forgiving those who had forgotten what happened. Even now, four years later, for-giveness was elusive and difficult. She still didn't know *why* her brother was taken, or *why* he was hurt, or *who* was responsible. Still, there *had* to be someone to blame. Someone needed to make amends.

Wendy tiptoed across the quiet room. She had seen the new kid arrive, but she didn't want to get too close. She wasn't looking for a friend. She wanted information.

The boy on the bed snored and sighed in his sleep. He hiccuped and gulped as though he was crying. She tried leaning in to peek at his face, but he had gathered the blanket in the crook of his elbow and draped it over his head like a shroud. She couldn't risk waking him to get a better look. His right hand was gathered into a tight fist, and his forearm was covered with red welts, as though he had been recently scratching at mosquito or chigger bites, but there were none that she could see. Maybe he was just nervous.

She'd have preferred to see his face, but there would be time enough for that, she decided. In a small town, it's no trick to find the new kid. What's more, it's nearly impossible for anyone to hide. If his face was familiar, she'd know it when she saw it.

His bags littered the floor, opened but unpacked. She crouched down, pulled the piles apart gently so as not to disturb the order and arrangement.

New sneakers, she noticed. Pressed shirts still creased from their packages. Stiff jeans. Either he rarely went out or his mother had recently shopped. Maybe both. A thick, new book. Only the art supplies looked well used. And there were lots of them.

Wendy noticed there was nothing electronic that she could see. Still, that didn't prove anything.

Outside the door, the Fitzpatricks' cats scratched and murmured and whined. *I know, I know*, she whispered. *Just give me a second.*

She peeked into the open backpack and pulled out a small photo album—the kind drugstores handed out for free. She moved to a square of moonlight on the floor and flipped the pages. The first five pictures showed a woman who looked like a younger version of Mrs. Fitzpatrick. "So that's your mom," Wendy breathed. She looked closer. The woman was pretty—glossy hair, perfect makeup, nice clothes. She looked, Wendy thought, like she should be on the news. Or maybe in a shampoo commercial.

The next five pictures were of a man and the same woman with their arms draped around each other. And the last pictures were family portraits—the same man, the same woman, a little boy with reddish gold hair and freckles, and something else: A miniature drawing of a boy with dark hair and black glasses had been carefully taped onto each photograph, tucked in with the rest of the family. Wendy looked over at the bed. She still couldn't see his face, but she could see the back of his dark-haired head—and his black glasses resting on the nightstand.

Why, she wondered, would someone paste a figure of himself into a family photograph? And why wasn't he in any of the pictures in the first place? Having no answer that satisfied her, Wendy removed one of the pictures and slipped it into her back pocket. She replaced the album and tiptoed back to the windowsill, pausing to get one more look at the figure on the bed.

She still couldn't see his face.

"Who are you?" she whispered into the darkness.

Having no answer, she swung her legs out the window and slipped into the night.

Chapter Six
The Letter, and the Other Letter

FOR THE NEXT FOUR DAYS, JACK DIDN'T LEAVE HIS ROOM except to go to the bathroom, or that's what he told his aunt and uncle anyway. Really, he just stayed in his room while they were home. Mabel brought his meals up and set them on the desk by the north window. "No sense letting the boy starve," she said. With each meal, she left a little note: *We love you, Jack*, or *I know the divorce is hard, but their split brought you here to us, and I can't help but be happy about that*, or *Be brave, honey*. And while Jack thought the notes babyish and embarrassing, he didn't throw them away. He flattened each one and slid it into his notebook, and he found himself doodling pictures of his aunt along the sides of the page—Mabel standing at the edge of a field, Mabel covering her face with her hands, Mabel holding a tiny baby in one palm.

Clive, on the other hand, didn't like it much. Jack could tell. More than once, he found his uncle standing in the hallway just outside his room, raising his index finger as if about to say something, and then thinking better of it and shuffling back to his office.

Once, Clive came in without knocking, hauling in a stack of nonfiction books on horticulture and dropping them with a thud on the desk.

"You *do* have nonfiction," Jack said, looking up from his drawings. "Finally, something *good*."

Clive didn't respond to this and sat on the chair, opening one book to a photograph showing a fruit tree with a cleft of bark cut away and a green bud held in place on the bare wood. "Have you ever seen an apple tree, Jack?"

"I don't know," Jack said, shrugging. "Maybe."

Clive nodded. "When I was a boy, my father kept fruit trees. To keep the orchard productive, he took shoots from different kinds of trees and grafted them onto a mother trunk. You see here?" He pointed to the photograph. "He took a very sharp knife and, right in the middle of the season, cut the skin of the tree, placed the tiny shoot on the wound, and bound them tight. The shoot would grow into the mother. And though they'd look like one tree, they weren't at all. They were two very different species, growing on the same trunk."

"Oh." Jack looked at his uncle for some clue as to where this conversation was going. "Okay."

"Well, you see, he had this one tree. An heirloom pear. Very old and rare, with lovely yellow fruit. He wanted to make it grow on one of the apple trees, so he grafted a bud onto an apple mother and hoped for the best." Uncle Clive pressed his hand to his mouth and paused for a moment, as though searching for the right words. "But there was a terrible thunderstorm, and the tree was hit by a bolt of lightning, splitting it in half, all the way down to the root. The pear shoot had only just attached, you see, so it was small and weak. But we had to remove it in order to save it. We had to graft it back onto its original tree. Indeed, by the time my father reached the injured apple tree, the pear shoot had already begun to detach. It couldn't hang on to something that was broken, so it freed itself."

Jack stared at the old man. His arms itched. His neck itched. He swallowed. "Did it die?"

"Everything dies, boy. But sometimes when things become…detached, we bring them back to the source. Do you understand what I'm saying to you?"

"Not really," Jack said. "Can I call my mom?"

Clive sighed, stood, and shuffled toward the door, fidgeting all the while. "Of course you can, son. Though I daresay you might find it difficult to reach her."

Jack tried to call five times that day. Each time, the message from her cell phone said that her mailbox was full and to try again later. Jack sat down to draw a picture of himself, and though he didn't mean to, he drew himself with an angry wound on his side where his old life had been only just ripped away.

Jack snapped his notebook closed and decided to take a break from drawing for a while.

Fortunately for Jack, Mabel worked every day in her art gallery, and, though the college didn't hold classes during the summer, Clive still had to show up for faculty meetings with the other professors from time to time, which meant that, for at least a few hours every day, Jack was left alone. Except for the cats. And the bird.

On his fourth day in Iowa, Jack wrote a letter to his parents:

Dear Mom and Dad, he wrote. *Iowa is worse than I thought. Dad was right. Aunt Mabel and Uncle Clive are kooks. Please let me come home.* Please. *I promise I'll try to be more like Baxter. I won't be too much trouble. Love, Jack.* Baxter, Jack's brother, had a summer job to keep him occupied and what seemed like thousands of friends to stay with if he needed to. So Baxter was allowed to stay home in San Francisco. And Jack wasn't.

Jack folded the letter neatly and slipped it into an

envelope. The cats watched him do it. They bobbed and wobbled their heads in time with his writing as he printed the address. They hissed at the stamp.

"What's the matter with you?" Jack asked. "You're the weirdest cats I ever met."

They hissed again, this time at Jack.

He brought the letter downstairs, the cats worrying at him as he went, every once in a while leaping up and taking a swat at his rear. "Knock it off," he said.

Lancelot was outside, standing on the mailbox.

"What are you doing—guarding the mail?" Lancelot fixed a bright bead of an eye right on Jack. Jack watched the hooked beak nervously. "Go on now." His voice was shaky. "Shoo." Lancelot waited for a long moment. Finally, with a squawk that clearly said "I'm only leaving because I *feel* like it," the bird flew away.

Jack sighed in relief. He opened the metal door and stopped dead. There was a letter sitting faceup with his name on it. No address, no stamp. Just *Jack*, written in a spidery, thin script. He left the note to his parents in the box and sat on the porch to open his own letter.

Inside the envelope was a very old piece of paper—a letter to someone who wasn't named. Just *Dear Professor*, and signed by a man named Reverend Marcus Weihr.

"Eighteen forty-nine?" Jack looked at the date on the letter. "It has to be fake. It should be falling apart if it's that old." While the paper *looked* old and *felt* old, the ink was clear, and the folds were still strong. The letter read:

Dear Professor,

I have followed with Great Interest your extensive Studies of the Supernatural and its intersection with the Natural world. If your assertions are correct, there is no end to what ancient mysteries Science might yet one day reveal! We may well one day learn that Magic is simply another tool of Nature, and subject, therefore, to the same Laws that govern the Earth and the Stars in the Heavens!

"Huh?" Jack said out loud. People in the olden days took a long time to get to the point, he thought. Plus, they used way too many capital letters.

I therefore think you will find Ample Subjects for your Research in my little Parish on the prairie. Our Settlement is located, I believe, on one of the Eruptions that you describe in your papers. I am sure of it. If I may, let me describe some of the Incidents that have occurred in my time as shepherd of this Flock, as well as some of the tools I have used to make contact with the Lady Herself.

The next part of the letter was...ridiculous. The letter told the story of a couple who knocked on his door in the middle of the night carrying a tiny baby—about the size of a man's fist. It had leaves for hair, and its skin was like the bark of a tree, and it fussed and cried in its acorn cradle. They wanted the Reverend to baptize the child and to tell everyone that the child was *theirs*. The Reverend wrote:

> *I did not know at the time the power of the declaration of Ownership. To call something* Mine *carries a great significance anywhere, but infinitely more so on the site of a Magic Eruption. Here, the words* Mine *and* Yours *carry a terrible significance—the consequences of which I am only beginning to understand.*

"What a load of garbage," Jack snorted.

"No, it's not," said a nearby voice. Jack yelped and jumped up, his heart racing. On the far side of the porch, a head popped up—a tall boy with a head full of hair so blond it looked as though it might glow in the dark. The boy grinned.

Jack, recovering himself, tried to take a casual stance. *It's easier to be casual*, he thought, *when no one's looking at you.* "How do you know?"

The boy shoved his hands into his back pockets and leaned back on his heels. "Me? I don't know nothin'," he said. "But it doesn't look like garbage. It looks like a letter. I'm Anders, by the way."

Jack's head reeled. He had spent his whole life imagining the kinds of conversations that he'd like to have with kids his own age. No one ever talked to him at school. *No* one. Even at home, Jack sometimes went days without exchanging a single word with his parents. And his brother was always so busy, he hardly even noticed that Jack was in the family at all—let alone in the room next door. Jack had gotten very good at inventing long and fascinating conversations in his imagination, and he had been eager to have a discussion one day with someone his own age about...well, anything, really. Still, this conversation was nothing like the conversations in his head. Jack changed the subject. "Hi," he said, trying to sound normal. "I'm—"

"Jack. I know. Your aunt called my mom. Plus, I saw your house wobble when you arrived."

"No, it—Wait a minute. Did you—" Jack stammered, not knowing which sentence to start with first, only to have all three tumble out at once.

"Long story. It happens when a house sits on an eruption point. Anyway, I gotta get back." He shrugged. "Chores. I'll see you around, Jack."

And before Jack could reply, the boy called Anders turned and disappeared into the thicket of branches at the back of the yard.

"Yeah, well," Jack began. But it seemed silly to start a sentence when the person he was talking to had already left. Still, he couldn't help himself. "*Eruption point?*" he called out. "There aren't any volcanoes in Iowa!" But the boy called Anders was already gone, and probably couldn't hear him.

Jack looked down at the ancient paper in his hand. *Why,* he thought, *did someone give this to me? And why not just hand it to me? Why the envelope?* He wondered whether it was part of a game, or a section from a book (*fairy tales,* Jack thought derisively), or maybe even a joke. It surely couldn't be *real.*

Later that day, Jack watched the mailman arrive with a stack of letters. He opened the metal door and slid the letters in. He took nothing out. Jack hurried downstairs to catch the man before he left. Obviously, Jack thought, he just didn't see the letter to his parents. No big deal.

"Wait!" Jack called, sprinting out the front door, opening the mailbox and reaching inside. The mailman paused but did not turn around. "I need to send this—" Jack stopped. There was no address on the envelope, no return address, and no stamp. "Oh. I guess I…um… never mind." The mailman didn't turn and didn't acknowledge Jack. He just shook his head and kept on walking.

I could have sworn I wrote the address on here, Jack told himself. He sat down on the porch steps and looked closely at the envelope, checking for the imprint of his pen. He found nothing. Gog and Magog snaked out of the house and sat on either side of Jack. They eyed the envelope suspiciously.

"You saw me write the address. Right?" The cats just gave him an icy stare. *Great*, Jack thought. *Now I'm talking to cats.* He opened the envelope and pulled out the stationery paper. The letter had been wiped clean. He stared at the blank piece of paper, shaking it a few times, as though the writing might jostle its way to the surface. It didn't. The paper didn't look touched. Even the folds had vanished.

How? Jack wondered. *Letters can't just erase themselves.*

The next day he tried again. By the time he reached the bottom of the stairs, the letter was blank.

Jack tried writing to his parents eight more times over the next four days. Each time, both envelope and paper stayed in the mailbox, perfectly clean and unblemished by any writing. By the fifth day, he had given up. It wasn't just that the disappearing letters were odd—obviously they were odd. But they were *wrong*. And the *wrongness* of that wobbling house with its indignant cats and possibly murderous parrot and its casual mentions of magic was more than anyone could stand, as far as Jack was concerned. And he, for one, had had just about enough.

Jack started packing.

Chapter Seven
The First Escape

THERE WAS NO MOON, AND THE STARS CUT THROUGH THE inky black sky like glinting shards of glass. Jack squinted. Having grown up in a foggy city, he had seen stars appear only rarely, and when they were visible, they were just dull hints of light. But here they flashed, hailed, and beamed. Jack crept down the stairs, his teeth clenched tight, his footfalls light as cotton on the treads. The last thing he needed was to wake the bird. Or the cats. Or even, Jack shuddered to think of it, his aunt and uncle.

There wasn't time to pack much—and anyway, it

wasn't like he was attached to most of the things his mother had packed for him. Half the clothes in the bag he'd never seen before. It was as though his parents had walked into the boys' section of the department store and thrown the first things they found into the suitcase. So Jack only took his notebook, pencils, and a change of clothes and shoved them into his backpack.

He didn't have any money, but he hoped that wouldn't be a problem. After all, he had never needed to pay for bus fare or a train ticket in his life. He'd simply climbed aboard and sat down. No one ever noticed.

He laid a note on the couch, and held it in place with the book that Clive had given him. He wasn't going to need it. There was *nothing* he wanted to know about Hazelwood, Iowa, secret or not.

Don't worry, the note said. *I'll be fine.* He hoped the words would stick. The words in his notebook stuck, after all. And if they didn't, well, it couldn't be helped. Eventually, his aunt and uncle would notice Jack was gone, and they'd figure it out.

The floorboards moaned and sighed under his feet. The door felt hot and reproachful. Jack shook his hand at his side and slipped into the night.

He wasn't afraid of the dark. Not usually anyway. In fact, for as long as he could remember, he had been sneaking out of his family's apartment—not running away exactly, but just *walking*. He liked the way the evening mist would gather in great tufts around the shoulders of the buildings and drift slowly to the street. Sometimes, the mist and fog fell so thick and fast that it erased the buildings, then the cars, then the other people walking by, then his own feet, then hands, as though there was nothing left but a cool, white space.

Iowa, though, was different. Here the night had voices.

In Iowa, the grasses breathed and murmured and sang. Crickets whispered in shadowed shrubs; mosquitoes hummed in clouds. Somewhere a cat tipped open its jaws and let loose a loud, feral howl. Jack checked his watch. *Three fifty-two*, he thought, hiking his backpack higher on his shoulders. *The faster I move, the farther I'll get.*

He quickened his pace.

Under the porch, four yellow eyes glowed softly in the dark. Once the boy reached the end of the block, Gog and Magog crept out of their hiding place. They paused briefly, their heads tilted upward, their tails straight and tall like spears, before leaping forward and sprinting down the street.

Anders was out of bed too.

Though the night had been dreamless so far, he woke

up agitated and worried, with a strong urge to stretch his legs. He slipped out of bed, pulled on his jeans, and tiptoed downstairs. *Three fifty-two*, the clock on the microwave read.

But something wasn't right. It didn't *feel* right. Very quietly, Anders lifted the back door's latch and slipped outside.

Mr. Avery should have been in bed hours ago, but he couldn't sleep.

He paced the perimeter of his Retiring Room, pausing every so often to page through the ancient diaries that he normally kept on his polished shelves but that now lay open on his desk. The first Mr. Avery, his great-grandfather, despite his vast researches into some of the universe's deeper mysteries, had nothing to say on the subject of *this* sort of difficulty. It was possible that the Reverend Weihr *did* have something to say on the matter, but Mr. Avery didn't have the good Reverend's diary. It had been secreted away two generations earlier by the Reverend himself, though now it was, Mr. Avery was *sure*, in the possession of a certain Professor Clive Fitzpatrick. He had no proof, but the self-satisfied smirk on the ancient professor's face was evidence enough, Mr. Avery felt. Unfortunately, the old man, if he indeed possessed it, had hidden it cleverly—despite Mr. Avery's gift in finding things and getting things, he had never been able to lay his hands on the book or access its information.

What he needed, he knew, was an *opportunity*. But what he *felt* was panic. One cannot make good decisions while panicking, but he couldn't help it. He paced and fidgeted, and, like a little child, felt himself on the verge of tears.

He stopped at the window, leaned on the sash, and gazed outside. At the far end of the road, a figure walked into the lamplight. It was small, the size of a child, its shoulders hunched under the weight of the heavy pack slung over his back. Its eyeglasses flashed in the dark. The figure stopped, turned around as though checking to see whether it was being followed, then shrugged and kept walking.

"You!" Mr. Avery cried. *And alone*, he added silently as the beginnings of a plan—desperate, yes, and not without consequences, but a bold plan all the same—spread from his mind to his face and uncurled into a smile. He grabbed his keys from his desk and hurried out to the car. *Just get him out of town*, he thought. *If I send him away before She wakes up, then perhaps things can stay as they've been. It should be simple enough.*

From the shadow of the thicket of trees in Henderson's Gully, Anders watched Jack approach. There was something about that kid. Something *important*. Though *what* it was *exactly*, Anders did not know. He had a few guesses, but that was it.

Jack came closer. Anders withdrew farther into the trees. As Jack approached, the wind increased. The branches creaked and moaned, and their leaves whispered incessantly. Anders was about to get up, persuade the new kid that it was way too dangerous to try to make it anywhere on his own, particularly at this hour, when a car appeared at the top of the hill. Anders watched it inch up the hill and pause for a moment. Just before it took off down the hill, he saw something remarkable: two small figures on opposite sides of the car leaped into the open rear windows. They were sleek and muscular and, though it was dark and they were far away, they looked remarkably like cats.

But before he could wonder at it, the car started moving, and it was heading directly toward Jack.

She can't know yet, I'm sure She can't know, Mr. Avery thought as he drove down the road, his hands gripping the steering wheel. *She's not awake yet. Just waking. There's a difference.* His eyes slid from side to side, checking fearfully for evidence of . . . he shook his head. *Best not to think about it*, he told himself. *Just get the boy out of town, and everything can go back to the way it was. She can stay asleep*

forever, for all I care. He picked up speed. He might have even attempted a lighthearted chuckle if he'd had the chance.

Instead, he screamed in pain.

A set of long, sharp claws dug into the sides of his face while another set of claws, belonging to an identical cat, attached themselves to his thigh and started scratching his pants to shreds. Mr. Avery took one hand off the steering wheel and pulled at one cat, but the other bit and scratched even harder.

"Get off me," he attempted to roar, but the upper cat shoved its rump into his mouth, and his voice was muffled in the fur.

And at this moment, a thought popped—unbidden— into his head: *And this is why I have always, always hated cats.*

Jack heard the voice first. He froze, turned, and saw a pair of headlights speeding down the hill. But something wasn't right. The car swerved wildly from right to left to right again. The brakes squealed and the engine roared as the shiny black car fishtailed down the road. Jack stared at it. He couldn't move.

"Get out of the way!" a voice screamed at him from the side of the road. But he couldn't. Jack felt his legs turning to lead. The car was closer…it was about to…

Jack reached out his hands toward the oncoming lights. He gasped and closed his eyes.

Anders pounced, grabbed Jack, and pulled him to the side of the road. Jack fell backward into the gully, his palms pressed hard against his eyes.

"Stopthecarstopthecar," Jack said over and over.

The car made one last squeal as it took a hard turn to the right. Jack screamed at the sound. The car wobbled, whined, and tipped over on its side, leaving a shower of sparks trailing behind. Once it had stopped, Anders left Jack panicking on the ground and ran over to see whether anyone was hurt.

Mr. Avery was inside, his body curled under his arms as a protection from attacking cats. "GET THESE CATS OFF OF ME!" he shouted.

"Don't worry, sir," Anders called. "I'll wake someone up and get help." He ran to the nearest house, but he left the cats. Even Anders, who got on well with most animals he met, knew better than to cross *those* cats.

Jack lay in the underbrush, his hands still pressed against his eyes, a clammy sweat slicking his skin, his breath ripping in and out in panicked heaves.

That car nearly killed me. Why did my mom leave me in such a dangerous town? He swallowed, sighed, and tried to get a hold of himself. He dropped his hands to his sides, blinked a few times, and looked upward at the sky. *And someone pulled me out of the way*, he thought. But he hadn't seen who it was. Who on earth would be just walking around at that time, he wondered. Jack had no idea. The ground beneath him was surprisingly warm, and the leaves, quite damp with the early-morning dew, pressed against his skin. He didn't push them away.

"I want to go home," he whispered. "I just want to go home."

His glasses itched terribly under his nose, but when he tried to adjust them, he realized that he couldn't move his right arm. Or his left. Tendrils of grass and ivy slithered along his side. They twined around his ankles and wrists and held him tight.

"What's going on?" Jack squeaked, but a wave of moss covered his chest, and a tangle of roots pulled him into darkness. "Help me!" he yelled. "Somebody *help* me!" And in that last second—when the sky above him was reduced to a spot the size of the head of a pin—only one thought remained:

Home.

Chapter Eight
Alone and Not Alone

JACK HAD A DREAM THAT THE HOUSE WAS MADE OF EYES — heavy lashed and pretty, but eyes nonetheless. Eyes that followed his every move, winked at his jokes, and welled up with tears for no good reason. In his dream, the eyes blinked in sequence, fluttering like waves from one end of the house to the other.

And the eyes sang.

Or maybe the house sang. In either case, it was beautiful, both hopeful and lonely all at once.

He woke with a start and groaned, covering his face

with his hands to block out the glare of morning light blasting into the window.

He was alive.

Thank goodness.

He gave a skeptical glance around the room. Which part, he wondered, was the dream? He brought his hand to his head and felt a hard, painful lump about the size of a walnut. He winced. Also, he was still wearing his muddy shoes, and his bed and body were covered with grass and moss and leaf bits. Strands of vine clung to his arms and legs, their spiraled filaments pressing against his skin, their papery leaves curling inward, like scrolls.

How? he wondered again and again and again. *How?* His skin had been itching terribly since he arrived in town, but the dirt and mulch made it a million times worse. He tried brushing the debris off of his arms and clothes, but there was too much of it. He covered his face with his hands and groaned. Rubbing his eyes, Jack rolled over, misjudged the distance to the bed's edge, and fell with a thud on the floor. The floorboards squeaked and sighed. They were warm to the touch.

"Ouch," he said out loud, rubbing his left elbow. He paused and waited, but no one came running up to check on him. He stood, and the floor whined, as though sorry that he should have to go. "Anyone home?" Jack called. But no one answered.

The shelves in his room, like the rest of the house, were crammed tight with books. Only one book sat alone, separated from the others by a handful of dried flowers in a glass vase on one side and the wall on the other. Jack slid the book off the shelf and let it fall, fluttering, into his hands. It was, he noticed, the same book that his uncle had given him on his first day at their house—the same book that he left on the couch when he took off the night before. Which meant that Clive and Mabel had read the note.

Jack felt sick.

The floorboards under his feet gave an impatient squeak. Jack sat down on the bed and flipped through the book.

"*The Secret History of Hazelwood*, by Clive Fitzpatrick," he read out loud. "Oh, sure. Just give me a book that *you* wrote," he said, the weight of the obligation pressing against his chest like a stone. "I don't know why he's making such a big thing about it. It's not even a *regular* book." The house shuddered and groaned. The windows rattled. *A storm, I'll bet*, Jack thought, and started reading.

The pages were thick, gold-edged, and handwritten in an elegant, spidery script. Many pages had things glued on—pictures, old newspaper articles, old letters, maps, and pages from diaries. Clive had arranged the clippings in the center of the pages with a heading on the top and an explanation on the bottom. Sometimes his writing went on for several pages. Practically every page talked about magic. Some of them even read like fairy stories.

"*Once there was a man who learned magic*," Jack read

out loud. "*After five years of study, he learned how to make one coin into two, how to make a thousand into two thousand. This wealth he did not share, and he became very rich and reasonably happy. The Magic did not notice.*"

"What *is* this?" Jack asked.

"*After thirty years of study, the man learned how the Magic moved from water to root, from earth to animal, and from the center of the earth to the stars. He learned how to locate Magic's eruption points on the earth's surface. He learned how to crack the Magic open like a melon and split it apart—separating the good from the bad. There is, the man learned, unlimited power in the spaces between* good *and* bad; *between* yes *and* no. *This, the Magic noticed—which is to say, the Lady who guarded the Magic noticed. The man approached the Lady and offered a swap:* My son for Your son. *And then things started going very wrong.*"

"Why does Uncle Clive want me to read fairy tales?" Jack asked himself. His hands were shaking and his temples were starting to sweat.

Some of the pages were covered with an odd filmy layer that had a bit of a golden sheen to it. *From the diary of the Reverend Marcus Weihr* was scrawled at the top in faded black ink, and *Do not remove the film* was written in red in a different hand. *Why?* Jack wondered. But the book didn't explain. In any case, it was the same man who wrote the letter he'd found, though the dates in the diary were later than the letter to the professor.

Jack sighed loudly and turned the page. More fairy

tales. He flipped the pages even faster, glancing at photographs with half-faded people, the landscape behind them visible through their torsos or faces. Jack leaned in closely and squinted. He assumed it must be a double-exposed photograph, but the fading didn't affect *everyone*. Just some people in the group. And in some photographs, there were shadows on the ground of a person who was not there. *Trick photography?* Jack wondered. He saw birth certificates and baptism certificates and school transcripts with missing names, missing dates, as though the people had been erased.

And then. On the last page. Jack stared for a long moment at the photograph. It was recent—the edges crisp and the colors bright—and mounted on the page with gold edging. It showed a little boy with straight black hair and pasty skin that seemed to cling oddly to his small body. He had glasses and a pug nose and wide eyes—livid and frightened and sad all at once.

Jack swallowed.

"It's me," he whispered, and he knew it was true: a picture of *himself*—sitting in Clive and Mabel's living room—as a little boy. The only picture of him, as far as he knew, in existence.

Underneath, the same spidery handwriting scratched out an inscription, which read: *For Jack: A Beginning, an End, and all that's In Between. From the people who love you most.*

Chapter Nine
A Picture's Worth

JACK RAN DOWN THE STAIRS, TRIPPING ON THE BOTTOM LANDing and falling in a heap on the floor. His breath came in hot, tight gasps. Jack's home back in San Francisco was covered with pictures of Baxter—as a baby, as a toddler, smiling with his soccer team or basketball team or Scout troop. There were no pictures of Jack. Not on the wall. Not in an album. Not on a screen saver on the computer. Nowhere. He never questioned it, and though he told himself it didn't bother him, he had, on occasion, cut out figures of himself and taped them into the pictures. He never mentioned it to his parents, and they never commented.

He burst into the kitchen, grabbed the phone, and dialed his father's cell phone in a panic, panting as it rang. The voice-mail greeting—featuring, as always, his father using what Jack called his "captain of industry" voice—nearly sent Jack into hysterics. At the beep, he took a deep breath before he spoke.

"Dad," he said, "you've got to get me out of here. You're right. They're kooks and I can't stay another—" There was a beep, and a digital version of a concerned woman cut over his voice.

"I'm so sorry," the digital woman said. "I didn't get that. If you'd like to leave a message, please press one."

Jack pressed one on the keypad and waited for the second beep. "Dad," he said, "it's Jack. I think Uncle Clive is crazy. He's got this book and it has—"

"I'm so sorry," repeated the digital woman. Jack pressed the button again.

"Dad, your stupid voice mail won't—"

"I'm so sorry," she said again. Jack pressed one.

"He's got this book and it's dedicated to me. Why would he dedicate—"

"I'm so sorry," the digital woman said. "I didn't get that." Jack pressed one.

"Dad, *please* pick up. I've *got* to get *out* of here. And why does he have a picture of me? You don't even have a picture of me. How can—"

The digital woman was sorry once again, and Jack hung up. He scooped the book in his left hand and hurled it across the kitchen, where it hit the screen and sent Lancelot flying with an enraged squawk. That he'd managed to annoy the bird was of little consolation. The book had fallen onto the counter, its open pages facing down.

"He wasn't talking about me," Jack said out loud. "That kid looks nothing like me. Too pale." He waited expectantly, as though the house might answer.

But the floor was suddenly still, and cold as any stone.

Later that evening, Mabel had just set Jack's supper on a tray when he entered the kitchen. He folded his arms.

"Jack," Mabel said with a start. "Did you want to join us for supper?"

He didn't answer, but sat down anyway. Mabel busied herself arranging the table settings while Clive grinned broadly. "Marvelous, marvelous," he said, patting Jack on the shoulders. Jack didn't smile back. He wasn't even sure he'd eat anything. He just wanted answers. Clive and Mabel dished out the salad and meat loaf, poured water, and set in on making nervous small talk mostly, Jack noticed, about the weather. After a bit, the conversation fell away, and the three ate in silence.

Finally, Jack couldn't stand it. "Why haven't my parents called me?"

Clive choked on his meat loaf. Mabel nervously drank her ice water.

"I've been here for more than a week. Why haven't they called me? Don't they care?"

"Well," Clive said slowly, "have you"—he cleared his throat—"called either of them? Successfully, I mean?"

Jack looked at Clive, his black eyes, the pleasant crinkles across his forehead and fanning down his face. *He knows*, Jack thought. *He knows and he's not telling me.*

"If you're having trouble, perhaps it's time to start asking—"

"You're not answering the question," Jack said, staring at his hands. He couldn't look up.

Mabel took Jack's hand. "Honey, I know how hard this is, and I know how you feel that things are, well, *unraveling*." Jack flinched at the word, though he didn't understand why. He noticed the skin on his arms was prickling painfully into goose bumps. *What's happening to me?* he wondered.

"But that's all normal," Mabel continued. "They are figuring things out and so are you. Everything will find its own place in its own time." She paused and leaned in closer, her gray eyes crinkling at the edges. "Do you understand what I'm saying, honey?"

Questions hammered inside his head, jumbling his thoughts. *Why aren't we talking about how I took off last night? Why did you put that book back in my room? Why did my letters to my parents disappear when the notes to myself stay the same?* But he couldn't ask any of them. They were too strange, too...abnormal. *I just want things to be* nor-mal, Jack pleaded silently.

Mabel crossed her arms tightly across her chest and leaned against the back of her chair, "Clive," she said sharply, her eyes narrowing on her husband. "This has gone far enough. *Look at him.*" She pounded the table with her fist. "This is bordering on cruelty. The child is *suffering*, and he needs to know *something.*"

Clive shook his head. "Does a student learn the the-ory of relativity before he's learned to add? Does he read Shakespeare before he's learned his letters? Of course not." He turned to Jack. "My dear boy, if I was to tell you that a wellspring of magic exists right beneath our feet, what would you say?"

"I wouldn't say anything," Jack said. "Because that's *insane.*"

"Of course, my dear, of course. And if I was to tell you that, once upon a time, a creature—a magic 'Guardian,' let's say for argument's sake—used to move through all living things within reach of the wellspring? And She diverted the Magic into the land, and the land was abun-dant and green and good. What would you say to that?"

"That there's no such thing as magic," Jack said, put-ting deliberate emphasis on each and every word. "And, by the way, that you're—"

"Indeed. And if I was to tell you that certain people have attempted to manipulate that magic for personal gain, and in their attempts to turn magic into money and power, ended up transforming what once was *good* into something grotesque and rotten, what would you say to that?" He steepled his fingers and rested his chin on the tips, gazing mildly at Jack.

"I don't…" Jack paused, gritting his teeth. His voice wavered dangerously. His uncle was making fun of him, that much was clear. Taking a deep breath, he stammered out the rest. "Fairy tales *aren't* real. *Everyone* knows that. I don't know why you're telling me these things. I don't—understand—*anything*." He picked up his dinner plate, stood, and left the kitchen without another word.

As he walked up the stairs and down the hall to his room, he heard his aunt and uncle whispering.

"It's happening too fast," Mabel said. "It's unreasonable what you're expecting him to do. He's just a *boy*."

"For now," Clive said.

Chapter Ten
Lecture

Frankie pressed his hand to the side of his face, trying to dull the pain. This wasn't the first time that his scars had flared. That they'd started burning again, like... well, it was hard to say. It wasn't that Frankie *didn't* remember. It was just that the memory was dark. And terrifying.

Still, there was a question that needed to be answered.

His mother and Wendy were in the other room shouting at each other.

"*Do you want your father to lose his* job?" his mother shouted.

"*Do you want Frankie to be tormented for the rest of his life by — by —* bullies?" Wendy shouted back. Despite the bloody nose and the hunk of meat on her blackened eye, Wendy wasn't about to back down.

Their mother calmed her voice. "Wendy, your brother is *special;* we all know that. There's no reason to think that he under—"

"Don't tell me he doesn't understand. He *does*!"

"I know you think so, honey, but the doctor—"

Wendy screamed in frustration.

It was a long-standing argument, one that neither mother nor daughter had ever been able to resolve. It had started, as usual, when Clayton Avery — not only the son of the richest and most powerful man in town but also the son of her father's boss — threw rocks at Frankie and called him Freak Show. This inspired Wendy — once again — to shove the Avery boy to the ground and bury her fists in his fleshy, horrible face. Fortunately for Clayton, Mabel Fitzpatrick happened to drive by. She grabbed both by their collars, told them off, and drove Clayton and Wendy and Frankie to their respective homes.

"If anybody insults my brother—" Wendy began.

"Then you will have to fight an awful lot of people," her mother countered calmly.

It wasn't often that Frankie was able to slip out from under his mother's hawkishly observant care. The only time that Wendy commanded her full attention was when she was in trouble. Frankie, on the other hand, was watched, monitored, and loved to bits. His mother spent most of each day talking to him or reading to him or trying new exercises to stimulate his damaged mind. Each day she would kiss his scars, then press her palm to her mouth and turn away, her eyes bright with tears.

"Listen, Wendy," their mother said in the other room. "This is important." Frankie seized his chance.

He slipped out the back door before he heard any more. His mother, he knew, was about to launch into a lecture that Wendy liked to call "The Value of Good Sense," or "How Not to Be a Pain in Your Mother's Rear End." He figured he had at least forty-five minutes — maybe more. He eased the screen door shut, hopped on his bike, and rode swiftly to the edge of town.

Someone watched him.

She had been sleeping — a long, troubled sleep. And *something* — She did not yet know what — had woken Her. Partially. She couldn't move, though. Not yet.

She watched the boy with the knot of scars approach. She felt him breathing. It was bad business, She knew, what had happened with that boy, but the details escaped Her — the memory had broken into glinting, painful shards, and the world had gone dark. She tried to yawn, but She had no mouth. She had no body, so She could not stretch. She wanted to stretch. Mostly, She simply wanted out.

She watched the boy with the ruined face. The boy was *interesting*.

She had been told he was an imbecile. She had been told it was *obvious*.

She watched his scars. They curved inward and out, like the inside of a snail's shell. She knew they followed the exact curves of snail shells. She knew a lot of things. She had administered the scars Herself. The boy hadn't even winced.

An imbecile, of course, was not suitable for a trade. Of course the deal was off, but something had gone wrong and She had fallen asleep. She *disliked* sleeping.

The boy spat on the ground and used his finger to draw curves in the mud, curves that split apart and came back together. Curves that met in the center. Like a snail's shell. Suddenly, She felt a shock, or not a shock but a wave.

She gasped.

The boy looked up. Saw Her. Saw right through Her. He stood, turned, and ran.

If She had a mouth, She would have screamed.

Chapter Eleven
Freak Show

AFTER CRAMMING HIS BREAKFAST INTO HIS MOUTH, JACK went back up to his room. The morning light filtered and greened through the increasing thicket of leaves outside the window. A few strands of vines had pushed through the gap between the screen and the sash and had started snaking their way across the wall. It couldn't be good for the wall, but still, he liked the look of it, so he left it there.

He pulled his duffel bag out of the closet and threw it onto the bed. At the bottom, surrounded by T-shirts and tied tightly in a towel so his mother wouldn't know about it, hid the skateboard. Jack pulled it out, sat down on the bed, and laid the board on his lap. Every edge was scuffed, the wheels were worn, and the stickers, blaring the names of bands or slogans, curled at the corners, barely hanging on. Still, it was rough and heavy and real. Something to believe in.

And Jack *did* believe in the skateboard.

The night before Jack's trip to Iowa, when, over dessert, their parents told Jack and Baxter about their new apartments and their new, separate lives, and that Baxter would be spending almost the entire summer with two of his best friends while the households were separated (they didn't mention Jack, nor did they look at him, and Jack had the distinct impression that his parents had forgotten about him altogether), Baxter did something amazing.

Baxter — normally very good at ignoring his brother — put his hand on Jack's shoulder. "But," he said, "what about Jack?"

After a few moments of confused silence, some clearing of throats, and a hasty dash to the back room, where they conferred for a while in low voices, his parents said, "Iowa. Aunt Mabel and Uncle Clive. Won't it be wonderful?" And with that, Jack's mother dashed to her desk to purchase airline tickets on her computer.

Later that night, Baxter came into Jack's room with the skateboard. "Don't let Mom see it," he said, handing the board to Jack. "I had to hide it until I broke my elbow, and even then I told her that I just tripped in the street. If she sees it, she'll just start spewing statistics about how many kids break their necks and other nonsense. Anyway, it'll give you something to do in Iowa."

Jack stared at his brother—the sunburned, freckled face, the strong chin, strong shoulders, strong back. It was the only time that Baxter had ever given him anything, and though Jack was sure he must have had other conversations with his brother, it was the only time that he could remember Baxter talking to him directly.

"Thanks," Jack said, finding his mouth had gone quite dry.

"Don't forget me," Baxter said, turning to leave.

Jack frowned. "How can I forget my own brother?" he called, but Baxter was already in the hallway and didn't respond.

Jack left the next morning. Baxter forgot to say good-bye.

Now, with his mother thousands of miles away, Jack would learn how to ride his skateboard. *Honestly*, he thought, *how hard could it be?*

He set the board in the center of the room, stepped on, and balanced. Normally, Jack had excellent balance and could climb trees and walk casually down their long limbs as easy as anything. But balancing on the plastic wheels was something different altogether. *Better try it outside*, he thought.

Jack walked quickly down the shadowy hallway, his skateboard clutched in his left hand. When he passed his uncle Clive on the stairs, he immediately hid the board behind his back, standing perfectly still, an evasive maneuver that almost always worked on his parents. Clive carried a tall stack of leather-bound books with gold lettering on the spines. Though the books were large and heavy, he barely looked winded, and instead bounced from stair to stair.

"Off for a run on the skateboard, then, Jack?" he said from behind the stack of books.

"Um, yeah," Jack muttered guiltily, his eyes focused on the worn red carpet. He clutched the skateboard in his fingers, silently determining that Clive wouldn't take it without a fight.

"Splendid, splendid. I'll be up in the study if you need me. Your aunt is off to the gallery this morning, but she'll return by lunch. I do hope you'll join us. She has made a lovely Jell-O mold." He lowered his voice. "She stole the recipe from Mrs. Emmer, but you didn't hear it from me." He winked and disappeared into his study, shutting the door behind him.

After trying for two blocks, Jack realized that there was more to this skateboarding business than he had originally thought. Already, he had the beginnings of a large bruise on his left hip and an angry scrape on his right elbow, and both of his hands were red and raw. In truth, he was glad to make his first attempt here in Iowa rather than in San Francisco, with its unforgiving hills.

There had to be a rhythm to this thing, he told himself. Push, push, balance, balance. Push, balance, push, balance. Trouble was, he found himself traveling this way and that, forcing him to think about changing direction rather than staying upright. After his fifteenth fall, Jack got up, brushed off his shorts, and dislodged the bits of gravel that had embedded themselves into the skin of his knees and elbows. He wiped his nose with the back of his hand.

He stopped when he reached the park at the end of the road, walked to the swings, and stepped onto one with his left foot and began swinging standing up. He pulled and leaned, closing his eyes into the wind of his own creation. This felt good. It was something he could do.

Without warning, something knocked Jack hard on his back, launching him into the air for one brief, thrilling moment, before he fell with a thump on the dusty patch of bare ground.

"Welcome to Hazelwood, Four-eyes."

It was a boy, Jack noted from his vantage point on the ground. And while most, if not all, boys his age were bigger than he was, this boy was huge: big feet in big leather shoes; wide, muscular thighs; chunky arms; and a chunkier middle. He had a baseball hat pulled low, but Jack could see that he had two blackened eyes peeking out from under the brim.

Jack stood up, brushed the dirt off his pants and out of his hair. The boy on the other side of the swing stayed as still and solid as a hunk of rock. Jack waited. In the silence, the whine of cicadas in the nearby trees seemed deafening. Neither boy spoke. Finally, Jack couldn't stand it anymore.

"Hi," he said, offering his hand for a shake. "I'm Jack."

The boy stared at Jack's hand as though it were a bizarre animal species that had just crawled out from under a rock. Slowly, Jack lowered his hand and shoved it into his pocket.

"I don't remember giving you permission to speak, Wart-face."

"No, actually it's *Jack*—wait, are you...*oh*," Jack said, suddenly understanding exactly where this conversation was heading. Being the only kid in his class without any friends, Jack was no stranger to the occasional run-in with a bully. Not *often*, of course, as most kids didn't notice him for long enough to hassle him. Still, there had been a small handful of bullies—hasslers, insulters, punchers.

This boy, Jack could tell, was a puncher. *Rule one*, he thought, *Don't Make Eye Contact.*

"Well," Jack said, keeping his gaze firmly to the left of the kid's shoulder, "it was nice meeting you." He turned and began walking away slowly, head down, feet barely making a sound on the dirt and ragged crab grass.

"Hey, Pig-snot," the boy said. Jack kept walking. He felt his ears redden and grow hotter by the moment. "What's it like in that ugly house? My mom says they're into witches and hoodoo."

Rule two, he knew, was Don't Talk Back, but Jack couldn't stop himself. "They couldn't possibly be into either," he said. "They're Methodists."

The boy took a step back, clearly flustered. He also knew the rules and script in the bully/bullied performance and was taken aback that Jack had suddenly decided to improvise. The boy frowned. "So?"

"Well, they're different religions, aren't they? You can't be Hindu and Jewish at the same time. Or Muslim and Zen Buddhist. They're way too different. It's like trying to be tall and short, or fat and thin, or human and—"

"What?" the boy asked, clearly even more confused.

"Never mind," Jack said, feeling stunned at himself.

The boy removed his cap and ran his fingers through his hair, staring hard at Jack. "You getting smart with me, dork?" He took a step forward, curled his fingers into a fist, and looked eager to throw a good punch.

"Smart?" Jack asked, buying time. He paused, drew a long slow breath. "No, no…" *Obviously not*, he thought. His eyes slid across the ragged field, where Baxter's old skateboard lay in the grass. In his head, he tried to calculate how fast he would have to run if he grabbed it on his way back to Clive and Mabel's house. He certainly couldn't ride it back. But if he left it there, what were the odds that he could come back for it? He shook his head. Not good, he decided. *My brother gave it to me*, Jack thought. *And there is no way I'm leaving it behind.*

The boy advanced and Jack stumbled backward, his eyes darting between the boy and the skateboard.

"Listen, Worm-turds, I'm thinking I should teach you a lesson."

But Jack wasn't listening. With a burst of speed that, frankly, he didn't know was in him, he darted around the boy, grabbed the skateboard, and ran for the road.

He didn't make it far.

A pair of thick hands grabbed him from behind while simultaneously swiping a booted foot across Jack's calves. With a grunt, the boy launched Jack into the air. Jack kept his eyes open, regarding the patterns of thick green and sandy brown. He hit the ground suddenly, smashing his fingers between the wheels and the hard dirt, a fall made worse by the force of his body behind it.

"*Hey!*" A voice cracked the space above Jack's head. Jack rolled over onto his back, shaking his hands a bit, hoping that he hadn't broken a finger or two. Nothing creaked, cracked, or popped. Jack decided that this was good news.

A girl stood two feet from him, her feet planted firmly

on the ground, her hands pulled into tight fists that she swung at her sides. Jack tried to make out her face, but her body blocked out the morning sun, which licked around the edges of her silhouette as though she were on fire.

"Is it just me, Clayton, or do you get dumber every year?"

Clayton stopped, wrinkled his brow in concentration, and stuck out his chin. "No, I don't." He shoved his fists into his back pockets and hunched his shoulders. "*You* get dumber every year."

"Honestly," she said, reaching down and helping Jack to his feet.

"He really does get dumber every year," she muttered to Jack. "Seriously. There've been tests."

"Shut *up*," Clayton said. "And you." He pointed at Jack. "Gotta get rescued by a *girl*? That's how they do things in Sissy Francisco?" Clayton smirked while the girl sighed loudly, resting her forehead in her hand and shaking her head.

Jack said nothing. He didn't mind who rescued him, but what's more, he didn't mind the fact that he needed help in the first place. You have to care about a person, even just a little, in order to beat him up. It's when they leave you alone entirely—that's when you might as well not exist, and if you disappeared forever, no one would really notice.

The girl stepped away from Jack. "I'm not rescuing

anybody. I'm just telling you off. And maybe I didn't do a good-enough job last time."

Clayton instinctively brought his hand to his blackened eyes in a defensive gesture. "Shut *up*," he said again. But before he could say anything else, the girl took two giant leaps toward Clayton, grabbed the neck of his T-shirt, and yanked his face close to her own. Jack's mouth dropped open. Despite being bigger and heavier, the other boy was clearly scared of this wiry, sharp-jawed girl.

"Listen," she said. "You stay away from me. You stay away from my brother. And stay away from the new kid. The last thing we want is for him to think this town is filled with a bunch of—oh." She stopped. "I forgot." She released Clayton, turned to Jack, and extended her hand. "Hi. Wendy Schumacher."

Jack stared at her. Her hair was long and snaked down from her white scalp all the way to the middle of her back in a shiny, copper-colored braid. Her pink lips spread into a wide smile, revealing a small gap between her front teeth. Her yellow sundress flapped around her body, which was all angles and edges, and Jack noticed that the knuckles of her right hand were scraped up and scabbed.

"Um," Jack said, suddenly realizing that she was shaking his hand and that he should probably shake back. No kid had ever shaken his hand before. "Hi." He stopped, but realized that she was still staring at him, expecting him to continue. "I'm Jack."

Wendy nodded. "I expected you'd look different. Thought you'd be—" She pulled her lips into a downward curve, trying to find the right word. "I don't know. I thought you'd look different."

Jack wasn't sure how to take that comment, so he started brushing the dirt and dead grass off his shorts and shirt.

"Don't mind him anyway," Wendy continued, jerking her head in the direction of Clayton, who had taken this opportunity to start slinking away. Clayton turned back and shot a poisonous scowl at Wendy, who closed her eyes and shook her head.

"I'm so *telling*," Clayton yelled.

"*No one cares!*" she shouted back. "Seriously," she said in a lowered tone. "He's not worth minding."

She picked up Jack's skateboard. "Come on, I'll walk you home."

Chapter Twelve
Brave

THERE WERE TWO BOYS SITTING ON THE PORCH. ONE WORE a seed cap. It was green. The other wore a parrot. It was Lancelot.

"Why," Jack asked Wendy, "is my uncle's parrot sitting on that kid's shoulder?"

"That's my brother," Wendy said, and while she didn't answer the question, her voice had an oddly dangerous edge to it. Jack decided it was answer enough.

The boy with the seed cap stood up. It was the same boy, he noticed, who was sneaking around the yard the other day. Jack looked at the ground. For as long as he could remember, he'd wanted friends. He'd wanted people to see him. And *here*, apparently everyone could see him. And Jack wanted to hide.

It's just because I don't like it here, Jack told himself.

It's just because I wish I'd never left, another voice whispered in his head. Jack batted at his ear and shook the voice away.

"It's you," Jack said. "Anders."

"Yeah," the blond boy said. "I'm glad to see you're doing all right." His smile was wide, even wider than Wendy's, and like Wendy, he was taller than Jack. A lot taller, in fact. And what he meant by *all right*, Jack wasn't sure.

The other boy stayed seated and did not look up, but cocked his head slightly to the left and stared intently at the space right next to Jack's hand. Jack looked at him questioningly, but glanced quickly away. Half of the boy's face was a mess—all tangled and bumpy, like some sort of strange fruit that Jack would see in the open-air markets at home. He raised his hand for a quick hello and tried to fix his eyes elsewhere.

"Nice to see you again," Jack said to Anders, and not to the boy on the ground. As if to protest, Lancelot flew upward from his perch on Frankie's shoulder, flapped his wings in Jack's face with an indignant squawk, and flew back into the house.

"Frankie's my twin brother. He doesn't say very much."

"Oh," Jack said.

"He doesn't—" Wendy paused, turned to Jack, and looked very hard into his face. Jack winced. "He doesn't...well, you've never, um, *seen* him before, have you?"

Jack frowned. He peered into Frankie's unresponsive face. The left side bulged and rippled—a complicated network of red, rough, irritated scars. Jack wondered whether it was painful. Without realizing he was doing it, Jack reached up and rubbed his own cheek before forcing his hand back into his pocket. Frankie did not make eye contact, nor did he seem to notice that Jack was staring at him. "No," he said, surprised.

In truth, he could have *sworn* he had seen that kid before. But he couldn't have, could he? As far as he knew, he had never met a deformed person before. Or a mute. Or, for that matter, until ten days ago, an Iowan.

"Oh, I don't know," she said, hesitating. "It just looked like he knew you. Or, well, you know. I just thought—maybe on a trip or something..." Her voice trailed off, and the blond boy rolled his eyes.

"Nice try anyway," Anders said, patting Wendy on the shoulder. She scowled at her friend.

Just what, exactly, Wendy was trying, Jack didn't know, but before he could ask, he was interrupted by the blare of a police siren. The sound was loud and high and punched Jack's ear so hard he yelped. Frankie stood, and though he didn't look at the police car, or anyone else for that matter, he put his body between the squad car and Jack. With a scratch of gravel and a squeal of brakes, the car stopped and two police officers stepped out.

"Schumacher," the first one said, taking out a notebook and writing something down. "We thought we might find you here. Been hassling old man Avery's boy again, have you?" He shook his head and tutted. "Smarter girls than you would've learned their lesson by now."

Jack peered over Frankie's slumped shoulders. Anders had taken Wendy's hand, and Jack noticed the boy's fingers were white, tense, and immobile—and no matter how much she tried to wriggle free, Wendy couldn't twist her fingers out of his grasp. Instead, she jutted out her chin, threw back her shoulders, and laughed.

"As if," she said. "I suppose you haven't noticed—again—that kid outweighs me by, like, a hundred pounds or something."

The other officer leaned against the squad car and peered up at the house. "You're getting quite a record there, Miss Schumacher." Wendy hissed and made another jerk of her arm to free herself. Anders hung tight. "Your parents have been notified and the social worker—she'll probably stop by again. So nice of her to do so. Trouble is, once a file gets heavy enough, people start talking about removal." Jack noticed Frankie's shoulders hunch tight and heard the boy gasp. He leaned over and saw a tear leaking out of Frankie's left eye.

"I thought—" Jack began, but before he could ask anything, Frankie stepped hard on his toe. No one else seemed to notice.

"No one's removing me anywhere," Wendy said, but her voice had a tiny waver in it that seemed to delight the second officer.

"Well, I don't know about that," he said. "Seems to me that your parents just may have had enough of a delinquent kid who goes around beating up—"

"But that's not true." Jack stepped around Frankie. The officers looked around for a moment to see who had spoken, before finally focusing on Jack. It took them a minute.

"Wendy didn't beat up anyone. That—Avery, or whatever his name is—that kid attacked me." He looked up at the officers, who regarded him with wide-eyed fascination. Anders dropped Wendy's hand, and both let their arms dangle at their sides. "And," Jack puffed up his chest a little, feeling suddenly emboldened, "it was for *no reason*." Jack let that sink in.

"Who are you, kid?" the first officer said.

Jack shrugged. "Me?" he said. "I'm no one. I'm staying with my aunt and uncle."

The second officer looked from Jack to the house and back to Jack again. "So, you're *that* kid."

Wendy and Anders grabbed Jack by both arms. He stiffened, but acquiesced as they walked backward toward the house. "He doesn't have to tell you anything," Wendy said.

"He hasn't done anything wrong," Anders said. "None of us have." They pushed Jack toward the wooden stairs, and he fell with a thud on the bottom step. He gripped the edge of the wood. It felt warm under his hands, but it trembled. Or perhaps it was Jack who trembled. He couldn't be sure.

"Of course he hasn't," the first officer said. Despite his rounded belly, the first officer's face was thin and gaunt, with a scattering of sharp stubble across the chin. He leaned in, reached into his pocket, and took out a small camera. "Lots of folks are interested in you, son. You know that?" Jack looked at the camera and winced at the flash. "Very, very interested." And with a laugh, they both slid into the car and drove away.

Wendy reached down and grabbed a rock. Anders snatched it away. "Don't even think about it," he said. Wendy snorted and sighed. She turned toward Jack, crossed her arms, and looked him up and down. Jack felt as though he was being x-rayed. Wendy's wide eyes narrowed and sharpened into two bright black points.

"All kinds of surprises today, I guess. You've got more guts than I thought," she said with a slow nod. She paused, as though deciding carefully what she should say next. "Sorry you had to see that little display." She glared at the receding lights of the squad car. "I wish I could say it was out of the ordinary, but I can't. It's Avery's town, you see. Avery's cops and teachers and buildings and… everything else. This isn't…a *nice* town. I wish it were." She took a step backward. "Anyway, we'll probably see you around."

Jack didn't move from the step as he watched the three kids walk away.

He went inside and, without saying hello to either his aunt or his uncle, retreated to his room and shut the door. Sighing, he sat heavily at the desk and took out his notebook.

How, he wrote, *is it possible that an actual conversation with kids my age makes me feel lonelier than ever?* He stared at the page for what seemed like an hour, trying to find an answer.

He never did.

At supper, Jack was silent while his aunt and uncle chatted happily about things that Jack couldn't imagine caring about. Clive turned to Jack and smiled. "You met our Frankie, then? And Wendy and Anders?"

Jack couldn't take his eyes off his dinner. He peered into the lump of noodles and cream and canned fish that seemed to quiver on his plate like a living, disembodied brain. The whole thing had been sprinkled over with crushed-up potato chips and something else that looked like chips but smelled strongly of onions. Jack wondered whether it was supposed to be food. He assumed it probably was, but sometimes you never can tell. Gog and Magog looked up expectantly, balancing on their hind legs. They looked like they could swallow the whole plate in one gulp. Suddenly, Jack really loved those cats.

"Yes," Jack said quietly. "I met them. Wendy. She's kind of…" Jack searched for the word.

"Prickly, yes," Clive said. "Not entirely a bad thing."

"They're the nicest kids in the world," Mabel said. "And brave."

Jack tried the noodles. They tasted like paste. He winced.

"You think that's an unlikely descriptor for your new friends?" Clive looked at him, and Jack could have sworn the man's eyes were twinkling.

"No—it's just—you see, they're not—" Jack's voice faltered and sputtered out. Should he start with "No, it was just the awful casserole" or "No, they're actually not my friends"? Either way, he wasn't going to look very good. "I don't know," he said finally.

"There's a lot of things a person can be in this world, boy," Clive said very seriously. "Or in any world, really," he added with a wink. "Brave is as good a thing to be as any. Will you pass me some more casserole, my love?" he asked Mabel, who blushed. "It's absolutely perfect."

When they weren't looking, Jack fed his to the cats.

That night, Jack rolled and sweated in his sleep. All night, he saw eyes in the walls. All night, he saw a woman running across a field of young corn. Her hands were green; her face was green; her hair was yellow and sweet like corn silk. She hid a small boy behind a house, and then she was a house—a house with sleepy windows and a grinning mouth.

Jack woke with a start and got out of bed. The house was silent, as though it were holding its breath. A glass of water sat on the desk, its sides sweating with condensation. Jack grabbed the glass and drained it in four large gulps. He wiped his mouth with his pajama sleeve and realized that he was roasting hot. It was *never* this hot in San Francisco in the summer.

He took off his pajama top, used it to wipe off his damp face, neck, and torso, and tossed it onto the floor. He sat down at his desk and began to draw. Without meaning to, he drew a picture of a girl, hair wisping about her eyes, at her ears, and away from her neck. Her head tilted upward and her mouth was opened, as though calling out to someone. In each hand, she held a star. Next to it, he wrote *Wendy Underground*. Lying back down, Jack fell asleep at once.

When he woke the next morning, he had no memory of the time he'd spent drawing. When he finally noticed the picture as he tied his shoes, he was so confused that he tore the page out of his notebook and nearly threw it in the trash. On closer inspection, though, he couldn't help but notice that it was a very good likeness. And despite the fact that Jack was terrified of her, at least in the drawing she was — Jack faltered — well, not *ugly* anyway. He folded the picture, knelt down beside his bed, and slipped it into the pages of *The Secret History of Hazelwood*. The windowpane rattled and the floorboards hummed, though the morning was still and the house was quiet.

He tried calling his mother, but the lines kept crossing. A man from a sewer company answered the phone first. Then a lady from the City of Toledo Morgue. Then a child speaking a language that Jack did not know. None of them could hear Jack talking, and they hung up on him. He tried calling his father, but the line was disconnected.

Jack leaned back in his chair, rubbing his nose under his glasses with one hand and thrumming his fingers against the book with the other. The walls shivered slightly, and tiny cracks appeared on the plaster next to the window.

"I'm not going to read it," he said out loud. The floorboards shook, the table wobbled, and the glass of water fell with a crack on the floor. Jack held the book to his chest, slowly scanning the room. He took a deep breath. "Um," he said, "I might read it."

The floors calmed, the windows soothed, and the house seemed to breathe a sigh of relief.

Jack opened the book.

Chapter Thirteen
The Grain Exchange and Trust

ON THE FAR END OF MAIN STREET STOOD THE GRAIN Exchange and Trust building. It was a long, muscular building, standing squarely in the center of Main Street, flanked by two prettily maintained, though rarely visited, plazas. Its limestone face had been meticulously carved with symbols of the agricultural economy—corn, wheat, livestock, and apples. There were images of growing trees and broad shoulders and industry. Upon closer inspection, however, one could see the hidden likeness of a sleeping woman—so hidden, in fact, that her face could only be seen on a slant or with a casual flick of the eye. She hid in the leaves of the trees, in the shade of the corn, and sometimes among the animals—but she vanished when viewed head-on.

Like the college and the Avery house, the Grain Exchange and Trust also had been built by Mr. Avery's great-grandfather, whose portrait hung in most of the rooms. Each room had its own staff of well-groomed workers who performed tasks for the Office of Savings and Loan, the Office of Real Estate, the Office of Farm Development, the Office of Auctioneers, and the Office of Progress. It was in these offices that small fortunes of local farmers and merchants were calculated, housed, divided, and systematically squandered, while the Avery fortune swelled and bloated like an overripe fruit.

For the past four years, however, the fortunes of farmers stayed steady in their accounts as the Avery fortune, though still massive, began to shrink at its edges. People told stories of the terrible rages and even the tears behind locked doors. No one mentioned these rumors to Mr. Avery. No one at all.

Mr. Avery arrived just before sunrise, without his briefcase and on foot. He had several scratches across his face, a large bruise under one eye, and an arm resting comfortably in a sling. He knew that he would not have to remark upon any of his injuries. No one would ask him.

His attempt to remove the boy from town seemed pathetic to him now—both desperate and laughable.

Still, if he could avoid performing the swap…if he could prevent Her from taking his only…Mr. Avery shuddered, forcing the thought off. His face sweated prodigiously, but he did not wipe it away. And he ignored his underlings as they offered their meager morning greetings. He prided himself on his ability to aggressively ignore underlings.

Mr. Avery threw open the doors of the Grain Exchange and Trust and stomped across the opulent (though fraying) red carpet to his office at the end of the hall. Framed in the leaded-glass window of the polished oak door was Mr. Perkins, hunched at a desk before a ledger book, sweat dripping from his arched brow. He had already been hard at work for well over an hour, Mr. Avery knew. Mr. Perkins was punctual.

"*Perkins!*" he roared.

Mr. Perkins dropped his pencil on the floor. He stood quickly and shoved his right hand deep into his pocket, tightly gripping something inside. "Yes, sir," Mr. Perkins said, shuffling papers with his left hand and scanning the floor for his pencil.

"You have an assignment. I want you to get some information on that boy at the Fitzpatricks'. Follow him if you need to. Keep an eye on him. Wear something inconspicuous. And take notes. I want to know what he knows. I hope I am understood," he added dangerously. No one, ever, wanted to be accused of misunderstanding Mr. Avery.

"But, sir," Mr. Perkins began in a quavery voice. "The boy. He isn't—" Unconsciously, Mr. Perkins pulled a small length of braided rawhide from his pocket and pressed it against his cheek. He held on for dear life.

"Don't ask questions," Mr. Avery snapped. "And don't let yourself be seen. I will be leaving town in an hour. I shall return in a few days and will expect a full report."

He knew his meeting with the governor would be successful. The governor was...an impressionable young man. But first Mr. Avery had research to do. He was closing in on an answer...he could *feel* it. And if his suspicions were correct—or even *marginally* correct—then he would require the use of the Fitzpatrick house. He was certain, with a little legal wrangling, that he could possess the strange house at the edge of town, mysteries and all, by the end of the week. Two weeks, if the Fitzpatricks made things difficult. Best to assume two.

"No, sir—I mean, yes, sir," Mr. Perkins said, tripping over the wastepaper basket as he hurried to retrieve his rain jacket and umbrella, two things he carried every day, whether it was forecasted to rain or not. The door moaned sadly as he pushed it open and closed with a brittle slam.

Mr. Avery watched the hesitant profile of his assistant through the glass until his silhouette was swallowed in the bright mouth of the door, and the old man was alone. On his desk sat two small pictures. The first was from an instant camera and had been glued onto a piece of paper with some arrows and words scratched around the edges.

Original position of subject, with an arrow pointing to an empty space in front of the Fitzpatrick house. *Subject remains?* with another arrow pointing to a boy-shaped shadow on the ground.

Mr. Avery sighed. "I need more time," he whispered. His hands trembled as he reached for the other picture — this one a very small photograph of his wife and son — his only son. His father had told him to have two, that it would be easier that way. Mr. Avery shook his head. He didn't want *easier*. He just wanted his boy. He closed his eyes, pressed the small frame to his heart.

He could still feel the icy waves in the wood, coming faster and colder than before.

And though he wasn't there to see it, he knew that on the outside of the building, the limestone eyes of the sleeping woman in the stone slowly slivered open.

Chapter Fourteen
The Skateboard and the Thief

THAT SAME MORNING, JACK AWOKE AT FIRST LIGHT. DESPITE the early hour, he could hear the clank and slurp of Clive and Mabel's breakfast dishes and the low hum of their conversation. *Don't they ever sleep?* Jack wondered.

The Secret History of Hazelwood lay open on his chest. He glanced over the page that he had read the night before. While some of the book was made from the diaries of Reverend Weihr, most of it was written by Clive. This particular page—the one that had put him to sleep—was about the stealing of souls.

Can anyone really steal *a soul?* Jack wondered. It seemed ludicrous, but really, everything in the book was ludicrous.

"*When a person's soul is destroyed,*" Jack read out loud, "*the memory of that person is also destroyed. Or so the theory goes. But what if there is a deeper memory? What of the soul then? I am heartened by the case of the old school and its eventual abandonment. The exact number of children ensnared at that particular eruption point can never be known. Still, the fact that eventually the town built a new school in a safer location demonstrates that there truly is a deeper memory. The town, without knowing why, acted to protect its children. Which means that, perhaps, the souls of those lost children are not entirely lost. Perhaps the memory is not lost but blocked. Perhaps it is possible that they could one day be found and set free.*"

Jack closed the book with a slap. "This is crazy," he said. Still. There was something weird about the town, and if the book had answers, then he'd rather get them there than have to actually talk to his aunt and uncle. After all, Clive was liable to just say something weird or vaguely creepy; at least with a book, Jack could slam the covers shut. He had not brought up his attempt at running away, nor did he mention the dedication and photograph in the book to Clive, and since Clive hadn't either, Jack was hoping that the conversation might be indefinitely avoided. Why Clive had thought to keep a picture of Jack when his parents hadn't even done so was a mystery to Jack, but for the time being, *not* knowing was preferable to *knowing*. For now. Because sometimes, Jack knew, knowledge can hurt. A lot.

And, anyway, there were other questions to answer first. Jack opened the book at random to a page taken from the Reverend's journal.

> *This may be my last Entry in this Record of my years in Hazelwood. Tomorrow, I shall use the Portsmouth to return to the World-Under-the-World and attempt to make whole what treachery has divided. My soul, I know, may be lost as a result, but I cannot worry about that now. My one hope—if I should fail—rests in this diary, in my preserved research, and in the future hero who can use my findings to set things right. I pray that I have properly bound my words to the page, should my soul and memory slip into the clutches of the Lady. I, alone, bear the blame for the curse on this place. I will set things right, or die.*

Jack shook his head and opened his notebook. *It's obvious the Reverend believes what he's writing,* Jack wrote, *but does Clive believe it? Does Mabel? And if they do, why do they want me to know about it? What does any of this have to do with me?* Jack didn't know. He slid the book and his notebook into his backpack and headed down to breakfast.

To Jack's great relief, his aunt and uncle left him mostly alone. Mabel handed him a plate of eggs on toast, insisted on kissing his cheek, and left for work. Clive, just before hoisting up the biggest pile of books that Jack had ever seen in his life, handed Jack a hand-drawn map of town.

"I should have given you this earlier, my dear boy. Here: so you won't get lost. Your aunt's shop is marked. She'll be expecting you at lunchtime."

"Oh," Jack said, "I had thought that I would—"

"Be that as it may," Clive said, balancing the books in his arms. "It's best, in my experience, not to disappoint familial females. The ramifications are never pleasant. In the meantime, several other points of interest are marked on the map and should keep you marginally entertained until then." Clive kept talking as he walked up the stairs. "And while we're always fond of the youth of today taking it upon themselves to explore and thumb their noses at their well-meaning elders, mind you note the restrictions. There are certain things that I would rather not have to explain to your aunt." And with that he rounded the corner and disappeared.

Outside, Jack sat on his skateboard, tilting back and forth as he studied the map. It was detailed—so detailed that not only was nearly every landmark named, but Clive had chosen to give alternative names to many of them as well. For example, Clive's own house had been marked *Our house (your house) (Tertiary Eruption Point).*

And the large forested area had been marked *Henderson's Gully (Original Eruption Point) (Don't go here!)*.

"You really *are* crazy, aren't you?" As if to answer his question, Clive opened the front door with Lancelot on his shoulder.

"Now, now, Lancelot, there's nothing to worry about. No wicked spirits about today. Oh, hello again, Jack." He waved jauntily at Jack, who gave a nervous little shake of the hand in response. Clive offered a small leather envelope to Lancelot, who took it in his mouth. "Now, don't worry, it's not that far." The parrot squawked anxiously before gliding away.

"Remember," Clive called after him, "you have to go the long way. Just to be safe." The bird took a left and disappeared from sight. Clive waved at Jack once again. "Cheers, Jack," he said, and closed the door.

Jack stared at the map, particularly the words *Don't go here*. If there were *really* erupting volcanoes in the middle of Iowa, then Jack, for one, wanted to see them. Keeping the map in his hand for reference, he turned toward where the gully was supposed to be, shouldered his bag, and kicked the skateboard to a start.

It was easier today. His muscles now had a memory of that snaking balance, that tilt and sway of the hips and spine. His knees had a bit more spring to them, and his legs, though sore, seemed to respond better to the fluctuations in his feet. He kicked at the ground with his left foot, encouraging a bit more speed and long, smooth glides. It was beautiful, he thought. It was graceful. He was doing it! And more than anything in the world, Jack found himself wishing that Baxter—or really anyone at all—might see him skating cleanly down the empty street.

Clive, after closing the door, did not return to his office. Instead, he remained at the window, peering at the black-haired boy in the street. He smiled at the boy's efforts to control both his body and the tiny machine at his feet, and swelled with pride as the child skimmed down the pavement. A moment later, a small, bald-headed man in camouflage pants and a flak jacket huffed in pursuit of the small boy. Clive sighed, pressed his forehead to the glass, and brought his hands to his heart.

"Gog," he called. "Magog." The two cats snaked into the foyer, looking up at Clive expectantly. "Follow that boy and be quick about it. He's headed for the gully, and that idiot Reginald is following him." He cracked the door and the cats slipped out, leaped off the porch, and bounded through the grass. Clive ran his hand through his thinning hair and sighed. "We just have to hope for the best," he said out loud. "We have to be thankful he's a smart-enough boy." But the floor under his feet shivered and quaked, and a low moan blew between the rafters and the roof.

*　　*　　*

Jack pulled to a stop at the edge of the forest. The trees were large and old, with tangles of underbrush crowding the ground. He couldn't see a path.

"How could anyone go in there? There's no place to go." He reached into his bag and grabbed the map. It showed a network of trails, shaped something like a spiderweb, that spread through the woods, but if they existed at all, Jack certainly couldn't see them. In truth, it seemed a bit of a shame. The woods looked cool and shady, and the day was already hot. Jack picked up the skateboard and walked along the edge of the forest. The branches of the trees sighed and creaked in the light wind.

He crept up to the crowded edge of the woods, placed his hands on the slim trunks of two pale aspen trees, and scanned the undergrowth for a path. The sunlight dappled and glowed on the greenery, and for a moment Jack had half a mind to tramp through the branches and weeds, just to see what all the fuss was for. And he might have done so, had it not been for the bloodcurdling yowl of two cats and the panicked screech of a terrified young man.

"No," the man cried as one of the cats batted at the edge of his flak jacket while the other attached itself to his thigh. "Bad kitty. Baaaaad kitty!"

Jack left the skateboard on the ground and ran over.

"Sorry," he said, pulling one large cat off the man's leg. It was astonishingly heavy. "They're my aunt and uncle's cats. I don't know why they're so bad."

"*Phtt, phtt*," spat one of the cats indignantly.

The man stared at Jack, openmouthed. He was holding a notebook in one hand, and the other was shoved into his pocket. He stepped backward.

"People in this town sure stare a lot," Jack said, attempting half a smile. The man said nothing but took another step backward. The cats pressed themselves to each of Jack's legs. They purred dangerously. Jack stuck out his hand, offering it to the stranger. "I'm Jack. I'm Clive and Mabel's nephew." The stranger had a pale, thin face and a bony neck. He opened his mouth as though to say hello, but all that came out was a squeak. He gulped, and took his hand out of his pocket. There was something wound around his knuckles and fingers, some kind of leathery shoelace. Jack raised his eyebrows.

"Don't even think about it," the man said, trembling.

Jack pressed his lips into a frown. "Don't even think about what?"

"It's not yours to take," the man said, walking backward and nearly tripping on his own feet.

"What's not mine to take?" Jack asked, taking a step forward. "I haven't taken anything. I just wanted to shake your—"

"I know what you are," the man yelped.

"I already told you who I am. I'm Jack. I'm staying with—"

"Not one step farther. You can't have it!" He pushed past Jack. In a burst of speed that didn't seem possible with a physique like his, the man ran to the skateboard and flung it into the gully and, in the same motion, grabbed Jack's backpack and took off down the street. The cats, with a terrific yowl, followed close at his heels, batting every once in a while at the trailing straps.

"Hey," Jack yelled, taking off after him. "Hey! Give that back, you lousy—" but he couldn't finish his sentence, as he tripped on a small rock and fell, face-first, sprawling across the pavement.

Jack groaned, rolled over, and checked his glasses. One lens had cracked, and one hinge had been pulled far out of alignment. "Oh, great." He balanced the glasses on the bridge of his nose, trying to push them back into their normal shape. His shirt had torn at the shoulder, and his shorts at the pocket. "Just great."

"Jack," a girl's voice sounded behind him. "Is that you?"

Jack shook his head. "Just keeps getting better and better," he muttered. He turned and saw Wendy, once again, standing over him. He scrambled to his feet.

"Clive said you went off this way. I thought we were going to show you a...Wow," she said, looking at his torn clothing and broken glasses. "What on earth happened to you?" She reached into the pocket of her shorts and pulled out a handkerchief. Jack took it gratefully, wiping the dirt off of his face. He folded the map and slid it into his back pocket. He had half a mind to stay indoors for the rest of the summer.

"I tripped on a rock," Jack said, ashamed.

"All this for a rock?"

"No," Jack said defensively, walking past Wendy to get a view of where the man had gone, but he was out of sight by now. "Some guy jumped me and stole my bag." Wendy opened her mouth to speak, but nothing came out at first.

Finally: "Who?"

"How should I know? He was kind of bald and skinny and nervous. Bony neck. Camo pants. The cats attacked him."

Wendy nodded grimly. "Those cats are smart. That guy is Mr. Perkins. He works for old man Avery—you know, his son, Clayton, is the kid who beat you up yesterday."

Jack puffed up briefly. "He did not. I just—" He wanted to say, *Beating up isn't exactly what I would call it*, but he couldn't. After all, Wendy had been there.

"Avery's awful, *awful*. What was in the bag?"

"Everything. My notebook, my drawings, some art stuff. Oh, and Uncle Clive's book. He left it in my room, and I thought I'd look through it. *The Secret*—"

"*The Secret History of Hazelwood*?" Wendy grabbed the collar of his shirt in her fist. "What were you thinking, taking that book out of the house?"

"Well," Jack said, "I mean—"

"Don't you know what's *in* that book?"

"Isn't it just—"

"You haven't *even read it*?" Wendy stood, looked down the empty street. "He hasn't even read it," she muttered to herself. "And here you just handed it to *Mr. Avery*, of *all* people. Nice work, buddy. *Nice*." She slugged him on the shoulder. "That way, right?" She pointed.

"What are you talking about?" Jack said, rubbing his shoulder. Wendy didn't look that strong, but she punched *hard*. "It's just a—" But Wendy had already taken off running. Jack pushed his way into the dense undergrowth at the edge of the woods, grabbed the skateboard, and scrambled after her. He could hear the mewling screeches of the cats echoing through the quiet town.

Jack caught up to Wendy, keeping pace with her long-legged lope, though it was difficult, since Jack was shorter. As he ran, the skateboard slid and wobbled in his sweaty hands, and despite his efforts, it slipped from his grip and fell.

"Hang on," he called to Wendy. "Let me get my—" But he didn't finish, because the moment the board touched the pavement, it began moving on its own—a straight, sure path down the street. Jack, without even planning to do so, jumped on the deck and grabbed Wendy's hand to help her on behind him. They gained speed, the wheels purring beneath their feet. Though it wasn't necessary, Jack leaned out and kicked the pavement from time to time, if for no other reason than to keep up appearances. Whether or not this seemed strange to Wendy, she didn't say.

"Oh God, he's practically there," Wendy said. Up ahead, a broad limestone building blocked the road, casting an inky shadow in their direction. The bald-headed man—*presumably*, Jack thought, *Mr. Perkins*—made several attempts to scurry up the stairs, only to be buffeted back by two snarling, spitting cats.

"Shoo," the man cried, and Jack noticed that his pants had been torn to strips, as had the skin of his legs, which bled heavily into his socks.

Serves him right, Jack thought, though he instantly felt guilty for thinking such a thing.

"Bad kitties!" Mr. Perkins yelped.

The skateboard slowed to a stop and Jack jumped off, running to the man.

"Sir," he said, "I'd like my bag back, please." One of the cats pounced on the man's back and hung on tight. He staggered toward the front door of the Exchange.

"I can call them off, you know," Jack said, though he wasn't entirely sure it was true. "Toss me the bag and say you're sorry for stealing." *Nice*, Jack congratulated himself. That, he felt, was an impressive addition.

"Don't *you* give me your lectures about *stealing*," the man said as he reached the door.

Wendy couldn't stand it anymore. She ran up the stairs and tackled him. *"Give it back, you thieving—"*

The doors flew open and two policemen, the same ones Jack had seen earlier, came running out. *Do they work in the Exchange building?* Jack wondered. *Is it really true that Mr. Avery runs everything in town?* The cats reared up and hissed at the approaching men before bounding into the shrubberies on either side of the entrance, vanishing from sight.

"Wendy," Jack gasped. "Stop it. We're going to get in so much—"

"Trouble?" one police officer said. "I'd say so."

One officer grabbed Wendy's arm while the other grabbed Jack. "We'll take these two home, Mr. Perkins. Unless you'd like to press charges."

"That won't be necessary," Mr. Perkins said loftily, brushing off his jacket and pants.

"Can I have my bag back?" Jack said, keeping his voice steady and his eyes on Mr. Perkins, who shuddered under the gaze.

Recovering himself, he turned, holding the bag tightly to his chest. "I don't know what you're talking about, young man," he said without looking at Jack. "This bag is mine."

"*Liar!*" Wendy shouted.

"That's enough, Schumacher." And Jack and Wendy, their forearms firmly grasped in the broad fists of the officers, were walked to the squad car.

As the car pulled away, Jack looked back at the stone building. Mr. Perkins stood in the open door with an unmistakably smug expression on his face. He nodded, turned, and went inside.

However, as the door slowly closed, Jack saw something that Mr. Perkins did not: the shadows of two quicksilver figures darting inside, their tails moving like whips.

Chapter Fifteen
Another Break-in

BEFORE THE POLICE DROPPED WENDY AND JACK OFF AT their respective homes, Wendy leaned close to Jack and whispered in his ear.

"*Tonight, keep your shoes on,*" she said.

"What?" asked Jack.

"No talking," said the first officer. He pulled into the Schumachers' driveway while Wendy's mom — her face set and fuming, and looking ready to ground the next person who spoke, whether kid or adult — marched toward the squad car. All four occupants in the car braced them-selves for impact. Even the officers, Jack noticed with some satisfaction, were terrified of Wendy's mom.

Jack, on the other hand, was handed over to a grim-faced Uncle Clive. Jack didn't look at him, but went upstairs and shut the door. He spent the rest of the day at his desk star-ing at the spot where his notebook should have been. With nothing to draw *on*, he just used his finger and the desktop, drawing picture after imaginary picture—a house made of eyes, a woman uncurling out of the ground, a boy who looked like a tree. Or a tree that looked like a boy. Which-ever. Each image floated in his mind's eye for a moment before wobbling, fading, and disappearing altogether.

Later, after a silent supper, Jack paced in his room. He didn't have his notebook. He didn't have the *History*. His nerves jangled and rattled, and the whole world seemed to shiver and shake. When Wendy's head popped over the windowsill, Jack nearly fainted in terror.

"Oh, for crying out loud," Wendy said. "Haven't you ever seen a person climb a trellis before?"

Actually, he *hadn't* ever seen a person climb a trellis. Jack's life, he realized with a start, had been very sheltered.

"Can you climb down?" Wendy asked.

"I don't think so."

"Then we'll have to be quiet. Did you tell your uncle?"

Jack shook his head. "No. But I think he knew. He

asked where my bag was, and I told him I had already brought it home."

"Yeah," Wendy said, throwing her sun-browned legs over the sill and jumping into the room. "He probably does. Fortunately, Mr. Avery's out of town. He hasn't seen the book yet."

"How do you know?"

"My dad works for the Exchange. Which means I also have these." She reached into the pocket of her cutoffs and pulled out a set of keys. She jingled them, giving Jack a quick, wide grin. "We'll only be gone a minute."

The Exchange was silent and dark, its employees all home with their families. All except Mr. Perkins, who had no family, making his office at the Exchange about as close to a home as he had anymore. He paced his office, sweat slicking his neck and forehead. The book lay on the desk, opened to the middle. Though he was never privy to the broad spectrum of knowledge possessed by his employer, he certainly knew this: Most of the reliable information regarding the person, substance, and power of the sleeping Lady came from the letters a certain Reverend Marcus Weihr had written more than a century earlier to Mr. Avery's great-grandfather.

While Mr. Avery had the writings and studies done by

his great-grandfather (also a Mr. Avery—a scholar by trade, and later the most powerful man that the county had ever seen), as well as *many* of the good Reverend's letters, he did not have the diary. He had looked for it, as had his father, grandfather, and great-grandfather, but to no avail. The diary was believed to be lost.

Until now.

Certainly Mr. Perkins knew that Clive Fitzpatrick was a formidable adversary with far more magic at his disposal than he ever let on, but this was better than magic. This was *smart*. Mr. Perkins carefully leafed through the pages—it wouldn't do to damage the book—and marveled at the simplicity of Clive's solution: Detach the pages, change the order, intersperse them with other writings, other artifacts, and, most crucially, encase them in a paper-thin, flexible resin. Cut, paste, and bind into a new book—and it *becomes* a new book. Which meant that in each generation of powerful and magically inclined Averys, every location spell and retrieval spell and any other spell they could think of was useless. They had been unable to locate the first half of the diary because it *didn't exist anymore*. It had become Clive Fitzpatrick's book. It was brilliant, really.

Mr. Perkins had no doubt that his boss would praise him—even reward him—for finding so valuable an object, but would he ever know what Mr. Avery knew? Or would he be forever in the dark?

When Mr. Perkins was a child, his grandmother had warned him about the wicked Lady who lived underground—a creature of power so great and so hungry as to remove a person's soul. She told him that not everyone could feel the Magic that hummed through the land and through each living thing. She said that such things ran in families—like big feet or curly hair. She told him that the Lady had Magic Children—one every half century—and that these children were marked for death, and that it was a shame, but there was nothing that anyone could do about it.

Besides, who *knew* what would happen to those children if they grew up, or what they would become? They weren't like *us*, his grandmother told him, so what did it matter? Still, it was a worry. What *if* one of the Lady's children survived? Would it be like Her? Would it steal souls too? Would it ever be satisfied?

Mr. Perkins carried rawhide every day because of his grandmother. A man's soul, after all, is no mere trifle. And he chose to work for Mr. Avery. Best to stand in the shadow of the man in charge, he thought. It's *safer*.

Still, Reginald Perkins was a curious man. How does, Perkins wondered, a man become as powerful as his employer's great-grandfather? And how does that power extend from one generation to the next? *What have the Averys been doing all these years?* He didn't know, but he had a feeling it wasn't anything *good*. And he was fairly certain that the book might give him some answers.

Mr. Perkins pulled out his sketch pad and laid it out on the desk. The copy machine was out of the question, of course. Who knew what it would do to the ancient inks, and the last thing Mr. Perkins wanted was to damage even a single page. Best do it by hand. He couldn't copy out the entire book. That would be madness. But a page or two. Maybe ten. Or even twenty. What could it hurt?

> *It is true that any damage that befalls the Lady must befall Her Other as well. They are, after all, simply different manifestations of the same Person—like a hideous and grotesque mirror. An injury to one is an injury to both, and if I were to destroy both, then the Magic would have no Guardian at all, and while the old stories are vague and unreliable, their descriptions of the disaster and desolation that follows the loss of a Guardian are not to be taken lightly. The destruction of Atlantis, then Lyonesse and Camelot—all believed to be on eruption points and all lost. I cannot allow it to happen here.*

Mr. Perkins wrote quickly, with a sure, clean hand. He wanted it to be accurate. There was no reason why he shouldn't be allowed to know just a little bit. After all, he *deserved* it.

Atop the bookshelf, two pairs of glowing yellow eyes blinked through the gloom. Sharpened claws extended and retracted and extended again. The cats were ready.

Wendy and Jack kept to the shadows. She took him to the side door that the low-level employees were required to use. The front doors were for important people. The side door was next to the Dumpsters and the recycling center. It smelled like old lunches and waterlogged paper. Jack wrinkled his nose.

"Do you even know where his office is?"

"Of course I do," Wendy said. "He's Avery's assistant. You go through Perkins's office if you want to see Mr. Avery. But no one does that unless they have to. This way."

They turned from the cracked plaster and peeling paint of the maintenance staff's rooms into a pretty hallway with limestone walls and dimly lit green lamps stationed every twenty feet.

"Why are the lights on?" Jack asked nervously.

"Probably for the security guard."

"*There's a security guard?*" Jack hissed.

"Yeah, but we don't have to worry about him. My dad knows him. Nice, but slow. Plus, he drinks." Jack couldn't help but notice the lack of assurance in her voice. "And anyway, here we are."

They peered through the glass door. Mr. Perkins's office was dark except for a single desk lamp shining down onto an open book.

"There it is," Jack whispered. "And my backpack's on the floor."

They opened the door—*Why isn't this one locked?* Jack wondered—and ran to the desk. Wendy grabbed the book and tucked it under her arm. Jack noticed a stack of writing paper lying facedown on the desk. He was just about to flip them over when he heard the unmistakable sound of a toilet flushing, a faucet running, and a bathroom door opening. Mr. Perkins appeared in the doorway, drying his hands. He dropped the paper towel onto the ground.

"*You,*" he said, pointing.

"Run for it," Wendy yelled.

Mr. Perkins rushed forward but stopped in his tracks as two alarmingly large cats leaped from the top of the bookshelf and stood in front of him, their muscled shoulders flexed and ready, their hind legs curled under their bodies, ready to pounce. He rested his hand on the desk to steady himself, curling his fingers under the edge of the small stack of papers. He picked them up and held them close to his chest as though they were a shield.

"You call your cats off," Mr. Perkins yelled. "Call them off!"

But Wendy and Jack had already burst through the door and were tearing down the empty hall. As they turned into the back corridor and headed for the door, they heard a thud, then a silence, then the scream of the attack.

Wendy hit the back door at full speed, knocking it open with a crash. Jack, a few strides behind, watched her take the steps three at a time and sprint across the square. She threw her arms up and hooted at the sky. Then she turned and smiled at Jack.

"Catch!" she called, and threw Clive's book in a clean arc. Jack ran for it.

There's a lot that can happen, Jack thought later, *between a throw and a catch.* For days after their break-in at the Exchange, he replayed the scene in his mind, trying to pinpoint the moment when the world changed. He never could.

What he did remember was this: Wendy, running in the dark, the moon and streetlamps lighting the wisps of coppery hair that had escaped the braid; Wendy, halting on her heels, pirouetting with a flourish of scratched knees and sunburned arms; Wendy calling his name and letting the book fly away.

He caught it, and the ground shuddered under his feet (*a fault line*, he told himself).

He caught it, and the air shivered with a quick breath of cold that sliced through the thick, humid air.

He caught it, and Wendy's face froze, then fell.

"What?" Jack asked. "What is it?" But the ground

under his feet still rippled and waved, and Wendy looked at him as though looking at a ghost.

"How did you do that?" she whispered. She stepped backward, nearly tripping on the sidewalk.

"Do what? Come on, Wendy, let's get out of here."

"I'll see you—" she began, taking two more steps backward. "I gotta get home." She turned and ran, disappearing into the dark.

"Wendy!" Jack called. "Wendy, come back!" But she didn't come. And Jack stepped on his skateboard and sped home, listening to the rhythmic whisper of the wheels against the long, dark road.

Chapter Sixteen
Knowing and Not Knowing

THE CATS DIDN'T STAY LONG—ONLY LONG ENOUGH TO drive a fearful Mr. Perkins under his desk and give him a nasty scratch below his eye. In a blur of silver fur they were gone.

Mr. Perkins sighed, shuddered, and crawled out from under the desk.

"Oh God," he moaned. "What will Mr. Avery say?" He mopped the sweat off his face with his hand, then reached into his pocket to grab his handkerchief. But instead of the blue hankie, heavily embroidered with moons and stars by his dear, late mother, he pulled out a small bundle of handwritten sheets of paper.

Five pages, copied by hand, from the good Reverend's diary.

"What will he say, indeed?"

Mr. Perkins smiled.

Jack never told his aunt and uncle about the theft, and while the touch and weight of the book in his hands gave him some relief, there was, still, in the pit of his stomach, a kernel of dread. And he could feel it growing.

To ease his mind, he started heading out on his skateboard every day. What was once an awkward jumble of arms and legs barely balanced on four wheels was now an exercise in speed and fluidity. He moved easily from one end of the town to the other, going so fast and smooth, he felt he might be flying. Jack carried the book with him everywhere — sometimes in his backpack but more often tucked into his pants, with the belt cinched tightly. He read it faithfully now, often taking notes, and always sketching as he read.

This part was written by Clive himself, in his spidery, slanted script, on page 309:

In the center of the world, where the wide land spreads itself to meet the wider sky, there lived two Ladies, one good and one bad, each one hard at work spinning a magical cloth. Each morning, the good Lady gathered thread made from the excesses of joy. She gathered the shimmering remains of dreams, the debris of abundant hope, and the happy cries of children, echoing across the prairie. Her cloth was beautiful, but the work was painstaking and slow.

The wicked Lady, on the other hand, thought it was easier to lay traps for men, women, and children in the tall grass. She waited until they cried out in fear and pain, and offered to comfort them with a kiss. She took their souls as payment for their freedom and cast them aside as empty husks. Quickly, Her cloth grew in length and beauty. Only a few more feet, *thought She,* and I shall have enough cloth to cover the hill, the field, the land, and the wide, wide world.

In his own notebook, Jack wrote:

1. *Clive thinks that people disappear. So does this Reverend guy. And that...something takes their souls. (Probably not true. Maybe people leave out of sheer boredom.)*

2. *People keep attack cats. Are there attack cats in San Francisco?*

3. *Mr. Avery's in charge of...everything. And no one likes him. How does he get all that power? What does he have that no one else does? (Clive and Mr. Reverend Guy would say magic. But they're nuts. What is it really?)*

4. *When someone is split into a good half and a bad half, does that mean the person's brain is cut in half too?*

5. *This town makes me itch.*

That last one was becoming more troublesome by the day. It started as a mild irritation at the back of his neck and forearms. Now Jack itched all over. It was as though his skin had suddenly transformed into an infernally hot and scratchy wool sweater—a gift from a relative, perhaps, that he was obligated to wear. In any case, it seemed as though his skin was not his skin anymore, that his body was trying to be something...else. And he didn't know what. And it irked him.

It didn't help Jack's growing sense of discomfort that, for days after the break-in, he saw Mr. Perkins hurrying past him on a bicycle. Each time, Jack instinctively darted away, his skateboard easily outpacing the bike, but still he had the distinct impression that Mr. Perkins was laughing at him. That Mr. Perkins knew something that Jack did not.

But *Jack*, and not Mr. Perkins, had the book. That had to count for something — Jack was sure of it. Mostly sure anyway.

What do you know? Jack wanted to shout. He had already checked every page, and it didn't look as though anything had been ripped out. Still, Mr. Perkins had read *something* to make him this happy. And Jack was going to figure out what it was.

Mr. Perkins, Jack noticed, left the Exchange at ten o'clock every morning and rode his bicycle past the park toward a large, beautiful mansion right next door to the college campus. On the fifth day of watching the man go by, Jack decided to follow him. There was a tangled hedge that separated the park from the row of houses on its eastern side, and Jack crawled in, crouched down, and waited. The branches pressed around him gently, and though they looked like they might scratch and cut his skin, Jack was surprised at how soft they were. The leaves breathed as he breathed. He watched the road. Mr. Perkins paused his bicycle when he reached the park, planted one foot on the ground, and scanned the grounds. Jack held his breath. The branches of the hedge seemed to curl around him just a little bit tighter, shielding him from view.

"Hello!" Mr. Perkins called.

Why is he looking for me? Jack wondered.

"Only cowards and sneaks hide," Mr. Perkins yelled in a higher, squeakier voice. Tough words, Jack thought, from the guy who had worn camouflage clothing while following him.

Mr. Perkins reached into his pocket, pulled out a small brown strap, and stroked his face with it before kicking at the pavement and pedaling down the street. Jack eased his body out of the hedge (Was it his imagination, or did the branches seem to hang on to his arms and legs? Did the leaves curl themselves on the curve of his skin?), dropped his skateboard on the ground, and followed him.

The skateboard noiselessly skimmed the road without so much as a push from Jack, eclipsing the distance between him and the peddling Mr. Perkins. Jack tried dragging his foot on the ground, but he continued to pick up speed. The mansion at the end of the road—Mr. Avery's house, according to the map his uncle had given him—loomed closer and closer.

"Slow down," he pleaded. "Slow down." But the skateboard did not slow down, and if Jack didn't do something soon, he'd hit the bicycle's back wheel. Thinking fast, he stepped hard on the back deck, tipping the board up and sending sparks flying behind. He leaped off lightly, caught the board in mid-spin under his arm, and hid behind a parked car. Mr. Perkins paused and turned, but too late. Jack was already hidden. Mr. Perkins stood in front of the mansion at the end of the road and waited.

A very old, very rusty station wagon pulled to a halt, and a tall, well-dressed man stepped out, his lips curling in distaste. He brushed his hands along his suit, as though trying to wipe away dirt and germs.

"*Perkins!*" he roared.

"I'm right here, sir," Mr. Perkins said, letting the bicycle topple to the ground and holding out the manila envelope. "Welcome home, welcome home! We have been lost without you, sir, utterly lost. I'm sure you simply *forgot* to leave your itinerary with us, but I will say I had quite the time trying to rearrange your meetings when I didn't know—"

"ENOUGH!" Mr. Avery roared. "I have no interest in your petulance, Perkins."

"Of course, of course, sir. It's just that we've had a bit of a breakthrough, and I have been anxious to share my findings with you. I have something that I *believe* you will find—"

"Quit prattling. Just give me the information and be done with it."

"Of course, sir, it's just that we have, I believe, access to a veritable treasure trove of—"

"Oh, for God's sake, Perkins, go inside. No. Scratch that. Get my bags, then go inside. Make yourself useful. And should I ever require the use of your automobile again, I would appreciate it if you'd invest in a new one. Your car stinks." He waved his hand in front of his nose to demonstrate the point and went inside.

"Of course, of course," Mr. Perkins continued, even though the other man was gone. "I'd just like to direct your attention to these pages that I've copied—sir? Sir? From the book?" Mr. Perkins sighed, slumped his shoulders, and pulled the bundle of papers from his coat pocket. "Right here, sir," he said to the open doorway. "From the Reverend Weihr's diary."

"What did you say?" Mr. Avery's voice came from the inside of the house.

"The diary, sir. I managed to—"

"*Get in this house right now, you blithering idiot, before someone sees you!*" Mr. Avery roared. Two hands emerged from the doorway, grabbed Mr. Perkins by the shoulders, and hauled him inside.

Jack stood.

Copied pages? That can't be good. He shivered, turned, and was about to skate away when he heard the sound of someone crying. The voice hiccuped and sniffled and sobbed.

"Hello?" Jack said.

The crying continued, and the person crying didn't seem to hear him. Instead, whoever it was, was saying something in between the sobs. "Make it stop, make it stop, make it stop," the voice said. Jack picked up his skateboard and crept around the side of the house.

A boy was seated on a basketball, his head on his knees, his hands pressed against his ears.

"Clayton?" Jack said, realizing from the beefy back and muscled arms who the boy was. "Clayton, are you all right?" *What are you doing, Jack?* he admonished himself.

To be honest, he wasn't sure. Still, it didn't seem right to just walk away.

Clayton sat up with a start. His face was blotchy and wet, and his ears were bright red. "What do you want?" he said.

Jack stepped backward. "Nothing. I just heard you were...I mean, I noticed that you were..."

"No, I wasn't." Clayton wiped his eyes and nose with the backs of his hands.

"No, you weren't what?" Jack asked.

"Crying," Clayton said with a sniff.

"Oh," Jack said. "Okay."

"And anyway, what are you doing here? This is *my* yard." He said the word *my* with a certain relish that made Jack's skin crawl. What was it that Clive's book had said? That the word *mine* had a special significance...or something. Jack couldn't remember.

"I'm not—I mean, I was just—"

"You were spying, weren't you?" Clayton took two short, aggressive steps forward.

"No, I just—"

"You *were*. My mom *said* you would. I *knew* you would!"

"No, you see, I only wanted—" Jack started, but seeing the look on Clayton's face, decided that it would be better to turn and run away. Once he hit the street, he jumped onto the skateboard.

"Oh, you are so *dead*," Clayton said, but Jack was

already flying. After two blocks, he turned back to see if the other boy was following him. Clayton Avery stood in the middle of the road, perfectly still, framed on either side by the massive house behind him. For a moment, Jack had the distinct impression that the house was bearing down on the boy, or that the ground beneath him was bubbling up, that Clayton stood in the middle of two things that wanted nothing better than to swallow him whole.

"Clayton," Jack called, "*be careful.*"

"Whatever, loser," Clayton called back. He turned, ran into the house, and slammed the door.

Chapter Seventeen
The Schoolhouse

THE NEXT DAY, JACK WENT BACK TO THE PARK AND SAT down on the bare ground, Clive's book on his lap and his notebook open at his side. Mr. Perkins, as far as Jack knew, hadn't left the Avery house. His bike was still on the ground, and the car—the one that, according to Mr. Avery, stank—hadn't moved from its spot on the street, in front of the Avery house. Jack checked again and again—his office shades at the Exchange were drawn and the lights out, even during business hours. Just the thought of the smirk on the little man's face made Jack sweaty and anxious. At the top of the page he had written *WHAT DOES HE KNOW?* Under that he wrote *AND WHAT DOES HE THINK HE KNOWS?* And under that he wrote, in very small letters, *I have absolutely no idea.*

Jack sighed and turned the page.

He flipped until he found another page of the Reverend Weihr's diary.

"*It is my belief,*" Jack read out loud, "*that the Professor used cunning and trickery and convinced Her that the swap of one son for the other would be reversible. I don't believe that She intended the destruction of either the Magic Child or the Avery boy. But the Magic broke and surged, and both boys were swallowed up. And in that horrible moment when She realized what She had done, Her heart split in two, and She split in two — Her Wickedness and Her Goodness divided into two separate beings. And the consequences, I fear, will span the generations.*

"*The Lady bears a single Magic Child for every human generation. Would the Averys be so heartless to perform this swap again in the future? Would they do it forever? And what of the Lady's children? Her wicked half will sacrifice them, again and again, in order to stay stronger than Her good half. So many lives will be lost if I do not intervene!*"

Jack sighed and scratched at his neck. It was getting worse, and he would have liked nothing better than to pull his skin all the way off and shake it out. Or leave it off forever. "I don't understand any of this," he said out loud. Though if he was talking about the book, or the bizarre behavior of Mr. Perkins, or the itching, or the strange hot-and-cold house, Jack wasn't sure. He wasn't sure about anything anymore.

And this story...Jack wouldn't say it was *true*. Not *yet*. Still, the idea of a power surge when a magical being was split in half. It didn't sound entirely implausible. If he were a person who *believed* in magic. Which he *wasn't*. Still, not too long ago he had read a book about the making of the atom bomb—how a tiny atom could release unthinkable power when split in two. Could the same be true of a creature made of magic? A magic Guardian? Could he *believe* such a thing?

He supposed it was *possible*. If he believed in magic, that is.

Which he—

"Ready, Jack?" a voice said. Jack looked up, startled. Wendy, Anders, and Frankie stood around him, their bodies silhouetted by the wide blue sky.

"Where did you three come from?" Jack asked. "And how did you know I was here?"

Wendy shrugged. "Anders had a feeling. Don't ask me how—it's just his thing." Anders grinned, picked up the skateboard, and handed it to Jack. "Found the one grassy spot, did you?"

"What?" Jack asked. He looked down. He could have sworn that he had only been sitting on bare ground, but now the spot where his body had been was a lush circle of green grass, with a few small violets winking shyly in the shadows. "How did that—um—" Jack stammered.

130

"Yeah, I guess." He changed the subject. "Ready for what exactly?" He looked up at Wendy and narrowed his eyes. Given that he didn't really know what it was like to have friends, Jack didn't realize until that very moment that he had missed Wendy and that he had been very lonely for the last few days. In truth, he reasoned, he had probably always been lonely—for as long as he could remember—but he'd never really noticed it before.

"You've been *avoiding* me." His voice was tight, accusatory, and it shamed him. He cleared his throat.

Wendy took in a sharp breath. "Have not."

"I mean, whatever. It's fine. It's just that I thought... I mean, at home I don't have very many..." His voice trailed off. Jack felt his cheeks heat up, and he wanted to slink away.

"Fine," Wendy said. "I *have* been avoiding you. Happy? And, you know"—she looked at the ground—"I feel bad about it, I really do. Things are weird lately, you know? Plus, my mom is super mad at me. But I'm here now. You ready?" She didn't look at him straight in the face but took his hand instead, gave a quick, firm tug to pull him to his feet, and started walking without waiting for an answer.

"For what?"

"We wanted to show you something," she said, tugging his arm again. She didn't let go of his hand.

Jack tried to swallow, but he found, to his surprise,

that every drop of moisture had been suddenly sucked out of his mouth. Wendy's hand felt hot and dry against his own cold, clammy palm. There had never, ever in his life been a moment when a girl had thought to take his hand. Even his mother wasn't a hand-holding sort. Or, if she used to be, she certainly never was with Jack.

After a few steps, Jack felt that the entire universe had somehow compressed into the space between his skin and Wendy's skin, which, he decided, wasn't saying much about the capacity of the universe. After fifteen paces, Jack started to panic. How long, he wondered, was this supposed to last? Would he have to hold her hand forever? An uncomfortable trickle of sweat curled down his neck and slipped along the groove of his spine. He wondered whether it was the humidity, though somehow he doubted it.

Finally, he couldn't stand it. He snatched his hand back and shoved it into his pocket. "I need to tell you something," he said quickly. "It's about that book."

Jack explained Mr. Perkins's daily bike ride from the Exchange to the mansion down the road, and his infuriatingly self-satisfied smirk. He told them about the arrival of Mr. Avery—that Mr. Perkins didn't seem to know where he had gone or even how long he was going to be gone *for*—and about the copied pages. But he didn't tell them about Clayton Avery crying in the backyard. It seemed rude, somehow.

Wendy folded her arms as worry creased deeply into her forehead. Anders puffed his cheeks, let his breath hiss across his teeth, and shook his head.

"That can't be good," she said. "You don't know which pages he copied?"

Jack shrugged. "There's no way of knowing. He didn't take anything *out* of the book, if that's what you're asking." He glanced at Wendy and Anders, feeling defensive and ashamed all at once. "I mean, I checked."

"You've read it?" Wendy asked. "The whole thing?"

"No, not all," Jack said. "Just parts. Some of the handwriting is hard to read, you know? What about you?"

She nodded. "The same. Just parts. Some when I was pretty little, so it gets jumbly in my head. Anders, maybe we should forget about today." She put her arm around Frankie's shoulders. "Maybe I should take him home. It's just that I...I don't like this. I wouldn't want...It's just that we don't know..." She grimaced.

Frankie rested his head, bad side down, on Wendy's shoulder. He smiled vaguely at Jack. Or next to Jack. Frankie's eyes were two different colors, one blue and one brown. Jack wondered why he hadn't noticed before. Also, with the scars mostly hidden from view, Jack noticed how very, very similar their faces were—as though Wendy was a girl version of Frankie and vice versa. Except Wendy didn't have mismatched eyes, and Jack wondered vaguely if Frankie had been born that way.

Then Frankie winked. Right at Jack. He raised his eyebrows once, then went back to swaying back and forth with a dreamy expression on his face.

"Hey—" Jack began.

"It's all right, Wendy," Anders said soothingly, slipping his hand around Wendy's free elbow and easing her forward. She released Frankie. "We have some time. He should see the schoolhouse. Frankie will be with us. Jack has Clive's book right there. Everything will be fine." He jerked his head toward Jack and Frankie, indicating that they should follow.

"I have notes," Jack said helpfully, but Anders and Wendy didn't seem to hear him. Jack trotted faster, trying to keep up.

Jack sneaked a few glances at Frankie, who didn't glance back. He just hummed and wavered. He hardly seemed to know where he was. And yet he followed Wendy and Anders without being told and didn't wander off. *What exactly is* wrong *with that kid anyway?* Jack wondered.

Frankie didn't make eye contact after that, and Jack wondered whether he just imagined the wink.

There were more people outside than there had been on the day that Jack arrived. A few cars whizzed by; heavily laden trucks hauled supplies to the stores on Main Street; there were even some other kids. But no one stopped and said hello to the Schumachers or Anders. Or Jack, for that matter. In fact, twice Jack noticed someone crossing the street and continuing on their way. The others didn't mention it, so he didn't either.

They walked down the road to where the line of grizzled trees separated the eastern edge of the town from the fields. A little way off they could see the old school, a dilapidated building no larger than a garage, almost a mile outside of town. Faded red paint flaked slowly from the graying exterior planks, while the whole structure leaned slightly eastward on its river rock foundation. Raspberry bramble, dotted everywhere with fat pink buds, tangled wildly all around, as though trying to cover it up, like a quilt.

"Is it just me," Wendy asked, "or does it look different?"

"Roof is lower," Anders said, adjusting his hat as he appraised the building. "Probably not safe to go in there today."

Jack hugged his arms to his chest, and the hairs on the back of his neck stood on end. *Don't be ridiculous*, he told himself. *There's nothing here that can hurt you.* The ancient structure seemed to swell and retract with each surge of wind, as though it were breathing.

"It was supposed to have been torn down fifty years ago," Anders explained.

"Why wasn't it?"

"Honestly, I think people forget that it's here. My grandpa went to school here. Said that kids would disappear sometimes. Just vanish, like they'd never been there in the first place. Course, my grandma said that was a bunch of hooey, and she'd never even heard of any of those people. She said it was the corn whiskey talking."

"Was it?" Jack asked.

Anders shrugged. "*Maybe*. But I doubt it. My grandpa said that some people are more"—he searched for the word—"'*sensitive*.' That certain people notice the weird stuff when most folks don't. He said it was like living in a town full of colorblind people and trying to explain the color blue. So, he noticed people vanishing, and noticed that their memories seemed to fade away. No pictures, no funerals, no nothing. It was like they'd never existed. Though, he also, it's true, loved corn whiskey. So who knows?"

Jack narrowed his eyes and regarded Anders critically. Anders had broad hands that were turned open as he spoke, as though he were praying. His wide, happy face was intent and honest as he told his story. If it were anyone else, Jack would have assumed that it was a trick, one of those where someone tries to get the new kid so scared that he cries or—even better—pees. But Anders, Jack thought, was not that kind of kid.

"So," Jack said hesitantly, because he did not want to hurt Anders's feelings. "You really believe that?" He checked himself. "I mean, what do you think?"

Anders shrugged. So did Wendy.

"Folks talk about eruption points, you know? That

there's...something. Underground. Magic or power or life or whatever. And it sort of bulges up and leaks out."

"What," Jack said. "Like a pimple?"

"*No*," Wendy said derisively. "Not like a *pimple*."

Anders thought for a minute. "Actually, yeah. Kind of like that. Anyway, it's not that big of a deal if the stuff leaking out is used for good things — making farms grow or cows give milk or helping the lambs when they're born. People've been using all kinds of charms and tricks for stuff like that since forever. But sometimes good things can get turned around by bad people, you know? Like your skateboard is *good* unless you decide to whack someone on the head with it. Then it's bad. Do you understand?"

Jack shrugged. "Sort of." He paused. "So you mean to tell me that you...both of you...believe in—"

"Magic?" Anders said with a grin. "You would, too, Jack, if you lived here." Anders paused a minute to think that over. "Actually, who knows? Not everyone notices. My grandpa used to say that it ran in families. Like having green eyes or double-jointed thumbs or something."

Frankie smiled and bent to the ground, picking up a few pebbles, each no bigger than a dime. He walked up to the school. He started to climb the rotting stairs toward the doorless entrance that stood wide open like a surprised mouth. He took the pebble and tossed it inside. They heard it tap on the floor. He turned and looked at

Jack. Or, Jack thought, he looked *near* him. In any case, Jack noticed that Frankie had just pulled something out of his pocket—something round and vaguely shiny—and shoved it back in again. He turned to the schoolhouse and took a step forward.

"Frankie, stop it," Wendy said, pressing her lips into a thin line.

"I do believe," Anders said to Jack, "but it's okay with me if you don't. Most people don't. Or, at least they say they don't."

Jack shoved his hands into his pockets, thinking of the handmade book in his backpack. "Yeah," he said, turning his eyes away from Anders and surveying the fields and the sky. "I kind of gathered that. Anyone disappear in there lately?"

"Well, not for a while. Wendy and I've been there a bunch of times and we're fine. But it's like something's asleep, you know. Been like that ever since—" He waved toward Frankie with a jerk of his chin.

Frankie stood on the top landing and launched three more pebbles. Two taps sounded. He took a step closer to the door.

"Him?" Jack asked. "So what happened to—"

"*Frankie*," Wendy said sharply. "Don't go in there." Frankie stood just inside the doorway. It seemed to Jack that the entire structure sagged a little more, as though it were hugging Frankie in toward itself. Frankie didn't seem to notice. He walked slowly into the front cloakroom, its old metal hooks glinting strangely in the low light. He turned, and Jack could have sworn the boy looked *right at* him. Jack squinted. Frankie was deeply shadowed and difficult to see. But Jack *thought* he saw Frankie reach into his pocket and pull something out. He extended his arm to the archway separating the cloakroom from the classroom, and, with a shudder, he *disappeared*.

No, Jack told himself. *He just stepped into the shadow.*

Wendy stood on the first step. "Frankie," she said, more loudly now, her voice sounding like a big sister's, though, in truth, she was only fifteen minutes older, which isn't enough to count. The stair under her feet cracked suddenly, sending up gray-brown clouds of dust and dirt around her feet. She nimbly hopped to the third step, which collapsed immediately, sending her down through broken wood to the ground. Anders and Jack ran to either side of the old wooden stair, held out their hands, but she ignored them. She righted herself, stood her ground, and looked up into the darkened hole where her brother hid.

"Franklin James," she shouted, "come here right now or I'm telling Mom." There was no answer. She looked to Anders. "Can you give me a boost? I'll get him out of there myself."

"I don't think you should go in there," Anders said, eyeing the roof and the bulging walls.

"And I don't think you should be telling me what to do," Wendy said with an upward tilt of her sharp chin, her hair streaming away from her body like a flag. She looked as though she should be holding a sword, leading an army, or killing a dragon. With one quick motion, Wendy grabbed the edge of the top stair and kicked her feet up and around, scrambling gracelessly to the top landing. She crouched there, looking in, moving slowly as though afraid to move too fast and fall through again.

"Frankie," she said quietly into the dusty silence. "Come on now." Her voice was hushed, barely a whisper. "You guys, I can't see him in there."

"Maybe he's hiding," Jack said.

"Where? It's just a room. Four walls, four corners. There's nowhere to hide." She stood, grasping the flaking trim of the old door just in case. "Frankie," she called. "Frankie!" Her voice scratched the sides of the walls, sent breezes flooding into the old schoolhouse and rushing out the gaping entrance. And, from behind them, the sound of someone laughing.

"Who is that?" Jack asked, turning around. "Is that Frankie? Wendy, I think he snuck out and he's back... *there* somewhere." He waved his arms toward the green field. Nothing moved. "I swear I heard something."

"Yeah," Anders said, peering across the road. "Me too."

Crack. The roof shivered and drooped. A whoosh of dust fell from the outside walls and out through the doorway. Wendy rubbed her bare arms. "It's cold in there," she said. "Why is it cold?"

"Wendy," Anders said. "Get out. Now. The roof is sagging even more." Another crack. And a long, slow sigh.

"Frankie's hiding," Wendy said, her voice steady and toneless, as though dreaming. "I just have to find him and then we can go."

"Wendy," Anders said, "listen to me. Frankie isn't in there. You don't see him and there's nowhere to hide in there. I don't know how he got out without us seeing, but he did, and, well, that's Frankie for you, isn't it."

Dry wood snapped and squeaked. More dust poured from the glassless windows and doorless door.

"I'm just going to check—"

"No, Wendy!" Anders and Jack yelled together.

The building cracked again. Anders jumped up on the disintegrating stairs, grabbed Wendy by the arm, and pulled her onto the grass. She screamed. The schoolhouse closed in on itself, like a hand rearing into a fist before punching. The roof buckled and curled, and the sides shivered and crumpled down like an accordion left on its side. All that was left was the doorless entrance, the post and lintel red with peeling paint, dust pouring out of its open mouth.

Chapter Eighteen
More Secrets

JACK, WENDY, AND ANDERS STARED AT THE CLOUD OF DUST that had been, just a moment before, a schoolhouse. Wendy scrambled out of Anders's grip, scraping her knees on the gravel.

"Frankie!" she screamed. She turned to Anders and grabbed a handful of his shirt, giving him a good shake. "Get him out of there," she ordered.

"But," Jack said reasonably, "he wasn't in there. You said so yourself."

"Well," she said, rounding on Jack. "Where was he,

then?" Her face blazed and Jack squinted. He felt himself crumple in front of her, like a piece of tissue paper that's too close to a very hot fire.

"I dunno," he mumbled. "Sounded like there was *someone* somewhere behind us." Or in front. Or underneath. Whatever. Another thing that defied any kind of explanation. *Nothing in this town makes any sense*, Jack thought, rubbing madly at the back of his neck. Everything itched. He tried desperately not to think about it.

"It doesn't matter where he was," Anders said, putting a hand on each of Wendy's shoulders and turning her away from the schoolhouse. He got her to walk back toward the road. "We can't get him out by ourselves, even if he *is* in there. Jack, do you think you can find your aunt's shop on your own?"

Jack fished in his pocket to see if the map that Clive had drawn for him was still there. It was. He opened it up and saw the old man's neat little drawings of the house, the college, Wendy and Frankie's house, and the gallery. There was even a little picture of the schoolhouse. Underneath were the words *Don't go here*.

"Ah," said Jack. "Yeah, I can find it."

"Good. Then run. Tell her what happened. She'll know what to do. Wendy and I will go get her mom."

Jack ran. He ran past houses with little old ladies sitting on front porches and yards where little kids played jump rope and hopscotch. It seemed to him that everything moved in slow motion. It seemed to him that the whole town was staring at him. It seemed to him that everyone *knew* that Frankie had somehow vanished from a creepy, collapsing building and, worse, that no one really cared. And suddenly it was as though the world was made from molasses or glue and was slowing imperceptibly to a stop.

Even without the map, Jack would not have had a problem finding the gallery. Aunt Mabel's gallery was not one to blend in. It was neither nondescript nor ordinary.

The gallery announced itself.

The windows had been painted with twisting vines and heavy blossoms, while the door broadly declared THE FAERIE QUEENE in elegant, curved lettering that glinted gold in the sun. He threw open the door and ran inside.

A man stood in front of his aunt. A very tall, very broad man who had to stoop to look her in the eye. His arm extended toward her, and a long, pale finger pointed. Jack stopped in his tracks. He had a wild notion to push the man down, make him point that finger somewhere else.

He knew exactly who the man was. Jack had seen him squeeze out of Mr. Perkins's awful car and head into the nicest house in town. Mr. Avery. Jack shuddered.

"I'll give you a week, Mrs. Fitzpatrick." The man's voice was rough and without kindness. "One week and that's it. After that, you're going to wish that you had taken my offer."

Aunt Mabel smiled sweetly. "I'll keep that in mind. Thank you so much for stopping by, Mr. Avery."

Jack stood still, watching his aunt. Though her voice, as usual, was warm and sweet and comforting as good food, her eyes glinted, sharp as knives. Jack told himself to never, ever make Aunt Mabel mad.

The man turned to walk out and saw Jack for the first time. "You!" His eyes went momentarily wide and livid before narrowing into two thin slits. "You, young man, while you are"—he cleared his throat—"*with us*, you will stay away from my boy. He has nothing whatsoever to do with you."

Jack stepped backward. "Um," he said, his voice wavering. "Hello, sir. It's…nice to actually meet you."

The man pinched his mouth into a tight downward hook and flared his nostrils, as though to let Jack know that *nice* would be the last word he would ever use to describe this meeting. He strode to the door, his polished shoes clicking crisply against the wood floor, and he was gone.

Mabel pressed her hands flat on the long counter and closed her eyes. For the first time, Jack noticed that she looked old. Also for the first time, he noticed that someone else was in the room.

"Frankie?" he said, his mouth open in disbelief.

Mabel looked up. Instantly, the tired expression fell away as her face curved into a smile. "Yes, he likes to show up now and again." She sat heavily on the rocking chair positioned next to the cash register, and sighed. Frankie crossed the room and stood next to Mabel. He laid his hand on her shoulder and fixed his mild eyes on Jack. For a moment, even though his lips didn't move, Jack felt as though Frankie were speaking. But he couldn't understand a word of it.

"What is it, Frankie?" Jack asked, utterly exasperated, but the moment was gone. Frankie was just Frankie once again.

"He is my big helper around here," Mabel said. "Some days I don't know what I would do without—" The door opened, swung so hard it hit the opposing wall with a rattle and a clunk. Wendy rushed in with a woman who Jack assumed must be her mother.

"Oh, thank God," the woman breathed, and strode across the room, enveloping Frankie in a bone-crushing hug. Frankie still managed to peer through the nook between her neck and shoulder, to peer directly at Jack, who was starting to feel slightly unnerved.

"Mrs. Fitzpatrick," Anders said. "It was the schoolhouse. It...collapsed."

"Again?" Mabel turned quite pale. "Was there anyone..." She gulped. "Is anyone..." She couldn't continue.

"Frankie was inside," Anders said. "And then he was gone. And we thought..." He stared at Mabel, who had gone from pale to quite gray. "But nothing...*bad* happened, you know?" He glanced nervously at Wendy, who was staring hard at her brother and didn't notice.

He seems more worried about Wendy than Frankie, Jack

thought. *In fact, he's not that worried about Frankie at all. I wonder why.*

Mabel stood. "Tea," she said with a shaky finality, and Mrs. Schumacher nodded. While Mabel poured from the pot under an embroidered towel, she motioned for Mrs. Schumacher to sit in the rocker.

"It's not that hot, I'm afraid, but it will do. I had a feeling I would need some a little bit ago, but Mr. Avery paid me a rather unpleasant visit and my sense of timing is all off."

Mrs. Schumacher didn't sit, but insisted that Frankie sit down instead. Kneeling in front of him, she inspected his eyes, his ruined face, and his palms. She peered into each ear as though looking for explosives, felt his forehead, and checked his pulse.

"You," she said to her son, her voice a fierce combination of exasperation and worry and love, "are going to give me a heart attack. You hear me, young man? You are *killing your mother.*" She shook her head, ruffled his hair, and kissed him loudly on his bad cheek. "You're a good boy, Frankie. Most of the time." She turned to Mabel. "You got anything stronger than cream for that tea?"

Wendy crouched down on a painted stool that Jack thought must be for sale and laid her forehead on her knees, shaking slightly. Jack walked over and, feeling that he should be doing something but not really sure what that something should be, gave her a little pat on the shoulder. He considered saying something on the lines of "there, there," but, fortunately, Wendy, in a violent jerk of her shoulder, forced his hand away.

"I'm not crying," she said, her red eyes pouring out tears. Jack looked over to Anders, who shrugged.

"Okay," Jack said.

Mabel glided over with a plate of cookies and told them to grab a pop from the fridge if they felt like it. Wendy claimed she wasn't thirsty, but Anders said, "Come on, now, Wendy," and helped her up by her elbow. Wendy continued to sniffle.

Frankie stared at Jack. Not next to. Not above. He stared at Jack full in the face, his mismatched eyes boring into Jack's head. Frankie reached into his pocket and pulled something out, held tightly in a closed fist. Jack raised his eyebrows, and Frankie nodded his head ever so slightly. Jack walked over to the rocking chair and leaned down. Frankie took Jack's hand and placed something hard and heavy and warm into his palm, closing the fingers around it. It felt like a rock. Stretching upward, he put his lips next to Jack's ear.

"*Don't lose it*," Frankie whispered, clearly and audibly. Jack nearly fell down.

"Wha—Ouch!" Jack began, but Frankie pinched him hard on the arm.

"What was that, dear?" Aunt Mabel said from the back room.

Frankie pursed his lips, his eyes wide and pleading.

"N-nothing, Aunt Mabel," Jack said. "Nothing at all." Without taking his eyes off Frankie, he put the object in his pocket. Frankie nodded and gave a grim smile. He jerked his head toward the back room, where the others gathered and drank and looked meaningfully at Jack. Slowly, Frankie's mouth began to form silent words.

Don't tell.

Chapter Nineteen
Normal. Or Not.

THAT EVENING, JACK ATE HIS DINNER ON HIS OWN IN HIS ROOM while his aunt and uncle were at the neighbors' to meet with a lawyer about...well, Jack wasn't sure. Something about the house. Jack hoped they'd see a contractor, too, because the house was moving more and more each day. It swayed and shivered so much that cracks were starting to form on the ceiling and walls, and the doorways heated almost to burning every time he laid his hand on the trim.

"You've got bad wiring, I think," he had told his aunt

and uncle before they left. "It's a miracle we haven't gone up in flames. Or been crushed by the roof."

Clive and Mabel smiled mildly, and Mabel kissed him on both cheeks.

"Jack, honey, I think it would be best if you didn't answer the door while we were out," Mabel said.

"When has anyone come to the door?" Jack asked. And now that he thought about it, it was rather odd. The only people who had visited since he arrived in Iowa were him and his mother and Wendy. But Wendy came in through the window. Didn't Clive and Mabel have any *friends*, Jack wondered.

"And, additionally, son," Clive added, "I think we'd like you to stay close to home. No more night wanderings. Your mother wouldn't forgive us if—"

He shook his head. "My mother wouldn't notice." And before they could respond, he turned, hurried back upstairs, and shut the door of his room to keep out the bird and the cats.

The windows were open wide as the sun went down and breezes blew in—hot, heavy, and sweet—in waves. The vines outside the window had completely broken through the screen and had tumbled into the room, spreading in all directions on the wall. They snaked across the floor under the bed and sketched shapes along the ceiling. Jack supposed he should do something about it, but he liked the growing green in the room. It made the house's strange quirks seem more…*normal*, somehow.

He leaned back on his pillows, opened Clive's book on his lap, and laid his notebook next to him on the bed.

Clive wanted me to read the book, he wrote in his journal. *And I did. Mostly. And after what I saw today … well, parts of it might not be … completely made up. But what does this story have to do with me? Professor Avery — a grandfather to Mr. Avery? a great-grandfather? — obviously, being a scary bully runs in the family. But I'm nobody.*

Jack shivered and itched. It was getting worse, the itching, and while he never saw any bumps or rashes, his skin was red all the time from his constant rubbing. He looked down at the open book. It was another page from the Reverend's diary, this one dated 1854.

> *What happened to the child? Dear God, after all these months, the question remains lodged in my heart like a sliver of ice!*
>
> *Professor Avery, along with his young son and his colleagues, stayed with me for several weeks, asking about the Lady who lives underground—in Her World-Under-the-World. I told them that She is the Guardian of the Magic, but further than that, I did not know. Was She fairy or angel or god? It was a mystery. What I did know was that for a creature of power, the choice to do good is its own kind of magic.*

They took samples and measurements and spent long hours combing through the pages of my journals. They were particularly interested in the incident following the loss of Her son—the child in the acorn cradle. We discussed my theory about a magical swap—the power of the words mine *and* yours *on an eruption point. God help me! I did not know!*

I watched them leave at dawn and go down to the gap at the bottom of the gully. Not two hours later, the sky turned black and a column of light shot up from the center of the bluff. A storm blew in, the likes of which I'd never seen, and the world shook. Then, instead of one column, there were two—a column of light and a column of darkness. And suddenly the storm ceased.

The men returned without Professor Avery's young son.

—Where is the boy? *I asked. The men smiled—and, oh! How my blood ran cold!*

—What boy? *they said, their mouths curling into wolfish grins.* There has never been a boy.

Jack hunched his shoulders, his eyes straining to read the fragile lettering in the half-darkness. He could hear his aunt and uncle returning—their slow footsteps, their murmuring voices. The sun, having only just set, wrung out color and dying light across the wide, cloudless sky. The room was still hot, and Jack paused every once in a while to fish out an ice cube from the glass on the windowsill and rub a cool slick across his forehead, on the back of his neck, and up and down his arms. San Francisco, he knew, would be cool and foggy and damp, and he wondered why he had never appreciated it before.

Is it possible that this story is—He stopped his pencil. He couldn't bring himself to write *true*. He gripped the pencil in his fist and pulled it away from the paper, as though it might write of its own accord. He slammed the book shut and dropped it with a thud on the ground. The floorboards vibrated with the impact and hiccuped under his feet.

"You should be nicer to that book," a voice said right behind him. "It's delicate." Jack jumped. He felt his voice snatch in his throat. He turned around. Wendy sat on the sill of the opposite window. Her hair was unbraided and fell lightly down her neck. Her face was reddened and hot. She balanced her elbows on her knees and leaned forward. "What's with the vines?"

Jack's voice turned to sand in his mouth. "Nothing," he managed to sputter. "How long have you been watching me?"

Wendy shrugged. "A while." Jack walked over to the

window and looked down. It was sickeningly high—at least for climbing. An orange-and-pink rose bush climbed up that side of the house on a white trellis. The air smelled sweet and heavy and good, and whether it was from the rose bush or from Wendy herself, Jack couldn't tell. He felt his breath constrict in his chest and took two quick steps back while nervously rubbing the back of his neck.

"Are there any thorns?"

Wendy showed him her hands. They were scratched and bleeding. "Yep," she said. "I want to show you something. Your aunt and uncle are downstairs in the kitchen, so the front door's out. Want to try to climb down? It's pretty easy."

Actually, he was pretty sure he *couldn't* climb down, but he certainly wasn't going to admit that. Besides, he might be fine. And anyway, Wendy didn't even wait for him to answer. With half a grin and a sigh, she leaned out into the night and swung her body over the edge.

Jack watched in horror. Wendy's arms and legs swished and pulled as she neatly negotiated her way to the ground. He sighed, gulped, and eased his body out the open window. Halfway down, he somehow wedged his foot in a particularly tight knot of thick, old vines and, with a panicked squeak, fell butt-first into a pile of grass clippings.

"Nice," Wendy said.

"Do I even need to remind you that it wasn't my idea to climb out a window in the middle of the night?" Jack said, standing up and brushing the grass off his shorts, rotating his ankle a few times to make sure it wasn't broken.

"It's not the middle of the night." Wendy took his hand and started walking. "It's barely dark." Jack followed obediently, the image of Clayton Avery's blackened eyes still vivid in his mind. Wendy, he decided, was not the type of girl he wanted to tick off.

The stone that Frankie had given him rested heavily in his pocket and felt warm against his leg. Why, exactly, it was warm, Jack did not know, but there was no one but Frankie he could ask about it, thanks to his promise, and any conversation with Frankie—well, who knew when or if that kid would open his mouth again?

They stopped at a pale green house with two porches and a low, gently sloping roof. "This is my house." Wendy released his hand and shoved her own into her back pockets.

"Oh," Jack said. "It's really"—he struggled for a word—"homey." He nearly slapped his forehead. *Honestly, Jack*, he admonished himself silently. *Be less lame.*

Wendy ignored the comment. "Follow me. It's over here." They cut across the yard and scrambled under the tangled branches of the hazel trees to the edge of the field. The corn was supple and young and moved gracefully in the light breeze. The papery leaves whispered as they touched. Jack rubbed the back of his neck.

"What am I looking at here," he asked, "besides corn?"

She ignored him. "When I was little, Frankie disappeared. No one knew where he was or what happened to him. My mom sorta froze up. She'd sit on the porch and stare out, and she wouldn't look at anyone or talk to anyone...." Wendy sniffed and rubbed away a few stray tears with the back of her hand.

"I'm sorry," Jack said.

Wendy waved his words away. "The thing is, right after he vanished, I started seeing this little kid in the corn." She pointed to a young oak tree a hundred yards off to the right. "That's where I saw him first. But he looked strange. He was little—real little, like a baby, but he wasn't shaped like a baby. He was shaped like a kid, just shrunk down. And his hair was rustley and green, like leaves."

Jack snorted, though he instantly regretted it when Wendy rounded on him, her face sharp and hot and livid.

"That's what I *saw*. I'm not saying I could explain it, or that I even believe it half the time. Anyway, he was wandering around and crying. Even when I couldn't see him, I could hear him crying. *All the time.* No one else could. I tried to tell my mom, but she was hopeless. My dad just got mad. And we had every cop in Iowa stomping around our house, and I tried to tell them too. They were useless."

"Yeah," Jack said. The story of the lost boy made him deeply sad for some reason. *Poor kid*, he thought. "So what happened?"

"I don't know. I finally told your aunt when she came

over with a bunch of casseroles and school clothes for me. Later she came back with your uncle, and he asked me all kinds of questions. It made me happy that *someone* was asking about it—that someone believed me." She rubbed her eyes with the back of her hand and sniffled a little. "See, it was like everyone had forgotten about Frankie. The cops stopped coming. My mom stopped talking about him. And even when I *asked*, people would go all cross-eyed, like they didn't know what I was talking about. And I was seeing that little kid in the corn more and more. It was like he was taking Frankie's place."

Jack's arms erupted in goose bumps, and the hair on his head stood out so straight, it felt like each strand was about to launch into the air. He *knew* this story from somewhere. But he couldn't put his finger on it.

"So, Clive and Mabel came over with weird cameras and books and other equipment. They said they were taking readings, whatever that meant. They came by every day to check on my family. They talked about Frankie over and over until my parents agreed that he really had existed. They told me to do the same. Then they found my brother. I don't know how—they just somehow knew where to find him. But, you know, he was…" Her voice trailed off.

"Broken," Jack said.

"Yeah." Wendy sniffed.

"What about the other boy?" Jack asked. "The one in the corn?"

"I never saw the lost boy again."

Wendy put her hand on Jack's shoulder. The sky was fully black now, and the milky moonlight lit Wendy's dark hair. She looked beautiful, Jack thought. She dropped her hand.

"I was just little, you know." Wendy crouched down and hugged her knees. She kept her eyes on the smooth stretch of farm in front of them. Jack sat down next to her, half expecting to hear a child crying in the corn. "So I thought all kinds of funny things. I don't know if half the stuff I remembered was a dream. But I thought that the kid in the field took my brother, or if he didn't do it himself that maybe he was responsible for it. So one night, before Frankie was found, I chased the lost boy into the field and threw a rock at him. He just caught it, and, as quick as blinking, he disappeared—and not just that. It was like a door opened up and roots of the corn slipped all around him and gathered him up and took him away. Like I said, I was just a dumb kid and thought all kinds of weird stuff. But I swear that's what happened."

"You threw a rock at the little boy?"

Wendy shrugged. "I was little too. I threw a rock at Clayton Avery in first grade once, and he never went underground. Anyway, when you came here, I thought…" She looked at the ground. "It's stupid, but I thought that you might be…well…" She swallowed and turned her face to Jack. "I thought that you might be able to tell me who hurt my brother. And mostly I wanted to know if it was you, if you were the one I should blame. I just...I thought that maybe you were actually—"

"But I—" Jack began, starting to panic. "I mean, I'm not—"

"I know, Jack. I *know*. Don't worry. I know you're just *Jack*. And you're a good person, and I'm glad that you helped us today, and what I'm trying to say is, well, I'm sorry I thought you were, you know..."

"Yeah," Jack said, rubbing the back of his neck. "Don't mention it." His skin itched uncomfortably, as though it was flaking off. He willed himself not to scratch.

"Anyway, this town is weird enough as it is. It's nice to have a friend who's, well, a normal person." She said this with emphasis, as though just by saying it, she could *will* it into being. She leaned over and kissed him very lightly on the cheek. She then gasped, pulled away, and ran into the darkness.

Chapter Twenty
Don't Panic

ALL THE NEXT DAY, JACK COULDN'T GET WENDY'S STORY out of his head. Granted, her parents were probably right that she had made up the kid in the corn—she was little, after all. Still, Jack could feel that kid's loneliness as though it was his own.

If there really was a kid out there, why would he be wandering around during the exact same time that Frankie went missing? Jack turned the questions around in his head, but couldn't find any answers.

Mabel knocked on the door and brought in a basket

of clean clothes. The leafy tendrils in the room had grown even more during the night, but if she noticed, Mabel didn't mention it. She stepped over the vines, laid the basket down on the bed, and gave Jack a long, hard look, pressing her fingers to her mouth.

"Jack, honey, are you all right?" She laid her hand on his forehead. Her fingers were cool and light, and though he wasn't about to say so, just the sensation of someone touching him made Jack so happy he thought he might cry.

"No," he said honestly. "I'm really not. But whatever. Don't worry about it." He turned away, blinking hard until she closed the door. After wiping his eyes with the hem of his shirt, he sat at his desk and opened the book.

> *When Her child went missing that first time, Her powers decreased. Corn withered, livestock died, dead birds fell in great flocks from the sky. The couple who had taken the child didn't have one of their own to offer as a swap. And the Magic dwindled, hampered by grief.*

"Jack?" Mabel opened the door.

"Huh?" Jack turned with a start.

Mabel had a wide, slightly forced smile across her face. "My sister is on the phone," she said.

"What?" Jack stared at her, openmouthed. He thought

for a moment, and narrowed his eyes. "But the phone didn't ring. Did *she* call *me*, or did *you* call *her*?"

Mabel shrugged and covered up the receiver with the heel of her hand. "Do you want to talk to her or not?" she whispered impatiently.

Though he strongly suspected that his mother had not called at all and, what's worse, that it didn't even occur to her to do so until Mabel placed the call for her, Jack took the phone anyway. He had a strong urge to call his aunt a busybody, but he resisted.

"Hi, Mom," he said, and Mabel left the room.

It was the first time he heard her voice in three weeks. This was not for lack of trying on Jack's part. In addition to his attempts at letter writing, he had also tried his mother's voice-mail system, his father's cell, his mother's cell and her other cell, and both of their assistants. Each time, either the numbers would scramble, or his voice wouldn't go through. Sometimes the cell towers failed or the phone lines went suddenly haywire.

He had so much to tell both of his parents—or, more specifically, he had so many questions to ask. So many, he kept a list of them in his notebook. The first question: *Why?* The second question: Also *Why?*

However, with his mom chattering away on the other line, Jack now found himself suddenly tongue-tied and embarrassed, his adventures so far seeming far-fetched and vaguely ludicrous, as though he had simply made them up on the spot.

"Mom," Jack said, "I've been trying to get a hold of you for weeks."

"What's that, honey?" His mother yawned. It was early in Iowa, so it was insanely early in San Francisco. What was his mother doing up that early, Jack wondered. He sat down at his desk and took out his notebook and started to draw. At the corner of the desk, the small round stone that Frankie had given him sat and glinted. It was still warm to the touch, and Jack was simultaneously unnerved by it and fascinated too. He picked it up and held it in his left hand.

"Is Dad there?" Jack asked.

"No, honey. Your father's at his new apartment. Honestly, dear, the housewarming was just yesterday. I thought you were having a nice time."

"What housewarming? *You* might have been there, but *I* wasn't, Mom." But on the other end, the kettle screeched and the microwave beeped, and Jack wasn't sure if she'd heard him.

"The decorator was here until late last night," she said, "and you won't believe what this place will look like when he's done with it."

She went on for a long time about fabrics and furniture, about tasks done and undone. She told him about specific details at work, about people he did not know. She spoke like a boss giving updates to an employee. Jack kept drawing. He liked to draw pictures of his mom.

She was tall and stately, with wide-set eyes and long brown hair that she always kept swept off her neck.

"But, *darling*" — his mother yawned again — "you simply *must* tell me what you've been doing...."

If his mother had been truly interested, Jack would not have known where to start. Fortunately, she wasn't interested at all and didn't allow him a moment to speak. Jack stopped listening to her words and focused his attention on the sound and rhythm of her voice as his pencil made curves and shades and emerging shapes in his notebook. He finished the sketch of her and stopped when he noticed he was making a figure coming through a darkened doorway.

He turned the page. He started a new picture, of the schoolhouse, but it made him shudder, so he turned the page again. He drew another picture of Frankie with half his body faded into a pale gray cloud. Jack drew the stone that Frankie had given him — the shimmery pearl color shot with blue veins swirling randomly across like clouds. He reached across the desk and hefted the real stone. It felt good — solid, reassuring, and strangely warm.

"And just *wait* until you see your new room. I know you're going to say you're too old and you don't want your mother decorating your space for you, but you should see what I have picked out."

"I'm sure whatever it is —" Jack began.

"I've put up picture rails so you can finally hang up

those photographs that keep littering your desk, and I've set up a whole rack for your trophies and team photos."

Wait, Jack thought. *What photographs? What trophies?* But he did not speak.

"I want you to walk into a room that just sings *Baxter*."

Jack dropped the phone onto the table. He felt his blood leave his face for a moment before rushing back. He felt cold, then hot, then sweaty, then clammy. He picked the phone back up and cradled it next to his ear.

"Mom," he said, trying very hard to force down the sick feeling that bubbled in the back of his throat. "Who do you think you're talking to right now?"

"Hmmm?" was his mother's musical reply.

"Who do you think this *is*?" Jack stood. He still held the stone in his hand. It heated quickly until it became uncomfortable. He didn't care. He just held on tight.

"Darling, it's too early for this sort of—"

"I'm not *Baxter*, Mom, I'm *Jack*. Jack! *Why aren't you listening to me?*"

And she *wasn't* listening. She was singing—a high, light sound with words so quiet that he couldn't catch them.

"Mom," he said, trying desperately to calm down. "It's Jack."

She paused. "Ja-a-a-ck," she said, very slowly, as though saying the word for the first time. "*Handy Pandy, Jack-a-dandy*," she crooned.

"What?"

"*Jack be nimble, Jack be quick, Jack jump over the candlestick.*"

"Mom, what are you—"

"*Jack and Jill went up the hill.*" Her voice was high and reedy, like that of a small child singing a song she just learned. "*To fetch a pail of water.*" She paused. "You know, that one never did make much sense." Her words thickened and slowed as though swimming out from a heavy dream. "You can't go *up* to get water. You have to go *down*. You have to go *inside*. Poor Jack. Poor Jill."

Jack held the stone tightly in his hand. He couldn't stand it anymore. Bringing his fist to the desktop, he shouted, "*Clair!*"

"There's no need to shout, dear. I'm right here."

"And where am I, Mom?"

"Well, don't be silly, honey. You're at your father's house." She gave an impatient sigh. "*Men's night,*" she added derisively. "What's gotten into you anyway?"

"Thanks for calling me, Mom."

"What are you talking about, Baxter, dear? *You* called *me*."

She told him about the little old lady on the first floor who claimed she could give the evil eye. She told him about her new driver, about the upcoming election, about his dad's new place.

I don't exist for her anymore, Jack thought. *I'm the grafted branch that's been ripped away.* There was a lump in his

167

throat sharp as a fishhook. He tried to swallow it down. He tried to spit it out. But his sadness hooked deeply into his flesh and wouldn't go away.

Jack didn't ask her any more questions, and after a while he stopped listening altogether.

Chapter Twenty-one
Freedom, and Other Security Risks

IT WAS STILL LIGHT AFTER WENDY AND HER FAMILY HAD eaten, but her mother had already fallen asleep on the couch watching the early news. Wendy tiptoed upstairs to check on her brother. As usual, he slept on his back, his eyes loosely closed, his lips a thin line, and his breathing so gentle you had to know him to know he breathed at all. She slipped on her shoes and checked the time. Her father, who, in addition to his job at the Exchange, sometimes worked the swing shift as a janitor for the college, didn't get off until nearly midnight.

She had time, she told herself as she shut the door as silently as she could and tiptoed down the squeaky wooden steps. She was, after all, the one no one worried about. Wendy had known from the time she was very young that this lack of worry translated to an abundance of freedom. It also gave her time to think.

She went back in her mind to the day that Frankie disappeared, when the lost boy appeared in the cornfield out back, the boy only Wendy could see. The cops had assumed she was lying. They called it *attention-seeking*. The psychologist called it *transference*, and the minister said that she was constructing a hero's narrative in her hope of finding her brother alive. Adults, Wendy knew, said a *lot* of things. And while it wasn't polite to tell them their ideas were completely idiotic, it certainly didn't stop her from *thinking* it.

Wendy had seen that boy each day that Frankie was gone. She had called to him, yelled at him, left bowls of cereal and milk at the edge of her yard, but she never saw him up close. When Frankie returned, scarred and silent, she didn't mention the boy in the cornfield. And anyway, after she threw that rock, the boy had disappeared, so it didn't much matter anymore. Some things were better left unsaid.

And, more importantly, some things were up to her to find out, because if she waited for the grown-ups in her life to tell her the truth, she would probably wait forever.

Two months before Frankie disappeared, when they were both eight years old, Wendy, Frankie, and Anders were all playing with some boys in the schoolhouse, throwing rocks into the open door, and screaming with laughter when they didn't hear the rock land. On a dare, one boy named Anthony went through the door. He did not come out. The children ran home, crying that the schoolhouse had collapsed with Anthony inside, but when a pack of panicked parents arrived at the scene, the schoolhouse was leaning on its dusty foundation, unchanged.

By that same evening, the adults had forgotten about Anthony. They accused the children of making the story up and inventing an imaginary boy. By the end of the week, most of the children had forgotten about the missing boy—only Frankie, Wendy, and Anders seemed to remember—or, at least, they were the only ones who claimed to remember. People said they were nuts.

Then Frankie disappeared. And though it took a little longer, well over a week, people started forgetting about him too. Wendy had to repeat his name again and again, show the fading photographs to their parents, hang on to his memory by sheer force of will. They remembered, though barely.

In the years that followed, Wendy would return to the schoolhouse with Anders. They ran their hands along the walls and floors, looking for . . . well, anything really. A door. A trick panel. A clue. But there was nothing. The schoolhouse had gone quiet. Just an empty, dusty space lit by daylight seeping through missing slats on the roof and walls, and no answers anywhere. And it had never done anything overtly *odd* until yesterday.

The schoolhouse, then, Wendy decided.

If only, for no other reason, to finally know.

She *had* to know.

Chapter Twenty-two
The Rock

IT WAS NEARLY THE MIDDLE OF THE NIGHT, AND THE MOON shone like a spotlight into Jack's room. The wind turned suddenly cool and dry and whipped through the wide windows, flipping the pages of his notebook, which lay open on the desk. Jack mumbled and rolled, hooking his pillow under his arm and folding it over his head.

There was, he noticed, a tapping sound.

No, he thought, more like a *thunk* coming at regular intervals. *Thunk*. Pause. *Thunk*. Pause. *Thunk*. Finally, there was an extra loud *thunk*, followed by a sharp pain on Jack's shoulder. Jack sat up, looked around, and saw that the pain had been caused by a rock that someone had thrown at the window, sailing easily through the hole in the screen. He climbed out of bed and shuffled to the window. Outside, the wind quieted the crickets. Half the sky was lit by the bright moon and pale stars. The other half had been covered by a velvety blackness that moved slowly across the sky. Soon, the moon would be obliterated. Soon. But not yet. Standing in the yard, lit by a bright patch of moonlight, was Frankie. He looked up and waved.

"Frankie," Jack whispered loudly. "*Frankie.*" He did not respond. "Oh, for crying out—Don't move. I'll be right out. I'll take you home."

He pulled on shorts and a clean T-shirt, and was just about to head for the window when he could have sworn he heard a voice say, "*The Portsmouth.*"

"What?" Jack said, spinning around but seeing no one there.

"*The stone. Don't forget it,*" the voice said again in the faintest of whispers, like the rustling of leaves.

"But who—" Jack said, but didn't continue. It didn't matter who had said it, he decided. It was just good advice. He grabbed the stone—it was warm to the touch—and put it in his pocket and, with a deep breath, attempted once again to climb down the trellis. He hoped it would be easier this time. It wasn't.

Once on the ground, Jack knew it was a mistake not

to wear a jacket. He rubbed his arms briskly and shivered and approached Frankie.

"What's going on?" Jack asked, realizing afterward that Frankie wouldn't respond. Frankie, his body rocking forward and back and his hands fidgeting at his sides, kept his eyes on Jack's window.

"What?" Jack said. "Oh, you mean the rock? Look. I have it." Frankie had, Jack noticed, very red eyes.

Frankie shook his head impatiently, stepped back, and brought his hands to the back of his head, screwing up his mouth.

"Frankie, what's wrong?"

Frankie grunted, kicking at the curb. Finally, taking a deep breath, he squatted down in front of a patch of thin dirt at the edge of the road. With his finger he wrote *Wendy?*

"Wendy?" Jack asked. "What about her?" But in reply, Frankie fell forward onto his knees with a guttural cry of pain. He brought his hands to his face and clutched at his scars.

"Frankie, for the love of—what's happening to you?" Jack asked, alarmed. He leaned down to help Frankie up, and his hand touched the patch of dirt with Wendy's name on it. The dirt was ice-cold. "What on earth?" he said, wiping his hand across the name, smoothing it away. Instantly, the cold abated and the dirt felt normal again. Frankie fell backward against the curb and groaned.

"I'm going to get my uncle," Jack said, standing up,

175

but Frankie grabbed his wrist and shook his head quickly. The silent boy stood, paused for a moment, narrowing his eyes a bit as though thinking, before giving Jack's arm a quick tug and walking quickly down the darkened street.

"Frankie," Jack called, "hang on a sec, I'm just going to get my—*Frankie!* Come *on* now." But Frankie was already halfway down the block. The moon was gone now, and so were most of the stars. On the western edge of the sky, flashes of light, with the occasional bolt, pulsed and flickered. Jack trotted to keep up.

"Is this the way to your house?" he asked. Jack didn't think so, but kept walking. Frankie said nothing, nor did he acknowledge that Jack had spoken. He continued to walk in sure, long strides.

They walked until they came to the Avery house. The house was dark except for one room on the left-hand side. Light poured out of the windows and pooled strangely on the surrounding grass. But it was like no light that Jack had ever seen. It was cold, and green, and heavy, like metal transformed into light. Jack looked away. Something about the light made him feel ill.

Frankie crossed the yard, grabbing a chair from the patio and positioning it at the side of the house.

"I don't think we should go over there." Jack did not move. His skin crawled and itched.

Frankie stopped, turned around, and grabbed Jack by the arm, pulled him toward the chair, and stepped up.

Frankie laid both hands on the wall and looked at Jack expectantly.

"What?" Jack demanded. "You want to push the wall in? That'll be subtle. Why not just use a hand grenade?" He raised his arms. The rain began.

Of course, he thought. *Of course it's raining.*

"Seriously, Frankie. Let's go. You can sleep at Mabel and Clive's if you don't want to go home. Okay? It's fine with me."

Frankie shook his head and shoved his hand into Jack's pocket.

"Hey! What are you doing?"

Frankie smiled and handed Jack the stone and brought both Jack's hand and the stone to the outside of the house.

"Um, now what?" Jack shook his head, and Frankie stamped his foot impatiently. "Look, Frankie, just show me whatever you want me to see and we can get out of here. Mr. Avery gives me the—oh!" Jack stopped. The stone grew hot. Frankie pressed his hand tightly over Jack's clenched fist and held it closed, preventing him from dropping the stone. A small door appeared in the siding. As though it had always been there. An old, low door that looked like it was made of barn wood. Jack could have sworn that he had seen something like it before, but for the life of him, he could not remember it.

Frankie reached over, pulled the rope handle, and swung it open.

Inside was a beautiful room. A wide mahogany desk, shining with oil. Paneled walls. Overstuffed leather chairs on delicately curved feet. An intricately carved fireplace with a strangely cold-looking fire emitting an eerie green glow. Jack shuddered.

A tall man leaned back in his leather desk chair, breathed in deeply through his extraordinarily large nose, and brought his fist onto the table with a deafening crash. The four police officers standing opposite him jumped in surprise.

"Perkins!" Mr. Avery roared, and the officers jumped again. Mr. Perkins came in through the door, holding a tray loaded with food, knocking some of its contents onto the ground.

"I'm terribly sorry, Mr. Avery. I just wanted to assemble the sandwiches."

"Will you quit blubbering about sandwiches!" Mr. Avery bellowed. "Frankly, Perkins, I find your lack of consideration utterly shocking."

Perkins sniffed. "Well, sir," he said in a quavering voice. "I'm here now. Shall we begin?"

Mr. Avery grunted. He closed his eyes for a moment before opening them slowly as he inhaled through flared nostrils. He steepled his fingers in front of his face, framing each side, making his eyes look wider, with a strange, cold sheen in the green firelight. He had a sharp chin and prominent cheekbones, which were so pale that they looked like actual bone.

Jack stood outside on that chair, the light, cold rain soaking his T-shirt, shaking uncontrollably. He felt suddenly grateful for the reassurance of Frankie's hand against his clenched fist, and he couldn't help but notice that the other boy was shaking too.

After another moment, Mr. Avery spoke.

"Mr. Fitzpatrick was given the option to relinquish the house to us," Mr. Avery said, his voice booming in the small room. The officers, despite their nightsticks and sidearms, hunched their shoulders and pressed close to one another, like frightened children. "Three times we offered and three times he refused. There is a power in three, and that power is now on our side."

The officers looked at one another, confusion on their faces.

"You mean the governor?" one officer asked.

Mr. Avery paused. "Sure," he said, using the same voice that adults often use to lie to children. "Of course. The governor."

Jack turned to Frankie. "He's lying, isn't he?" he said. "He's talking about magic." The word stuck like a thorn in the back of his throat. He swallowed. "Isn't he?"

In response, Frankie squeezed Jack's hand a little tighter, giving the tiniest of nods. He didn't take his eyes off the men in the room.

Mr. Perkins cleared his throat. "With all due respect, sir, *he* has been given the correct number. *She* has not. We only asked Mrs. Fitzpatrick once."

Mr. Avery snorted. "The wife is not our concern. She has nothing to stand in our way."

"And what of the boy?" one officer said, in a faint hiss of a voice. Jack imagined that this is what a snake would sound like if a snake could talk.

Mr. Avery paused. "The boy is the key. The boy is the reason there will be no swap in this generation. Once the boy is…" He paused. "*Out of the picture.* That's the moment that the Lady's Other will be weakened to the point of possible defeat. Grief, love: those are the Other's weak points, and easy enough to exploit. But simultaneity is key. We must have the boy called Jack in our possession now. Tonight. Without him the plan will fail. Alert your officers—"

Jack dropped the stone. The door disappeared. "What?" he yelled. He looked at Frankie's astonished, shaking face. "What?" he yelled again. It took Jack a couple of seconds, but he realized with a start that Frankie's mouth was forming silent words.

Shut up, the mouth said.

"What was that?" shouted a voice from the house.

"Someone's out there!" shouted another.

Frankie reached down, grabbed the stone, and shoved it into Jack's pocket. The sky flashed, split open, and poured down.

"*Run*," Frankie shouted.

Chapter Twenty-three
The Descent

THE SCHOOLHOUSE APPEARED, ITS EDGES SHARP AGAINST the shimmering sky, and Wendy slowed down. Her worn canvas shoes seemed to grow leaden, and the thought of going forward suddenly seemed like a very bad idea indeed. She stopped, shoved her fists into her back pockets, and stared across the field. The uppermost leaves of the corn reflected the unexpectedly vibrant colors of the sky—some patches shone in pale pink, others dark purple, and others in a vivid red.

Underneath, shadows unfurled in every direction and

rippled away from her in waves. It was only July, and the corn was still low. Wendy could see from one end of the field to the other. In a few weeks, it would reach the top of her head, and in a month and a half, the road would look like a tunnel—a very dark tunnel.

She kicked at the gravel in the road, told herself she was being very silly, told herself it was just a stupid, broken old building.

Still, the mystery began in the schoolhouse, and it was never answered. And still, in the end, she had to know.

Wendy stood in front of schoolhouse stairs. They were repaired, rebuilt, repainted, and gleaming. *Who?* Wendy wondered. *And why?* The multicolored sky lit the schoolhouse walls and the land around it with mottled colors that spilled over and around themselves like a quilt.

Suddenly, Wendy felt tired. Very tired. So tired that she knew if she tried to stand for another second, her legs would give out. Slowly, she lowered herself to the ground, but instead of weeds and gravel, she found herself sitting somewhere soft—a chair, where only moments ago there had been none.

She propped her feet up on the schoolhouse stairs and sank deeply into cushions made of feathers and silk. As she sank, she found they gave off an intoxicating smell—flowers or perfume or something else entirely... and she found herself feeling sleepy.

And perhaps she slept and perhaps she did not.

She heard the sound of kids laughing and shouting, the thud of a ball being kicked, the clatter of a metal bucket hitting the gravel yard, the rhythmic chanting of jump rope rhymes with the regular thud of feet. But no one was there. The voices gathered in front of her and seemed to shift this way and that in the sweet-smelling breeze. They echoed across the field. But when she opened her eyes, Wendy could see no one. Just the schoolhouse, so white it seemed to gleam in the high sun. It had become three stories tall, with a bell tower, both narrow and sharp, that rose high in the air as though trying to puncture the sky.

Wendy squinted and shaded her eyes. As she stared, letters started inscribing themselves over the door, as though scripted by an invisible pen.

"*W...E...L...*" Wendy read along. "*Welcome, Wendy.*"

"*You musn't leave me,*" a voice whispered from the softness that surrounded her. "*You musn't go away like he did.*"

Wendy smiled.

"*I belong here,*" she whispered dreamily. "*Just like Frankie did. And I'll never, ever leave.*"

Chapter Twenty-four
Again

JACK AND FRANKIE HELD HANDS AS THEY RAN BLINDLY through the dark and the rain. Or Jack ran blindly. Frankie, thankfully, seemed to know where he was going.

Four times Jack stared wildly over his shoulder to see if they were followed, and four times he only saw the wet road, the shadowed houses, and the dripping trees. Through the thundering of the rain, they could hear a police siren. Then another. Then another. Howling like wolves and circling near.

They turned onto a road that had houses on one side and a cornfield on the other. Frankie's footfalls slowed a little as he peered around the side of someone's garage. He gripped Jack's hand even tighter and ran behind the first available house. Within seconds, a pair of headlights moved slowly around the nearby corner and oozed down the street. Frankie and Jack darted into the dark nook between the house and the toolshed. They pressed themselves against the sodden bricks, barely daring to breathe.

Jack set his teeth and peered around the far side of the house. The car had pulled over about three houses up, and two men got out. One of them had a cigarette hanging out of the side of his mouth, and it gave a dull glow in the dark rain. Both men stared at the cornfield on the opposite side of the road.

Jack crouched down, tried to keep himself in shadow. The rain poured heavily off the roof of the house and onto his head. He was wetter, he felt, than he had ever been in his life. The men stood staring for what felt like hours, but what was more likely only a few minutes. The man without a cigarette turned to the smoking man and shrugged. The smoking man shrugged, too, and threw his cigarette into the darkness. They both slid back into the car and drove away.

"They're leaving," Jack said. Before the words had completely left his mouth, Frankie already started pulling him to the next yard. They moved in short bursts, from yard to yard, peeking over the side of the houses for more cars. None came.

When they came to the last house on the block, Frankie stopped at the back door, checked the latch, and pushed it open. He jerked his head at Jack in what Jack assumed must be a welcome.

Normally, Jack would have felt profoundly uncomfortable going into someone else's home. In fact, aside from Clive and Mabel's, he had never been invited into anyone else's home for as long as he could remember.

Frankie led him through a cramped mudroom into a wide, clean kitchen. Even in the dark, Jack could tell it was normally sunny and pleasant. And warm and dry. Frankie grabbed a handful of small towels that were hanging over the handle of the stove, and the two of them began drying their faces. The lights flipped on and a woman in a bathrobe stared at them from the doorway. Her cheeks were so pale they were almost white, except for two bright red splotches under each eye. She folded her arms across her chest. She opened her mouth to speak, but no words came out. Frankie reached over and grabbed back on to Jack's hand.

Finally, Jack spoke. "H-hello, Mrs. Schumacher. S-so sorry to wake you up."

"I," Mrs. Schumacher said in a voice that was barely louder than a whisper, "have not yet thought of an appropriate punishment, young man." Jack noticed, with some relief, that her eyes were on Frankie and not on him.

"But make no mistake, something will come to me." She lifted her chin and looked past them to the darkened doorway to the mudroom. "That goes for you, too, young lady. You think you can hide from your mother, but you can't."

Frankie and Jack looked at each other, and then at Mrs. Schumacher. Jack cleared his throat. "Um, Mrs. Schumacher, Wendy isn't with us."

"Oh, she'd like me to think so, wouldn't she? *Wendy! This minute!*"

"No, I mean it." Jack stepped forward. "I woke up and looked out the window and Frankie was there. I don't know. Just standing there. I came out to bring him home and we got caught in the rain. I don't think Wendy was ever with him." Jack noted that this was not a lie. It wasn't the whole truth, either, but he had prided himself on never lying before, and he was happy that he didn't have to start today.

"So where was Wendy in all of this?" Mrs. Schumacher placed her hand on the edge of the counter and leaned toward it. Jack wondered if she was about to fall over.

"Nowhere. She wasn't anywhere. I just thought—" Mrs. Schumacher pushed past Jack and started hunting around in the mudroom, pulling the coats off their hooks as though Wendy might be hiding behind.

"Wendy," she said. "Wendy!"

Jack stood shoulder to shoulder with Frankie, feeling

the other boy's silent sobs crash across his body like waves.

"This is why you were out," he hissed at Frankie as Mrs. Schumacher tore through the main level of the house. "You thought she was with me, but she wasn't. And then you thought Mr. Avery...why would Mr. *Avery* know what happened to her?"

Very slowly, Frankie brought his hand to his scars. They looked, Jack noticed, even worse than before—puffier, redder, and slightly weepy, as though they might be infected. Frankie looked directly into Jack's eyes for a brief moment before squeezing his mismatched eyes shut and letting tears leak out.

"So you don't think Wendy is...I mean, she couldn't be..." Jack couldn't finish. He supposed he should do something, maybe look in the cupboards or under the drapes, but it seemed fairly useless anyway. His hands hung motionless by his sides, his eyes did not blink, and even though his wet clothes made him freezing cold, he couldn't even shiver.

Mrs. Schumacher ran back into the kitchen, followed closely by a man who Jack assumed must be Frankie and Wendy's father. He was unshaven and wore a flannel shirt with undershorts and slippers. He stopped in front of the refrigerator, which was covered with papers from school and photographs and shopping lists and coupons from the local grocery store. With trembling hands, Mr. Schumacher removed a photograph of Wendy from its magnet. The photograph showed Wendy on a soccer field, wearing a green jersey and holding a ball under one arm. She was smiling. What the photograph did not show was the bottom half of Wendy's body. The cleats were gone, the shin pads were gone. Even the scabbed-up, knobby knees were gone. The upper half of Wendy floated in midair. She was half erased.

"Margaret," the man said. His voice was heavy and scratchy with sleep. "Oh God, Margaret. Not again. *Not again!*"

Mrs. Schumacher said nothing. She turned away. Jack noticed that her shoulders were shaking. She opened the back door.

Nothing was visible.

Nothing but the rain.

Chapter Twenty-five
Mostly True

THAT NIGHT, ANDERS WOKE FROM A TROUBLING DREAM. His room was dark, its silence rippled by the open-mouthed breathing sounds of his two brothers at the other end of the room. In his dream, Wendy sat on a chair that was a chair if you looked at it one way—and a very large hand if you looked at it another. In his dream, Anders himself sat on the steps of the old schoolhouse. He was very small, he noticed. No bigger than a mouse. He jumped up and down and waved his arms, trying to get Wendy's attention, but she was soft and dreamy and didn't notice him.

The steps rumbled and shook. He heard the sound of yawning and was nearly knocked down by the worst morning breath he had ever smelled. Slowly he turned around.

There were two windows on either side of the door. For as long as Anders could remember, the windows had been covered by two large pieces of wood that had been marked with graffiti by kids who had done so on a dare. The boards were gone, the graffiti was gone, and even the windows were gone. Instead, he saw two very large, very sleepy-looking eyes—eyes that were just starting to open. In his dream, Anders took one flying leap off the bottom step and landed hard on the gravel, pitching forward and cutting his knees.

He didn't stop. He ran to the chair (or was it a hand?) and grabbed Wendy by the shoe.

"Wendy," he yelled—but even in his dream he knew his yell was no louder than a squeak. "Wendy, you have to get up. We have to get out of here."

Wendy didn't hear him—or if she did, she didn't show it. Instead, she snuggled deeper into the chair. The eyes on the schoolhouse snapped open, and the door no longer looked like a door. It was a very large, red-lipped mouth.

"I'm *awake*!" shouted the mouth.

"Yes," murmured Wendy. "Isn't it wonderful?"

And before Anders could shout, *No, actually, it certainly is not*, the chair closed tightly around Wendy and pulled her under the ground. The spot where both chair and girl had been began to ripple and swirl like water, its waves knocking Anders off balance and tumbling him to the ground.

"Wendy," he whispered, but she was gone.

Anders woke in a tangle of sheets. He sweat and shook. "Come back," he shouted, but his voice cracked and rasped with sleep. He sat up and noticed his knees. They were sore and bleeding. His hands were scratched too. He flexed his fingers. This sort of thing had happened before—injuries from dreams appearing on his body the following morning. His grandfather suffered from a similar malady (though Anders's grandmother said it was hogwash). He'd wake with scrapes, bruises, concussions—once, a broken finger. Anders knew that some dreams were dangerous. Some dreams were *real*. Which meant that the eyes in the schoolhouse, the Wendy-snatching chair, the ground swirling like water...

"Oh no," he said, his heart beating faster and his stomach turning to lead. Wendy wasn't just gone. She was *gone*. And there wasn't much time to get her back.

Chapter Twenty-six
Poor, Poor Reginald

Mr. Perkins arrived at the Fitzpatrick house very early in the morning, as decided by the group—which is to say that Mr. Avery decided and everyone else knew better than to disagree. The demolition order, tucked in a manila folder in his briefcase, had to be personally delivered. Once the Fitzpatricks had the order, they had six hours to vacate the property. Since time was of the essence, it was crucial to hand over the papers as quickly as possible.

"Catch 'em when they least expect it," Mr. Avery had told him, leaning his sharp face very close to Mr. Perkins, so close that Mr. Perkins could see the curled hairs in his very large nose. "The boy hasn't been seen coming back to the house. Let them think we have him. Let 'em *know* that we have the upper hand. They can step aside or they will be crushed. Progress will not be stopped."

Mr. Perkins paused at the front door. After a rainy and miserable night, the morning was lovely. The road stretching away from the Fitzpatrick residence had been washed so clean by the rain, it looked new. The cornfields beyond were deeply green, and the brightening sky was the kind of blue you only see in paintings.

Mr. Perkins sighed and reached into his pocket for his piece of rawhide. He held it tightly in his fist as he knocked on the door.

The door opened before he could knock three times. Clive Fitzpatrick stood in the doorway, looking unshaven and slightly rumpled, as though he had not slept all night—or if he had, he had slept in his clothes. And from the look of him, on the floor as well.

"Hello, Reginald," Clive said wearily. "It's been a long time, hasn't it?"

"Yes, sir," Mr. Perkins said, feeling suddenly flustered and shy. "I mean, Professor Fitzpatrick. Yes, it has."

Mr. Perkins had taken Clive Fitzpatrick's Magical Thinking in Western Literature course before he was forced to withdraw halfway through. Clive—or Professor Fitzpatrick—had generously refrained from giving Mr. Perkins an F, as most of the other professors would have done. Instead, he listed the course as "Incomplete" and sent young Mr. Perkins a note saying, *Should you ever return, you will surely pass.* He did not sign it.

"Well, boy," Clive said, turning and padding through the living room. "It wouldn't do to chat on the threshold. Do close the door behind you. We would be delighted if you would please join us in the kitchen for tea." Mr. Perkins stood in stunned silence. He had not anticipated an invitation for tea. In fact, Mr. Perkins could hardly remember the last time he was invited for anything. Ordered, yes, but never invited.

"Thank you," he said quietly, and shut the door behind him.

The Fitzpatricks' kitchen was one of those bright, pleasant kitchens that face east to catch the morning light. Sunlight streamed through the many windows, spilling across the blue tile countertops, the wide planked floors, the polished tabletop.

Clive had already taken his seat next to Mabel, who looked equally tired and worn out. A very large parrot fluttered down from the top of the refrigerator and landed on the table, between Mabel's teacup and Clive's untouched toast. He turned his head and stared at Mr. Perkins with an outraged—and possibly murderous—look in his black button eye. He opened the hook of his beak and let out a squawk that sliced into Mr. Perkins's skull and made him wonder if he would ever hear properly again.

"That'll do, Lancelot," Mabel said. Mr. Perkins wondered if this was an admonishment or praise.

"Sit," Mabel said finally. Mr. Perkins sat. "Tea?" she said, pouring tea into a pale blue mug. Mr. Perkins tried to say *thank you*, but he was so overcome that it was little more than a gargle. Mabel rolled her eyes.

"Mr. Perkins," she said, laying her hands on the table as though to steady herself. She had, he noticed, beautiful hands. "We have had a long and unpleasant evening. I'm sure we don't have to tell you that our nephew is missing." She paused and fixed Mr. Perkins with a hard, icy stare. He was suddenly so cold, he thought his skin might crack. Mabel cleared her throat and continued. "Or that your employer has seen fit to cut off our telephone and electricity. *That* was a nice touch." She sipped her tea and set her cup back onto the saucer in a way that struck Mr. Perkins as being vaguely sinister. "Given that it is more than likely that we are facing a long and unpleasant day, I would appreciate if you could say what you came here to tell us so we can attend to our rather pressing business here."

"Although," Clive cut in, "we are very happy to see you." He gave Mabel a meaningful glance. Mabel sighed.

"Yes, yes," she said rather quickly. "It is always a pleasure to have former students at our table." She pressed her lips together tightly, as though she wanted to add something but thought better of it.

Mr. Perkins felt his eyes suddenly well up and his lower lip start to quiver. It was, by all reckoning, the nicest thing anyone had ever said to him. He cleared his throat.

"Of course, of course," he said, trying to sound as much like a businessman as he could. "There is always so much to do, isn't there? Busy, busy, busy, rush, rush, rush." He cleared his throat again. Clive and Mabel stared back in an embarrassed silence. Mr. Perkins pulled his briefcase to his knees and popped it open. "As you know, Avery Industries has generously offered to build a new road connecting the grain elevator to the town."

"And which grain elevator would that be, dear?" Mabel asked.

Mr. Perkins swallowed, but his mouth had gone quite dry, and the swallow got stuck in the back of his throat, causing him to choke slightly. He tried to calm it by taking a swig of tea, but ended up burning the entire inside of his mouth instead.

"Well," he said, wincing, "that would be the grain elevator that will be located on the piece of property where the old schoolhouse sits currently."

"Ah." Mabel poured cream into her own mug and sipped her tea. "So your employer is intending to tear down our house to build a road to a structure that has not yet been built." She laid her cup daintily onto her saucer in a way that struck Mr. Perkins as oddly dangerous.

"Yes, ma'am, yes indeed."

"And the other houses on the block. Are they slated for demolition as well?"

"Well, no, not currently, ma'am, but as the project—"

Mabel did not let him finish. "So you mean to say that, while the entire block stands in the way of this— I'm certain, very worthwhile—project, your employer has decided that, for now, only *our* house will be taken and destroyed. How, pray tell, will the road function with the other houses in the way? Will the trucks be expected to swerve?" She folded her hands together and laid them in her lap.

Mr. Perkins pulled out paper after paper detailing the project and the legal standing granted by the governor (under duress, of course, but granted all the same) that allowed his employer to take the Fitzpatricks' home. "You will, of course, be compensated." Mr. Perkins listened to the whine in his voice and felt ashamed. He cleared his throat. "Amply compensated," he clarified.

Mabel reached across the table and took hold of Mr. Perkins's hand in both of her own. Her hands, he noticed again, were warm and strong, and utterly lovely. "My dear Mr. Perkins."

"Reginald," Clive corrected.

"Yes. Reginald. You can tell your employer that we care nothing for his paperwork or his signed orders, and you can tell him from me where he can stick them."

She raised her eyebrows and, for one horrible moment,

Mr. Perkins worried that she might laugh. No one laughed at Mr. Avery and got away with it. No one.

"We will not leave this house. We'd rather die. Really, he's a fool to ask."

Mr. Perkins gasped. In the grasp of Mabel's hands, he felt his own start to sweat and shake. "You have no idea who you're dealing with," he whispered. "Or what he's capable of."

"My dear man," Mabel said. "Neither does he. His plans will fail. Indeed, they already have—he just doesn't know it yet. Now if you please, I'm sure you can see your own way out. My husband and I have much to do."

Mr. Perkins gathered his many papers and shoved them unceremoniously into his briefcase, shaking the table as he forced the case closed. Even then, there were several paper corners sticking out along the metal edging. He mumbled something intended to sound businesslike and vaguely dangerous but that ended up sounding more like *thank you*, and hurried to the door.

"I notice, lad," he heard Clive say as he skittered down the hall, "that you hang on to a piece of rawhide. Smart boy. The stories about rawhide aren't true, of course, but they're *mostly* true. It isn't the *thing* itself, but the *belief* in the thing that matters. Your soul is yours as long as you choose to hang on to it. If the rawhide helps you believe, then all's the better. Just *don't lose it*."

Chapter Twenty-seven
"Freeze!"

JACK SAW WENDY.

He called to her, but she didn't answer. "I'm over here," he yelled, but she fell to her knees. He was standing on one side of a clear, flexible wall that bounced back when he pushed it. He pounded, but he couldn't break it. He saw a woman wearing a dress made of spiderwebs and moss leaning over the girl, her locust wings fluttering in anticipation. He saw her reach her hands into Wendy's open mouth and pull out...*something*. He saw Wendy's body lighten, fade, and blow away like a dried-out husk. Jack screamed.

"*Mom!*" he yelled as he woke, his face dripping with sweat, his breath rattling around in his chest.

Although Jack didn't remember going to sleep at the Schumacher house, he found himself waking up in a room that he did not recognize. His shirt had finally dried during the night, mostly, and his shorts, too, except for his waistband and the small of his back. He was lying in what he assumed must be Frankie's room, on one of those guest beds that roll out from the space between the regular bed and the floor. Frankie was asleep, open-mouthed and sighing, with the telltale marks of dried-up tears all across his ruined face. Jack sat up.

There was something hovering on the brink of his memory. Something important.

He searched for his shoes, and found them, inexplicably, under the pillow, which explained the nasty crick in his neck. The stone in his pocket warmed and vibrated, forcing him to remember the flared nostrils of Mr. Avery. His bulging eyes. The sick, green light. The words *out of the picture* hanging in the room like a noose. There was no doubt what the old man meant by it.

Why would Mr. Avery want him dead, he wondered. What was he to Mr. Avery?

He glanced over at Frankie, who hiccuped in his sleep. The scars on his face looked new. *What kind of injury stays like that for four years?* Jack didn't know. He tiptoed down the stairs and out of the house.

The town was quiet; the streets, empty. Jack breathed a sigh of relief. To his astonishment, he found his skateboard sitting in the grass. Did he bring it with him last night to take Frankie home? He certainly didn't *remember* doing so. Still, it was quicker than walking. He hopped on, gave one quick kick, and coasted down the road.

He had an idea of where Wendy might have gone. After all, she was the one looking for answers.

Jack sped off toward the schoolhouse.

Anders left the house without his shoes. He thought it wise to do so. The road was wet, the grass waterlogged and sloppy. The muck squished irritatingly between his toes. But the morning was crystal and bright, and things would dry out soon enough. Besides, he needed his feet on the ground.

He cut across the neighbor's farm to the schoolhouse.

Or where the schoolhouse used to be.

It was gone. Completely gone. No cloud of dust, no pile of shingles, no collapsed frame or siding or ruined walls. There wasn't even a splinter or a stray nail to show where the school had once stood. Just a perfect rectangle of grass that was short and velvety like a golf course, and a bright, poison green.

Anders stood at the edge, wondering if he should

stand on the grass. He shrugged, and stepped inside the rectangle. It was warm and dry and pleasant. Very pleasant indeed.

He put his hands in his pockets. He leaned back on his heels, wondering if he should stay there all day. In fact, he thought it might be high time for a nap. The green curled around his feet, wound gently around his legs, and hugged him about the waist. There was something he was supposed to be doing—he was pretty sure anyway—but he couldn't remember what it was. He closed his eyes, tilted his head back to feel the heat of the sun. He saw a spangle of flickering light and a girl standing on the sky, staring up at the windy fields above her head. Anders felt a sudden, sharp shock at the soles of his feet and two hands gripping his shirt and nearly ripping it off.

"*No!*" the voice behind him yelled. *"Not Anders too!"*

Anders felt as though he were being pulled in two. Finally, the grip on his legs gave way, and he fell backward, rolling on the gravel. It hurt his elbows and knees, but he didn't much notice. What he *did* notice was that he was awake.

Also, he noticed that the person kneeling behind him was Jack.

"Are you all right?" Jack asked, staring hard at Anders.

"I saw Wendy," Anders said, looking back at the rectangle of bright green grass. There was no imprint of his body, no crushed blades where he had been.

"You were *sinking*," Jack said.

"You're not listening," Anders said. "I *saw* Wendy. She's here...somewhere. Underground I think."

Jack shook his head. "No, *you* aren't listening. It was like...quicksand or something. But green. And it was sucking you down. It was up over your waist by the time I yanked you out."

Jack was panting, and his hands trembled. The rectangle of grass *looked* solid enough, but it had rippled as Anders had sunk lower and lower. And what's more — when Jack pulled Anders out, *something* had tried to pull him back.

I know what this is, a voice itched in the back of Jack's brain. He tried to shrug it off, but it wouldn't go away. In Clive's book, there were references to some sort of trap — a snare for souls. But *how* could something take a soul? What do you *do* with a soul anyway?

Anders crouched next to the green rectangle. He inhaled a long, slow sniff and reached his fingers toward the grass, letting them hover less than an inch over the surface. Nothing happened at first. Then, one blade of grass unfurled, stretched, and grabbed on to Anders's fingertip. Then another. Then, a handprint-sized section of grass bubbled forward, erupting toward the outstretched hand. Anders snatched it away.

"You know," he said thoughtfully, pressing his fingers to his lips and resting his elbows on his knees, "my brothers like to catch rabbits. You ever had rabbit stew?" Jack crinkled his brow and shook his head. Anders shrugged. "Can't say I care for it much, but my brothers like it. Thing is, they've got too much to do, with school and sports and the farm. Doesn't leave much time to hunt, you know? So they started making these snares. And they're good too—they made this clever design. It never fails. But, it's not enough to catch *any* rabbit, you see? You want to catch the *fast* rabbits, the *strong* rabbits, the *smart* rabbits. You eat an idiotic rabbit and it doesn't taste very good, know what I mean?"

"Not at all," Jack said, growing more worried and confused by the second.

Anders sighed and stood. "In order to catch strong, healthy, clever rabbits, you have to really *know* how those rabbits operate. You have to *want* to catch them. This thing here"—he pointed to where the schoolhouse once was—"it *attracted* Wendy. And us. And other kids like us. *Curious* kids. Do you think that's on purpose? Do you think that She's looking for a certain *kind*—"

"She?" Jack said, starting to panic. "What are you saying?"

Anders shoved his hands into his pockets and leaned back on his bare heels. He scanned the fields, the road, and the sky. "I guess I'm saying that we need to get out of the open. And we should probably talk to your uncle."

"But why would we need to get out of the open—" Jack started, but he looked up. A police car sped around the bend and squealed to a stop. Two officers leaped out.

"*Freeze!*" they shouted.

"That's why," Anders said grimly.

Chapter Twenty-eight
Daybreak

"Target spotted," rasped the police transponder on the desk, "standing on the side of CR 20 with another juvenile male. We won't need backup. Over." Mr. Avery sighed loudly and clicked off the sound on the radio. He slumped into his large, comfortable chair. On most days, his chair felt like a throne, and Mr. Avery felt like a king. But not today. Mr. Avery felt quite a few things, but kingly was not among them. He hadn't slept in days. He wondered if he'd ever sleep again.

"*Horace*," said the face in the mantel. "*Hooorrrr-aaaacccee.*"

He winced. He hated the name Horace. Even when he was a child, people called him Mr. Avery.

"Horace," She said again, and Her lips were no longer the color of wood. Nor were Her eyes. Her lips blushed. Her eyes paled to gold, then brightened to a livid, poisonous green. She blinked, smiled, then blinked again before vanishing back into the wood. She was not awake yet. At least, not all the way. But the eyes had been blinking more and more, ever since the boy called Jack arrived. First here in the Retiring Room, then at the Exchange, and even in the grass, and on the walls of the college, and etched in the pavement on the street. Once, an entire cornfield rounded into a face, blinking its eyes and yawning deeply through its wide, sharp-toothed mouth. As though it wanted to swallow every soul alive. He shuddered. The mantel calmed and was just a mantel again. He brought his hands to his face and pressed gently at the eye sockets, trying to press the pain—and Her eyes—away.

The face in the mantel reappeared. She flexed Her cheeks, slid Her eyes from side to side. Her skin remained the color of polished mahogany. Her mother-of-pearl teeth were white as clouds. She smiled. Mr. Avery gasped and whimpered. Her smile was both beautiful and terrible. It could bring a man to his knees, rip his soul from his body, leave him nothing but a dry husk. In fact, it often did. Mr. Avery gritted his teeth and willed himself from falling apart.

"Clever boy, Horace, dear. Very clever boy. Your brother was clever, too, wasn't he? Oh, so clever."

"Not so clever," Mr. Avery muttered. Mr. Avery could hardly remember his brother's name, though he had watched the swap occur, long ago, when he was a boy. He remembered the baby in the acorn cradle lying next to his brother—a drippy-nosed child with a penchant for asking annoying questions. His father and the Lady said *yours* and *mine*. The ground shook. The light flashed. Magic surged over his skin like static electricity. And his brother was gone forever. That was how it was *supposed* to happen. Mr. Avery was *supposed* to have two children. *Supposed* to, but didn't. So much for his cleverness.

"No," She agreed, Her hair blowing around Her, as though in a wind. As it rippled, he could see corn and wheat and switchgrass, waving toward the horizon and the sky. He nearly wept at the beauty of it. "Not so clever after all." She closed Her eyes. Vanished. Reappeared. "I have been sleeping, Horace. I dislike sleeping."

"An unintended consequence."

"Of your negligence."

He bowed his head. "Of my negligence," he said, though to himself he added: *Of my lack of planning. Of my weakness.*

"Where is your son?" She asked.

"Not available," Mr. Avery whispered.

"I'm weak, Horace. I'm cold. This, dear, is your fault. My needs are few. A soul is all. Perhaps two. Perhaps a thousand. And your son. Remember? *Yours. Mine.* That was the deal. That has always been the arrangement. Your father wasn't this difficult."

"No," he whispered. His feet were cold, his hands were cold. Outside, he knew it was hot, but in Her presence his breath clouded out of his open mouth, and his teeth chattered. "I'm sorry, but it is out of the question."

"Fine," She said. "Bear your own consequences."

"There's a soul waiting for You underground." Mr. Avery felt it the moment the Schumacher girl fell into the snare. He *always* felt it, like a jolt in the power that flowed from under the ground and into his bones. Or at least it used to. The Magic, thanks to his botched swap, was a mere shadow of what it used to be. Still, when Wendy fell underground, he *felt it*. And though her soul, for the time being, was still intact, he knew he'd feel it—like a kick to the solar plexus—the moment it was ripped away. Already he braced himself.

"A girl," the Lady sighed. "Girls are *prickly*. Especially that one. I need to be stronger to take her soul. I need to *be…awake.* Tell me, dear, where, perchance, is *my* son?"

"Only half Yours."

"Indeed," She said. "A mother split in two. Still, I take what's mine, don't I, Horace?"

"He has been apprehended. If we eliminate him in

sight of Your Other, we can eliminate Her forever. Your powers will increase, and so will mine. No more...*misunderstanding*. I'm only thinking of what is best, my Lady. I am ever Your servant." He mopped his brow. Despite the cold, he sweated through his clothing—a heavy, drippy sweat, stinking with fear.

"Good," She said, vanishing sleepily into the wood. "I'll rest," She murmured. "But not for long."

Chapter Twenty-nine
Escape Routes

MRS. AVERY STOOD NEXT TO THE CLOSED DOOR, LISTENING. She was not supposed to listen, of course. But she did. She listened all the time. When Clayton was young, and it was clear that she would not have another child, she listened every day, crying silently into her hands, gathering enough information to propose a plan.

It was not, as it turned out, a particularly *good* plan, and it was a shame what happened to that poor Schumacher boy, of course it was, but a good mother must protect her own. Myrtle Avery never had any ambitions to become a particularly good *woman*; however, she was and would be a good mother. Her child would be protected. She would see to it.

She laid her fingertips on the polished face of the door to steady herself. She was a small woman, pale skinned, tiny featured, a birdlike body dressed always in brown, with large, round glasses that magnified her large brown eyes and made her look like a surprised owl. She blinked rapidly to beat back tears. Her husband's voice trembled. She had only heard it tremble twice before: first on their wedding day, and then later, when he transmitted her plan to a woman on the other side of the door. A woman Mrs. Avery had never been allowed to see. A woman whose voice haunted Mrs. Avery's dreams.

I have been sleeping, Horace, the woman's voice said. *I dislike sleeping.*

It wasn't my fault, Mrs. Avery thought desperately. *I demanded what any mother would demand.*

Where is your son? The woman on the other side of the door had a voice slick as a ribbon around a throat. It was subtle, muted, dark. Mrs. Avery shivered.

Not available, she heard her husband say. But his voice was weak, and *oh*, how timid he sounded.

She backed away from the door and crept down the stairs. She tiptoed into the kitchen, breathing hard and fast. She forced herself to remain calm. She forced herself not to scream. Throwing open the junk drawer, she rummaged hastily for her keys and sunglasses. She ran to the backyard, forgetting her shoes, forgetting her purse, forgetting to care about what she had forgotten.

"Clayton," she whispered. *"Clayton!"*

Clayton Avery stood next to the garage, throwing a softball against the door and catching it with a well-used glove. At the sound of his mother's voice, he hastily threw both ball and glove into the hydrangea bushes next to the garage. Throwing a ball against—or, for that matter, even standing near—the garage was against the rules.

Mrs. Avery opened the back gate and closed it quietly.

"Oh," Clayton said, giving his mother what he hoped was a winning smile. "Hi, Mom." He paused. "Where are your shoes?"

"Get in the car," she whispered, opening the side door to the garage.

"Why?"

"Shhhh." She looked over her left shoulder toward the house and shuddered visibly. "No talking. Get in the car."

Now, the last time his mother told him to get into the car without explaining why, it was because she was tricking him into sitting in the office for a whole hour with some lady doctor who wanted to know all about his *feelings*. After that, Clayton refused to accompany his mother on any driving trip unless she told him exactly where they were going and specified whether there were snacks involved.

But today. Today his mother's eyes were wild and red.

And she had no purse. And she would never leave the house without shoes unless it was an emergency.

Clayton got in the car.

Mrs. Avery had friends in Des Moines. Fellow librarians she would meet at conferences, and they would have lovely dinners where everyone talked about books and politics and trends in the larger culture. Since her marriage, she saw these friends rarely if at all. Still, she continued to send them Christmas cards every year and received them in turn.

If she showed up at their doorstep, surely they would not refuse her safe harbor. Surely they would not turn her away. One cannot, she reasoned, turn one's back on a mother with a child.

Clayton sat in the passenger's seat. He had, she noticed, very quietly unbuckled his seat belt, and slouched comfortably. He had shoved two pieces of a foul-smelling purple gum into his mouth and now chewed it greedily, blowing fat bubbles and letting them pop with a dull, wet smack.

"There's a trash bag right there. Let's get rid of the gum."

"No," Clayton said, turning toward the window. He had gum in his hair. As a librarian, Mrs. Avery was fundamentally opposed to gum and wouldn't mind it if it was simply banned from the town, or even the nation.

She turned to her son. Her beloved little boy. "*Now!*" she screamed.

"Okay, okay. *Jeez, Mom.*" The gum fell out of his

mouth. He missed the trash bag and it fell on the floor. Mrs. Avery breathed in slowly through her nose. She would not notice, she decided. There were other things at stake.

"Mom," Clayton asked, "why are we back at the house?"

"Clayton, sweetheart, we're on our way to Des —" She couldn't finish.

Inexplicably, she pulled the car back over to the house and put it in park.

"How bizarre," she said, shaking her head. "Here I am on automatic pilot. At a time like this." She put the car back in drive and sped away.

Five minutes later they were back at the house.

"Mom, why are we —" Clayton said with his mouth, once again, full of gum.

"No talking," Mrs. Avery said. She raked her fingers through her hair and grabbed a handful at the nape of her neck, holding on tight. "Just drive," she said to herself, "just keep driving."

She decided to head north. She didn't know anyone to the north, but she could get on the freeway and that ran away from town and not toward it. They could stay in a motel, maybe. Or sleep under the stars in a field. She gunned the engine and gripped the wheel with her free hand. The freeway was wide and fast, but after about a minute, she noticed that it started to curve — imperceptibly at first, but with a shrinking radius, until it was all she could do to stay in her lane. When they passed the sign that said WELCOME TO HAZELWOOD, it was all she could do to keep from crying. The road snaked up the rise and emptied into the town's streets. She drove slowly to the top of the hill, the tangled wood of Henderson's Gully stretching silently to their right.

"All right," she said, more brightly than she had ever said anything in her life. "Not a problem. No problems here. We'll just take Old Twenty. That meets up with—"

"Mom," Clayton said. "What's that on our house?"

"Clayton, what did I say about talking? There's nothing on our—Oh. My God, *what is that*?"

It was a cloud. Or, more accurately, it was clearly meant to look like a cloud. It was large and puffy, like a dish of ice cream, like the clouds in cartoons or storybooks. And it was floating right over their house. Mrs. Avery stopped the car in the middle of the street. Their house was in shadow. She could see that four windows were broken and the gutters on the northern side looked as though they had been ripped off by a strong wind. As they watched, the house seemed to be aging quickly. The paint—only six months old—peeled and flaked to the ground like snow. The boards warped. The porch sagged. Another window broke. And another.

The cloud above the house darkened, rumbled, and rained. Lightning hit the yard surrounding the house.

"Mom?"

But Mrs. Avery didn't answer. This had happened once before—the day she said that the woman on the other side of the door couldn't have her son. The day she made her husband alter his agreement. The cloud began circling around the roof, and then spiraling outward. She looked back toward the shadowed forest at the side of the road. There were stories about the gully, but those were just *stories*. No one knew about the woman whispering in the Avery house. The woman who wanted her son. If Clayton couldn't escape, at least he could *hide*.

Mrs. Avery felt a sob threatening to explode out of her chest. She gasped, and turned to her son, cupping his face in her hands.

"Run. Run *now*. Go into Henderson's Gully and get down low. Find branches and cover yourself, and don't move until I come calling for you."

Clayton's face went from white to red. He began to cry. Snot flowed from his pudgy nose, and Mrs. Avery wiped it away with the back of her hand. "But—"

"I'll keep driving. Hopefully, that thing will think you're still in the car and will follow me." She kissed the top of his head. "Run. *Don't let anyone see you*."

She reached across his body, briefly laid her thin hand on the curve of his cheek, and inhaled deeply at the very smell of him. Then she opened the door and shoved him out of the car. She pulled the door closed and drove away, leaving Clayton standing in the road, weeping and terrified. She did not let herself look back.

Chapter Thirty
Wendy Underground

WENDY WAS IN THE DARK. THE SKY WAS GONE, THE GRASS was gone. The chair and the red-nailed hand and the welcome sign and the beautiful schoolhouse were all gone, gone, gone. She coughed and spat. Dirt in her mouth; dirt in her nose.

A voice whispered in the dark—a dry, quiet, papery kind of voice, like an autumn leaf right before it crumbles away to nothing.

Is she...could she be...

"Hello?" Wendy attempted to say, but she choked

instead. Gravel between her teeth. Clay on her tongue. She spat again.

Is she like us? Is she?

No, child. That one's alive.

Like the boy? Is she like that boy?

He was a real boy.

I once was a real boy.

You, never!

I was! I know I was!

Hush! Don't frighten her. That last voice seemed older than the rest, and male, and slightly pompous, like a substitute teacher. The rest sounded like children.

"Where am I?" Wendy managed. She spat a few more times and began feeling around in the dark. She was leaning against a curved wall made of packed earth—though it wasn't packed very well. As she ran her fingers along the sides, she could feel a fine powder crumbling away in her hands.

It should be rather obvious where you are, girl.

Oooooh! She's a girl! I was a girl, I think.

You weren't neither.

You don't believe anyone.

I want to touch her.

Get back, all of you! She'll go away, and then you'll be sorry!

"Stop talking," Wendy said to the darkness. "Let me think." She shut her eyes as tightly as she could and opened them slowly. Nothing. Darkness. She tried it again. This time she could see pale glimmers of light— so faint that it was as likely as not that she was imagining them. Still, as it was better than nothing, she got onto her hands and knees and crawled slowly toward the limpid fragments glowing in the dark.

Come back here at once, young lady.

"I'm not convinced that you're real," Wendy said to the darkness. "I might be dreaming or I might be awake. In the end, they're kind of the same. No matter what, you only ever know about half of what's going on. And even then you only *mostly* know. I'll just talk to my*self*, thank you."

There's no difference, she told herself, between talking to your*self* and talking to imaginary voices. Either way it means you've gone crazy. She'd find a way out, she decided, crazy or not.

I do wish you'd stop and listen, child. I have questions.

"*You* have questions," Wendy snorted, bending close to examine the shards of light on the ground. They were made of glass. She picked two up and held them in her hands, though she gripped too tightly and cut the top of her left palm.

"Ouch!" she said.

Oh! Children! The older voice drew closer. He sounded breathless and excited. In the darkness, Wendy rolled her eyes. His voice sounded exactly like one of those overly pompous substitute teachers who made someone like Wendy want to throw something. *Observe how she can hold the Lady's mirror in her hands. Locomotion is one of the traits of those with both bodies and souls. See how delicate human skin is—one slice and it tears like a leaf and she bleeds.*

The childlike voices gasped. They gave a collective *ohhhhhh*.

Was ours like that? Did we bleed too? Another child's voice. Hushed and horrified. Wendy found it intensely annoying.

"It's not a big deal to bleed. Everyone does it."

We don't, several voices said sadly.

Wendy ignored this and examined the glass shards in her hands. If it was a mirror, it was unlike any that she'd ever seen. First, it created its own light. Wendy had heard of plants and animals having bioluminescence: strange, shy creatures that lived in the dark, making light on their skin like they were magic. But she had never heard of a bioluminescent mirror before. Second, the mirror appeared to have two reflective surfaces, not one. And third, the mirror wasn't reflecting anything in front of it. Instead, other images appeared in the glowing surfaces, and the images flickered and changed. She saw a brightly colored bird gliding over an empty street, its black eye scanning up, down, and sideways. She saw a purple house with ivy growing in and out of the windows, its tendrils fanning across the roof as though looking for something. And she saw two boys standing in front of a patch of green as a police car fishtailed to a stop right in front of them.

"Anders!" she yelled. "Jack! Get me out of here!"

Chapter Thirty-one
The Long Arm of the Law

"YOU KNOW," JACK WHISPERED TO ANDERS, "THIS IS THE second time I've been arrested since I got here."

"Shut up, kid," the officer said. He, like his partner, held a lit cigarette in his mouth, which bobbed up and down when he talked. Jack wondered whether their ashes flicked into each other's faces, and if they did, whether the officers minded it. The smoke curled around their heads and thickened the air.

"You got the Portsmouth?" Anders said in a voice so quiet it was barely more than a breath.

"What's that, kid?" asked the officer in the passenger seat.

"Nothing, sir," Anders said helpfully. "It's just that your cigarettes are bothering my allergies." He coughed a few times to prove his point.

"Right," said the officer in the driver's seat, taking another drag off the cigarette. "No more talking."

The squad car serpentined through the town, doubling back and looping around blocks so often that Jack felt dizzy. The officer in the passenger's seat kept talking on the radio, trying to figure out what he was supposed to do with the two boys, but something with the radio wasn't working right.

"Dispatch, this is car five-nine-oh. We—"

"It's inappropriate to use the dispatch system for grocery lists," said a woman's terse voice on the radio. "You may discuss boxes of Cheerios after hours."

"No, dispatch, we've picked up the boy—"

"We are not looking for a *toy*. We're looking for a *boy*."

"*No*, we're informing you that we've apprehended—"

"I don't care what you've pretended, Officer. This is no time to be playing games. We've got a manhunt going on, and all of our jobs are at stake."

And so on.

The officers in the front seat swore and complained.

"You watch," said the officer in the driver's seat, "they're just doing this so that we bring him into the *station* and *they* get the reward."

"Typical," said the other. "But we can play at that game. We'll just wait until we get a location on old man Avery. We'll deliver the kid to the Man himself." They turned up the radio and listened closely, though it was difficult as the static became worse and worse with each passing second.

Anders and Jack exchanged glances.

"This is ridiculous," the first officer said.

The second officer pointed to a squad car parked in front of a house. "Look. There's Johnson and Clarke. We'll talk to them."

"But they'll want a cut. I don't want to divide it four ways."

"Better four ways than nothing. And that's what we'll get if the jerks from the station get their hands on the kid. You think *they'll* give us our due?"

He slid the squad car to a halt and the two officers got out.

Anders turned to Jack.

"The Portsmouth," he hissed. "Do you have it?"

"*What?*" Jack asked.

"The stone. That Frankie gave you."

"But how did you—"

Anders shook his head impatiently. "Never mind that part. Do you know how to use it?"

Jack pulled the stone out of his pocket. It vibrated and heated in his hand, and the blue veins stood bright and livid against the pearly surface. "No," he said at last.

"It made, I don't know, a window or something. Frankie did it so we could hear a meeting." Though he knew the words were *true*, Jack was horrified at how unlikely they sounded. And how his voice sounded so very much like someone caught in a lie.

"It opens a door," Anders said slowly. "Press it against a wall and tell it where you want to go, or what you want to see."

Jack shook his head. "You do it."

"I can't," Anders said. "Not here anyway. You're going to have to pull me in after you. Frankie and I've tried it all over the place. Don't tell Wendy." Anders paled at the thought. "She doesn't know. And she'd kill me if she did. Anyway, Frankie could only make it work when he was standing right on an eruption point. I could stand a little ways off, but not very far. I'm pretty sure *you* can use it anywhere."

"What do you mean, *I can use it anywhere*? Why would *I* be different from *you*? And anyway, Frankie did it. *He* opened the window when we were outside Mr. Avery's house." Jack shuddered. The sound of Mr. Avery's voice saying *out of the picture* still rang in his ears.

"Are you sure about that?"

And Jack thought for a moment. Frankie pressed Jack's hand to the wall, but it was Jack, not Frankie, who held the stone, and it was Jack, not Frankie, who thought, *What's going on in there that he wants me to see?* Had *Jack* made the Portsmouth work without realizing?

"But"—Jack's mouth had gone quite dry—"why can't you guys use it? Why me?"

Anders shook his head. "Oh, Jack," he said softly. "Haven't you guessed? Don't you see that—oh! quick! They're coming. Open a door, Jack."

"But I don't know how."

Anders pressed Jack's hand against the back of the seat. "You *do* know how, even if you don't realize it. Tell it where you want to go. *Concentrate.*"

"Hey!" the taller officer shouted. "What are you two kids doing? *Hey! Knock that off!*"

"Now, Jack!"

Jack shook his head. There was no way. *I just want to see my mom*, he thought desperately. *I just want to be home.* He shut his eyes.

And a door appeared. It opened into the darkness. Jack and Anders tumbled inside.

Chapter Thirty-two
The Search Party

It took four hours for the police to arrive. In the meantime, Mr. and Mrs. Schumacher searched the entire house and the surrounding area while they waited for the police. At dawn, Mr. Schumacher went to the station, but only found a single harassed-looking dispatcher, who told him that the entire force was out on a manhunt and that he needed to sit tight until they could spare an officer to take down the report.

"Fill out the missing persons form and I'll call it in," she said kindly.

Mr. Schumacher sat holding the pen over the paper for a full ten minutes, trying desperately to remember Wendy's name. Finally, when the name returned to him in a flash, he filled out the form as best he could (How tall was she again? How much did she weigh? Did he know those things before?) and left the station in tears, repeating her name again and again and again.

Wendy, Wendy, Wendy. The entire family turned her name into a mantra. *Wendy, Wendy, Wendy.* Until at last the officers arrived.

Frankie couldn't help himself. He had forgotten about his carefully planned sighs and dreamy smiles, he had forgotten to keep his face empty except for the scars. He sat at the table next to his mom and dad as two police officers wrote down notes regarding the disappearance of Wendy. It was a waste of time, Frankie knew, and he couldn't stand it anymore.

"Have you noticed any changes in her behavior patterns in recent days, Mr. and Mrs. Schumacher? Is it out of the question that she may have run away?"

"No," Mrs. Schumacher said, balancing her forehead against the heel of one hand and closing her eyes tightly. She had her other arm looped around Frankie's middle, as though he might suddenly launch upward and fly away. "Not at all. I mean, she got into a fight not too long ago with that Avery boy."

"That's nothing new," grunted the other officer.

Frankie's father pushed his chair away from the table

with a loud squeak that made everyone wince. "I can't just sit here and wait. We've done this before."

"Sit," Mrs. Schumacher commanded, but he was already opening the drawer next to the refrigerator, rattling around the contents until he produced a set of keys.

"With any luck," he said, grabbing his seed cap off the hook, "she's wandering the streets looking for trouble." Mrs. Schumacher slammed the palm of her hand on the kitchen table, making the dishes rattle, but he was already opening the door. "I'm gonna bank on luck."

The officers didn't get up. The first officer picked up his mug and brought it to his mouth. "It's best to leave this to the professionals, Jed. You'll only muck things up."

"Seems to me, you told me that once before," Mr. Schumacher said with a hollow laugh.

Frankie looked directly at his father, something that he rarely did. His father had very large brown eyes that were often darkened with exhaustion or regret or even sorrow. Very slowly, Jed Schumacher adjusted the back of the seed cap and fitted it over his balding head. His eyes were on the knot of scars.

"Franklin James," he said, "you coming?"

"He most certainly is not," Mrs. Schumacher said, but Frankie was already on his feet and walking quickly to the door. His father shrugged.

"I'll feel better not to have him out of my sight. Call the Jorgensons and the Rustads and—and—who else?

Jan Hoveland. Tell them I'll pick them up and we'll go looking. And tell Clive Fitzpatrick too. I tried their phone already, so you'll have to go over there. He's a weird old coot, but he found Frankie, and I never forgot it."

"Frankie. *Franklin James.* You turn yourself right around, young man," Frankie heard his mother say, but his father closed the door behind them, and she didn't open it again.

At the second stop sign, Frankie saw Lancelot. He was perched at the top of the sign showing the intersection between Elm Street and Johnson Avenue. He was staring down the edge of his hooked nose like a hawk. Frankie waved at the bird, which waved back with both wings.

The bird, Frankie knew, was telling him something. *Here. Now. Come.* Frankie nodded.

And before his father could stop him, Frankie opened the door and sprinted through the yards, heading indirectly for Henderson's Gully. He could hear his father honking the horn, wrenching the door open, then closed, and swearing behind him. His father would attempt to chase him, but he would never catch up. Frankie may have been silent and hurt, but he was *fast.* He pounded across the yards, cutting a path that a truck couldn't follow, until the sounds of his father's shouting receded and he could only hear his own breath and the rustle and beat of Lancelot's wings. The bird, he knew, wouldn't leave him, and that was a comfort.

The scars on his face burned. She was angry. Frankie knew it in his bones.

Angry was good, he thought. Angry meant that they still had a little time and that all was not—not yet anyway—lost.

Frankie turned at the end of Elm Street and slid into the curtain of green that fringed the edge of the forest. The trees pressed close to one another, but Frankie didn't slow down. He knew the gap between each tree, each bush, each fallen snag. He knew the hidden paths, invisible to the eye but not the body. He scrambled and ran. All he could hear was the pounding of his feet, his rasping breath, and the constant drum of his heartbeat, reminding him that he was alive.

Even now.

Even *still*.

There was a door somewhere in that thicket of trees and vines and muck at the bottom of the gully. But where it was and how to open it, that was another matter indeed.

Chapter Thirty-three
Connections

JACK AND ANDERS WERE IN DARKNESS, TOTAL AND ABSOLUTE. They gripped each other's hands for dear life, the Portsmouth pressed firmly between their palms.

"You know," Jack began, but his voice sounded dreamy and far away, and he had forgotten what he was about to say.

It smelled like flowers. No, it smelled like baking bread. Jack had a sudden memory of a small boy lying on a bed made from petals and feathers, and wondered whether it was a painting he had once seen, and why the image seemed so real to him, and why it made him suddenly want to cry.

"Jack," a voice whispered. "Ja-ack."

"Mom?" Jack asked. "Is that you?" But of course it wasn't his mother. Jack's mother had a clear, sharp voice. But this voice was neither sharp nor clear. It was soft, velvety, and dark.

"Anders, did you hear that?" But Anders was silent. If it wasn't for the sensation of Anders's hand holding on to Jack's own, he would have believed himself to be alone.

"Jack, I've missed you," the dark voice said.

"Where are you?"

"Open the door."

"What door? I can't see anything."

"Open the door, honey."

Without warning, Jack felt his body slam against something hard and rough. He felt around for a handle.

"Anders! Help me!"

Anders moved nearer and helped to push.

"It's not supposed to be stuck like this," Anders said.

"What *is* it supposed to be like?" Jack huffed. The door gave its first creak. "Why is this so difficult?"

"Piecing together what's been broken is always difficult," the dark voice said. "But that doesn't mean it's impossible."

"I don't even know what that's supposed to mean," wheezed Jack.

"What *what's* supposed to mean?" Anders asked.

"Just open the door, darling," the dark voice said.

Fumbling in the dark, Jack ran his hands along the bumpy wood.

"I'm trying to. Ouch!" A splinter lodged itself deep into his index finger. Finally his hands found a deep groove and a metal latch. He lifted the latch with a slow creak, and felt the door jerk out of his hand, as though blown by a strong wind. Jack and Anders found themselves tumbling though space, through time, through door after door, until landing with a thud on a narrow strip of rug in a hallway crammed with paintings and bookcases. Clive and Mabel's house. They lay in a crumpled heap on the floor.

"Are we dead?" Jack asked, unable to move.

"I don't think so," Anders said. "Dead people don't care if someone's sitting on their knees. Could you please move, by the way?"

Jack tried to tilt his body upward, just as someone gasped.

"Oh! My!" a woman's voice said. "Clive, dear. He's back. And Anders is with him." Mabel knelt down next to Jack. Her eyes were very red, with dark circles underneath, and her cheeks were pale and streaked with tears. "Thank God," she said, and threw her arms around his neck so tightly that he choked.

But Jack was only half listening. The voice he heard in the dark was still speaking. It was muffled and quiet, as though it was coming from behind a very thick wall, but he could hear it all the same.

My darling, the voice said through the walls.

Be careful, it said from the floors, from the baseboards, from the ceiling.

Be brave, my brave boy. The voice thickened and choked. *My brave, brave boy*.

Jack laid his hand on the floorboards to prop himself up. They were hot. He touched the wall on his right. It was hot too. He didn't pull his hand away.

It's not heat, Jack thought. *It's love. This house loves me*.

Tentatively, he patted the floorboards with the pads of his fingers. The warm wood shivered at his touch. The books, the paintings, even the figurines on the shelves, all shook and rumbled.

"The house," Jack said slowly. "Why does it—" He stopped. He couldn't say it.

"Ah," Clive said as he came up the stairs. "He's starting to understand."

Chapter Thirty-four
When a House Is No Longer a House

GOG AND MAGOG POSITIONED THEMSELVES AT THE TOP OF the stairs, facing downward. Sunlight poured from the landing window, casting a long rectangle of light that draped over their hulking shoulders, giving their silvery fur a curious gleam. They sat perfectly still, and if it wasn't for the occasional lash of the tail, Jack could have sworn they were statues.

"Tea," Mabel said finally. "I'll make tea." She stepped over the cats and went down the stairs.

"Let me help, Mrs. Fitzpatrick," Anders said quickly,

scrambling to his feet and hurrying after her. The cats didn't move. Clive had lowered himself down to the floor and leaned his back against the wall. Sitting down like that, without his constant movements, Jack could see just how small the man really was. And how *old*.

"What does Anders know?" Jack said. "About me. And..." He faltered. "All this... weird stuff."

"Tough to say, really," Clive said, chuckling. "That boy always knows more than he says. Still. Probably everything. And, though it pains my professional ego to say this, he likely knows more than I. He'd never admit to it, though."

"Mr. Avery wants to kill me," Jack said. His voice was deadly calm, after the many hours of fear. Jack felt sure that he must still *feel* fear... somewhere deep inside himself. But after all this time, he could no longer *feel* himself feeling it.

"Indeed he does, Jack," Clive said, shaking his head. "He's wanted to kill you from the day you were born. Now, though, his motives are different. Before he wanted power, but now, I'm not convinced he even *wants* power anymore. Not like he used to. All he wants is his son — an understandable urge, of course, and natural, but the cost to the rest of us is terrible indeed. To save his son, he must kill you, or so he believes. If he kills you now, he'll kill your mother too. Or half of her anyway. The *good* half. Which means that what's left of the magic underneath our feet will be evil magic forever. No choices. No goodness. No hope. No nothing."

Jack sat up straight. "I have *no idea* what you're talking about. My mother is in San Francisco. She's smart and busy and just a person. There's nothing magic about her. And—" His voice caught in his throat, sharp as a fishhook. He swallowed. "She doesn't even know who I am anymore."

"That's where you're wrong, boy. Your mother knows *exactly* who you are. She knew the moment you laid your hand on her door. Indeed, that was the very moment that she began to wake up."

"This stupid house isn't *family*. It's not my *mother*." Under his feet, he could feel the floorboards hiccuping slightly, as though repressing a sob.

Clive looked at Jack steadily in the face. "Well," he said, "of course not." Jack relaxed. "At first glance, you are sitting in something made of wood and plaster and glass. A house has never given birth to a boy, and therefore we can assume that a house has never been anyone's mother." Jack stared at the wall. It was made of hand-smeared plaster, painted over many times, and the paint was thick and bubbly. It seemed solid enough. But two bubbles began to swell and green. They grew lashes. They blinked. They were damp with tears. Jack couldn't move.

"Clive—" he whispered.

"And," Clive continued, as though Jack had not spoken, "on the other hand, *of course she is*. Not the house per se, but inside—the fibers of the floorboards, the pebbles of plaster, the joists, the doors. Everything. She's, well, she's *inside*. And she's trapped. On some level, Jack, you knew. You've always known."

Jack laid his hand on the wall, and felt the wall press back at him. "I just don't—"

"Listen Jack, there isn't much time. Your friend Wendy is in terrible danger. So is Clayton Avery, though he doesn't know it. And so are you. There's magic underground. Quite a bit of it, actually. You know this already. I know you've been reading. I know you've been taking notes. And I know it's been *difficult* for you to believe, yet you *have* believed all the same. It's true there was a Guardian of the Magic who protected it from those who might want to manipulate it. But after a terrible lapse in judgment, the Guardian split in two and became the Lady and the Other, wicked and good—that's all true, Jack."

"But that's just—" Jack stopped. He was about to say that it was *just a story*, but he couldn't bring himself to do it. He wiped his nose with his free hand, but kept the other pressed against the wall. He could feel the shape and warmth of another hand straining at the wallpaper. "Even if it *is* true, it doesn't have anything to do with me."

Clive shook his head impatiently. *"It has everything to do with you."* He closed his eyes and breathed through his nose until he calmed. "For well over a hundred years, in each generation, the Lady has swapped Her new child with a son of an Avery, and each time both children—

one human and one Magic—were swallowed up in the transfer of power, and lost forever. You've *read* this, Jack. Four years ago, Jack, that child was *you*."

Clive paused. Jack shook his head. *Wendy said I was normal*, he thought wildly. *I felt normal.*

"I was there, Jack; I *saw* it. The Lady's Other—the *good* half—tried in previous generations to stop the swap, but as She could not *think* like Her wicked half, She couldn't make a plan. So She was doomed to fail. Four years ago, She came to me looking for assistance in hiding you. I knew a few spells, you see. Together, we infused magic into the very fibers of the house, created a little magical world sealed away from the Lady's knowledge or power. We hid you right under Her nose, and you grew. I know you have no memory of this," Clive waved Jack's protestations away.

"*Will* I?" Jack asked. "Remember, I mean."

"If all goes well, your memories will come back in time. Or that's the theory. My theories haven't been entirely accurate, I'm afraid." He shook his head and sighed. "I thought we'd be able to hide you until you were grown. But the Lady learned of our plans. She trapped the Other in this house—an unintended consequence of my earlier spells. Then, she took you and set off to perform the swap, intending to deal with me at a later time. She bound me with vines and forced me to come. She wanted to force me to watch the destruction of a child that I had come to love." Clive closed his crinkled eyelids, and big tears slid into the grooves of his cheeks.

The plaster pressed against Jack's back. He could feel the outline of hands. Jack closed his eyes.

"What the Lady did *not* know was that Horace Avery is a liar. He was not about to swap his only child. He kidnapped young Frankie Schumacher, gave him a sleeping draft, and told the Lady that Frankie was Clayton. The Lady laid you in your acorn cradle at the feet of Mr. Avery. 'Yours,' she told him. Mr. Avery set the sleeping Frankie in the Lady's arms. 'Yours,' he said. But Frankie wasn't his to give. The Magic backfired. The earth shook and flashed. The Lady screamed as a rip opened in the land, pulling both Her and Frankie inside. The vines binding my hands instantly loosed, and I leaped to the rift in the land. I tried to grab him, but I was too late. And you, frightened by the noise, ran away into the fields."

"I was the kid in the field." Jack whispered. He felt empty and hollow. A dry husk. "The one Wendy saw. That was *me*."

"It was you."

Jack closed his eyes and suddenly remembered a dream. Or the dream of a dream. He could remember a pair of hands guiding his small shoulders through a field of sunflowers. The hands were green, as was the face of the woman who owned the hands. Green hands, green face, green eyes, and a shock of yellow hair that smelled like the silk from corn. In his dream, the woman told him to run.

Mabel arrived with a tray of milky tea and handed mugs to Jack and Clive. Jack took a sip but couldn't take any more. The thought of eating or drinking made him sick.

Mabel knelt close to Jack and cupped his face in her hands. He flinched, but she did not move. Her hands were warm and soft on his skin and her face was kind and sad at the same time.

"We wanted to keep you with us, you know," she said, and Jack noticed that her large gray eyes were wet with tears. "We made you appear as a boy, only a bit younger than your brother, Baxter. We thought it would be simple enough to stitch you into the fabric of an existing family. We gave you memories and a life. You looked like a boy; you thought like a boy; but you weren't." She swallowed hard. "We didn't know how alone you'd be, Jack. Honestly, we didn't. Clair—well, she's my sister and I love her, but she is"—she paused—"*complicated*. And your dad, bless him, is a bit of an idiot. Neither had any capacity to prepare you for this. For what you'd have to do."

And I was so alone, Jack wanted to say, but the words wouldn't come.

Clive cleared his throat. "I've been studying this problem longer than anyone, but there are parts that even I don't entirely understand. I was pretty certain that both halves would stay asleep as long as you were far away from here. We thought, son," Clive said, "you would be safe until you were old enough to set things right. You are not old enough, of course, but your family unraveled, which meant that my spell binding you to *them* unraveled too. I'm not as clever as I used to be, it seems. Or, perhaps I was never that clever to begin with. Still, it doesn't change the fact that the only person who can release Wendy is *you*, and if you do not act quickly, all hope for her will be lost."

"But what can *I* do?" Jack asked, finding his voice, but neither could answer because someone was yelling downstairs.

"Mrs. Fitzpatrick," Anders thundered from down below. *"Mrs. Fitzpatrick!"*

And Jack realized that the thunder wasn't just from Anders's voice.

The ground underneath and the air above rumbled with the sound of wheels and hinges and steel. Diesel smoke poured in through the windows, making Jack choke. He peeked past the curtain and saw trucks approaching. And bulldozers. And a wrecking ball.

And under Jack's feet, the floorboards shivered in fear.

Chapter Thirty-five
Split

"What is this place?" Wendy asked.

Nowhere, a dozen voices answered.

Everywhere, a dozen more countered, the two groups of voices twisting into one.

"That's not very helpful," Wendy muttered. She sat on the dirt in front of a scattering of glass shards, each one casting a weak light into the utter darkness. Each one showing a quick flash of...something. People and places that Wendy thought she should know, but the world outside of this dark, tight space seemed farther and farther away from her with each breath. As though her memory was pulling away, unwinding like a spool of thread as it rolls across the ground. Hang on, she told herself. Hang on for dear life.

As the oldest resident here, the pompous, substitute teacher voice said, *I do remember that the Lady of the realm had a name for it. She called it the World-Under-the-World. I don't know what She calls it now. And anyway, it didn't used to look like this.* He sighed. *It's not much of a world anymore, I'm afraid.*

"What did it used to look like?" She could hear the dry, breezy breathing of…whatever those voices were, coming closer in the darkness. She hunched her shoulders and her skin crawled. Surely they weren't anything to be afraid of. Still, their *otherness* disturbed her.

It was as big as the world, one voice whispered

Bigger, said the pompous voice. *And twice as beautiful. Magic flowed through the Under-the-World and sprung outward. It blessed the land, you see, and everyone was happy.*

A handful of voices fell to weeping. *He doesn't remember,* one voice declared. A boy, Wendy thought, about her age. *He's just making it up. None of us can remember a thing. We don't even remember our own names.*

A sound like crumpling paper stopped the voices cold.

I remember, the pompous voice said. *I do. I probably remember more than the Lady Herself does. I…knew of Her. I…don't exactly remember the capacity, you understand. Or—*

I mean to say—that I don't know why I sought to know. Only that I did. I had a diary, and I thought it terribly important to write my findings down. It was all before, well, before—he searched for the word. *It was before this...* His voice trailed away.

Wendy reached down and picked up several more mirror shards. They clinked and shimmered in her hands. She could see how the shapes might be brought together, fitted neatly like a puzzle.

There wasn't much left to hold them up, I'm afraid. The Magic's been siphoning out of this place for years, the pompous voice said.

"But why? Where has it been going?"

For well over a century, there's only been half a Guardian. Her good half's been locked out, you see? It's a terrible way to run things. Only half the planning, half the insight, half the forethought and creativity. My guess is that the other half's been stolen. Turned into money, or human power. A waste and a shame, if you ask me. She's supposed *to keep that sort of thing from happening. It's Her* job. *The Magic is meant to bless the land, not to enrich greedy men. But, given that She's only* half *Herself, She can't see it. Just look what She did to that poor mirror.*

"You mean this?" Wendy let the shards spill to the ground.

Indeed. It was one of my first discoveries—and a very clever one at that. I had thought it would make me famous as a...a...well, whatever it was that I did. When She was whole,

She had a mirror that reached nearly up to the sky, where She could watch over the Magic as it poured out into the world. She could do so Herself, of course, and She often did walk about on the surface, keeping an eye on things. Still, though, it's hard for anyone to be in several places at once. Even a magical being.

So She would use the mirror to see. But, when She split the Magic—and Herself—into pieces, the World-Under-the-World began to shrink and fade. The first to go was the sky. Then the trees, and everything green. She broke the mirror, saying She couldn't bear to see the ugliness of the world above, but we knew better. She was ashamed.

"That sounds really stupid," Wendy said, looking at the shapes of the shards. "And a waste of a perfectly good mirror." They looked so sad all broken up like that. Wendy fluttered her fingers. Maybe, she thought, it would be a better light source if it was all put back together. If it was one, big, glowing object. Then at least she could see. And maybe she could see a way out.

Indeed. As I said, only half the planning. If this continues, I don't know what will become of all of us. Not that She cares. What's it to Her if we are all buried under the bluff? She has what She needs. Took our life force, abandoned what's left to this level of childish and trifling conversation until the end of time, I suppose.

Don't be like that, meanie, another voice said.

Yeah, Mr. Bad Breath, chimed another.

Do you see what I mean?

Wendy felt her skin run suddenly cold. "What do you mean you're what's left after She took the life force—" She stopped. "What *are* you, exactly?"

We had names once. And families. But that's all gone now, and we have been erased—or mostly so. I'm sure you know, my dear, what we are, even if you don't want to say it. Indeed, I daresay that you will be joining our little fellowship as soon as the Lady returns.

Wendy felt something dry and light press against her back and whisper in her ear.

We are souls.

Chapter Thirty-six
Journey Underground

FRANKIE HELD ON TO THE SAPLING TREES FOR BALANCE AS he negotiated his way down the steepest part of the gully. Lancelot, apparently tired of dodging branches, clung to Frankie's shoulder, and, though the claws made him wince, Frankie allowed him to stay. The bird clucked and murmured, a constant whirring of whistles and non-sensical syllables that Frankie felt he might be able to understand if he could only concentrate long enough.

But there was no time. No time at all.

By the time he made it to the mucky bottom of the

gully, his scars burned so hot and bright Frankie was sure they must be glowing. He wondered if it was possible for scars of this type to reopen, or if they were simply reliving painful memories.

If so, the scars weren't the only ones.

With each step, he saw more vividly the hulking figure of Mr. Avery standing next to a woman—or at least he thought at first that she was a woman. A woman with skin like the smooth bark of a maple sapling and softened by moss. Mr. Avery's voice saying, *Of course he is my son, he looks just like me.* And she reached out her hand and touched his cheek with her finger.

Her touch burned.

Burned.

It sliced curve upon curve into his skin, but he couldn't cry out and he couldn't move.

But someone screamed. A woman perhaps. Or something quite like a woman.

And there was a terrible rumble under his feet, as though the land had changed to water.

And then the light vanished and he was alone in a room littered with broken glass. There was a day—after innumerable days, with the bodiless whispers in the dark and fingers made of wood and root clutching at his face, holding him down—when a man appeared as though on the other side of a screen. An old man with a kind face that Frankie recognized from around town. *I can pull you out, boy,* the man told him, *but it will hurt.*

You've been tricked, Lady, the man had said. *The swap did not occur. See? I've brought it back to You.*

Frankie watched as the old man reached in and handed something to the Lady's woody, sluggish hands. The fingers released his face and cupped an acorn cradle — but it was empty. Her child — Her Magic Child — was gone.

A trick! the Lady's voice said. *Another trick!* Quickly, the old man grabbed Frankie by the back of his shirt and pulled.

A scream. Then silence. Frankie looked over his shoulder as the woody hands sank into the ground, and all trace of the Lady was gone.

Come back! Her voice seeped through the ground, through the walls of the underground cave. *Come back to me.* But Clive had already wrapped him in a blanket and didn't seem to hear Her. *Come back!*

And it did hurt. Terribly. And continued to hurt, though more dully thereafter.

You must stay silent, the man told him. *She is asleep, though barely. Your voice will not work now, I daresay, but in time it will come back. You must not use it. We can't afford the risk. Your silence will be useful. The time will come when your voice will also be useful, but that time is not now. Do you understand?*

The man wrapped him in a blanket and carried him to the police station where his parents were called. Later, the mayor, the minister, and the Ladies Auxiliary called for an ice-cream social to be held on the lawn in front of the town hall. Everyone came, except for the richest man in town, or his wife, or his young son. People noticed, but they did not mention it. They knew better.

Frankie pressed his hand against his scars. The burning was worse now, which meant that he was close. He winced, set his teeth against the pain, willed himself to keep from crying out. He wasn't altogether sure whether his voice would even work, should his resolve for silence fail him. Other than the few words he spoke to Jack — and even now they seemed barely real, like a dream, or the dream of a dream — Frankie had kept his promise to Clive and stayed silent.

He knelt down at the edge of a slow-moving stream and laid his hands on the muddy ground. It was under him somewhere — that dark place. Which meant, he was pretty sure, that his sister was under there as well. He would find her, and he would trade places with her. The trick, of course, would be to do it before She wised up to it. He'd have to act fast.

Lancelot circled a point in the grass about fifty feet in front of Frankie, and landed on a rock. The bird looked back at Frankie with an unmistakably pointed expression. Frankie dropped the handful of mud and wiped his hand on the side of his shorts. He stood and walked to the rock where the bird sat perched and looking down.

There was a hole.

It was not a particularly large hole — just small enough,

though, for a person to slip through, and, judging by the muddy footprints and the impressions of fingers scraping through the loamy muck, someone recently had. Frankie leaned over and squinted into the darkness.

"Oh, thank God!" a voice shouted from below. "Help! I'm stuck down here. My mom. Someone has to call my mom." The voice hiccuped with unrepressed sobs, and its consonants lisped and trudged through what sounded like a waterfall of snot. "And, and, the fire department. And a SWAT team. Just get me out of here." Frankie turned to Lancelot who opened his wings and shook them slightly. *My thoughts exactly*, Frankie wanted to say, but did not.

"And, and, oh my God. Is that you, Freak Show?"

Frankie sighed, shook his head, and stood up. Lancelot looked at him quizzically. Frankie wished he could talk to the bird. The bird had been, for as long as Clive had had him, Frankie's friend. Though he was sure it was only because Clive had instructed the bird to do that, Frankie appreciated it all the same. It's not every day that a person makes a friend. Especially when a person doesn't talk.

From down below, Clayton Avery's panicked voice echoed through the hole. "No, no, no. Sorry, sorry, sorry. I know your name isn't Freak Show, it's...it's...I mean I know it, I swear! It's...Frankie! Your name is Frankie! Ha! I knew it! Seriously, Frankie, I'm so, so sorry about the Freak Show thing, but you have got to go and get some help. I have, um, um — money! Yes! Money! Want some?"

Frankie leaned down and put his face right next to the parrot's bright beak. Lancelot closed his eyes and laid his head right on Frankie's scars. The scars, after heating steadily the closer Frankie came to the gully, were now blisteringly hot. Frankie wouldn't have been surprised if they were steaming. Startled, the bird squawked, backed up, and flew away. After waving sadly good-bye, Frankie dangled his feet into the hole and slid inside.

Chapter Thirty-seven
Joy, and Other Weapons

MABEL, ANTICIPATING THE TRUCKS, HAD ALREADY STOPPED BY at a few different houses with a few choice words. People were ready. Mrs. Schumacher activated the phone tree and Mrs. Nilsson rounded people up in her van. She also brought her barbeque trailer and a yearling hog for the occasion. Anders's father and two of his older brothers blocked three sides of the house with very large tractors. Neighbors arrived with blankets and picnic baskets and seated themselves on the grass. Mabel's friends from the Ladies Auxiliary moved through the crowd, shaking hands and kissing cheeks and patting backs. Everyone was glad to see them.

Jack and Anders stood side by side in front of the window and watched. Mabel walked toward the door. "Don't let them out," she said without looking back. Clive laid his hands on the boys' shoulders.

Jack rested his knuckles on the sill. It was warm and oddly soothing. He watched the faces of the neighbors who gathered on the lawn. Some chatted and waved at Mabel. They scowled at the oncoming bulldozers while passing around cups of coffee and paper plates piled with doughnuts and fresh fruit and fourteen types of pie. The children played tag, pin the tail on the donkey, and capture the flag. There was even a piñata.

There were others, however, who did not sit on blankets, but instead wandered about in a daze, vaguely bumping into one another as though sleepwalking. Jack turned to his uncle.

"Some of these people didn't choose to come out here, did they?"

Clive took a step back. "No, son. Not everyone."

Jack nodded. "So who did it? Aunt Mabel? The house?" Jack looked at his hands. "Did I do it?"

"It was the house, which is to say the Lady's Other, Her good half, *inside* the house. Ever since you came home, She's been able to send tendrils of Her Magic outward—not a lot, you understand. Thin roots and vines stretching out and retracting."

"Right." Jack looked very carefully at his uncle's face. Clive had an impish look to him, as though his face had been carved from the flesh of an apple and left out to dry, wrinkly and sweet at the same time. "If you don't mind my asking, Uncle Clive, what are you?"

Clive's face broke into a wide grin. "Me? I am a person. A man."

Jack looked at Anders, who stared, embarrassed, at the ground. He turned back to his uncle. "And what am I, then? Exactly, I mean."

"You, Jack, are *neither*. A creature of earth and Magic and the will of your mother—a Magic Child."

Anders removed his seed hat, ran his hand through his pale hair, and whistled.

"You knew, didn't you?" Jack said savagely, poking his finger into Anders's chest and making him flinch.

"A hunch," Anders said with a nervous shrug. He jammed his hands into his pockets and examined his bare feet. "I was never sure. But, truth be told, I was becoming more sure than not."

Outside, the closest bulldozer let out a tall plume of inky smoke. The driver opened the door of the cab and climbed down to the ground. He called something to the people on the grass, but they did not move. He waved his hand a few times, but they didn't even seem to see him. He removed his cap, rubbed his balding head a few times, and got back into the cab. The floor under Jack's feet felt stretched and taut, like a muscle ready to spring.

High above, the sky swirled green and red and purple. A dark black spot opened just over the horizon and began moving toward the house. Clive grabbed Jack by the front of his shirt and took Anders by the arm.

"Listen," he said, "if your mother—or the woman you've always believed to be your mother—had listened to us, you would know the stories and would, at the very least, be marginally prepared."

The ground rumbled beneath their feet.

"Stories?" Jack asked. "What does that have to do with finding Wendy?"

Clive shook his head. "Wendy doesn't need to be found. We already know where she is. She's been dragged to the same place where her brother was dragged. She has taken his place. If Mr. Avery succeeds in capturing you and destroying this house, then the Lady's good half—which is to say your mother's good half—will also be destroyed and scattered to the four winds. Only Her wickedness will remain. And nothing will prevent Wendy's soul from being ripped away—and with it all memory of her. We will only have a shadow, a gap that will itch in our minds forever."

Jack paced, holding his head. He thought he might be sick. He hadn't known Wendy long, but the thought of her *vanishing*—all memory, all everything—well, it was more than he could bear. Anders groaned a little. His face had gone quite gray and looked as though it had been twisted into a knot.

"That can't happen, Clive, it *can't*. What do I have to do?" Jack said desperately.

"Even the score," Clive said.

The floor rumbled and shook under their feet. Two vases fell off an end table and an entire bookshelf emptied its contents onto the floor. The walls shivered and quaked while spidery cracks unraveled across the plaster. All around was the sound of wind, and the sound of a woman's voice calling his name—*Jack, Jack, Jack.*

"But—"

"There is tremendous power, Jack, in the gap between good and evil. Tremendous power indeed."

Eight cars approached slowly, inching their way down the street. A very tall man walked in front. He mopped his brow with a handkerchief and dabbed at his eyes. Under his feet, the ground bubbled and swelled; it swirled in concentric circles and shimmered like oil.

"I'm going outside," Clive said. "Your mother's good half—the Lady's Other—lives and feeds on joy. All those happy people out there? That happiness is for *Her*. It spills out of us and makes Her strong. The Lady, on the other hand, has kept Herself stronger *in the past* by stealing souls—a deceitful, dirty trick if there ever was one. But effective. Right now, though, She's very weak. I daresay that's the only thing that's thus far saved Wendy—she's...a prickly girl, if you understand me. In Her current condition, the Lady wouldn't be able to get that soul if She tried. Wendy will fight Her for it, bless her."

Jack thought of the two dark bruises under Clayton Avery's eyes. And that was just for an insult. What would a girl like Wendy do to protect her *soul*? Jack shuddered. Whatever it was, Jack knew it would probably hurt.

"If I can lure the wicked half into the house, we have laid enough traps to pull the two together—or near each other anyway. You have a right, Jack, to face the two of them. They are *both* your mother, you see. But we can't fix the situation as long as Wendy is trapped in the hall under the hill." Clive looked at Anders. "Go through the back door. Cut through the field. Follow in Wendy's footsteps." He turned to Jack. "*Someone* needs to get her out, Jack. *Someone* needs to save her. But make no mistake, there will be consequences." And with that, he hurried out the door.

Chapter Thirty-eight
Another Door

DEEP UNDERGROUND, IN THAT SWILL OF DRIPPING WATER and mud and rotting leaves, Clayton Avery made two realizations:

First, he learned that he was not, as he had always believed, stronger than that freak Frankie Schumacher. Although the boy was so easily beaten up in earlier days (Clayton, in fact, had told his friends that beating up Freak Show was just no longer even a challenge), Frankie had handily dodged Clayton's fists after refusing (*refusing!*) to give him a boost out of the hole (after Clayton had promised—mostly—to help Frankie out afterward). And then, to add insult to injury, Frankie had launched Clayton into the air and brought him down onto the muddy floor with a sickening thud, and had forced him to march into a long, dark tunnel, presumably to his death.

Second, and probably more disconcerting, Clayton learned that Frankie was a dirty, rotten, lying *faker*. Frankie Schumacher, with his show-offy, ruined face, who dumbly accepted any and all taunts that Clayton could think of, without tears or threats or talk-backs— Silent Frankie Schumacher could talk. The fibbing *sneak*.

"I don't know why I have to go following a liar— ouch!"

Actually, Clayton was not following anyone. He was leading the way down the tunnel, pushed forward every now and again by a swift kick in the pants by Frankie.

Frankie, on the other hand, ever since his first *Snap out of it!* which he yelled—*yelled!*—right in Clayton's face, had not stopped talking. He was not, however, talking to Clayton—or anyone else for that matter. Sometimes he yelled at no one in particular—things like, "I'm back! You don't need her anymore!" Or: "I'll bet You feel pretty stupid for letting an old man and a little kid trick You like that! Why don't You swap out me and Wendy, and no one'll ever know!" But most of the time it was incessant muttering.

And regardless of what you called it, it was, Clayton

felt, incredibly annoying. Clayton wondered if perhaps, after not talking for so many years, Frankie simply didn't know how people normally did it.

"I want my father," Clayton whined.

"No, you don't," Frankie said, peering into the darkness ahead. "You think you do, but you don't. Trust me."

"Why would I trust—ow! No kicking!"

But Frankie didn't answer.

"*She sewed soul after soul into a quilt as wide as the world,*" Frankie muttered. "*And the quilt kept the Magic safe— mostly. But what the Lady did not know was that a rip had formed along the far hem.*" He ran his hands along the damp wall. "A rip along the far hem," he said again.

Clayton wanted to club Frankie over the head, use his body as a ladder, and peek out the top of the hole. He wanted his mother. There was dirt in his eyes, dirt in his mouth. And the worst thing—the *worst*—was the buzzing in his ear. A buzzing that had begun the day that the new kid came to stay with the Fitzpatricks and had never left. Except now, the sound had changed. Instead of the ringing of bells, it was a voice that said *Now, now, now!* Clayton nearly wept with aggravation.

"I'm allergic to something down here," Clayton said, tugging at his ears.

"Magic," Frankie said, hooking his fingers into a groove on the wall. "The Magic knows you're down here. Boy oh boy, is your dad in trouble."

"What?" Clayton asked, but Frankie did not answer.

All Clayton heard was a loud rip, as though someone was tearing a bedsheet from end to end. There was a rush of wind, and the wind smelled like wheat, like pollen, like the milk of raw corn kernels crushed under the thumb.

Clayton felt himself falling again.

And falling.

And falling.

And he felt as though he and Frankie would never stop.

Chapter Thirty-nine
The Price of a Soul

MR. PERKINS RODE IN THE CAB OF A BULLDOZER NEXT TO A man named Tim, who wore a gold earring in one ear and a tattoo on his arm with a picture of a pig with a crown of thorns and a halo and a slogan reading MEAT IS MURDER. Tim spent the ride over explaining how he works at the feedlot during the fall to pay the bills and has to wear long sleeves so his boss doesn't see the tattoo. Mr. Perkins did not care, but nodded politely as he gazed out the window.

He could see Mr. Avery walking behind them, the

ground rippling under his feet, a hankie pressed tightly over his nose. The fumes must be terrible, Mr. Perkins thought, and mopped the sweat from his brow and eyes and cheeks.

The ground under Mr. Avery's feet seemed to gather, shimmer, and unfurl like cloth. In fact, the more that Mr. Perkins thought it looked like cloth, the more it actually did—an unfolding, many-colored quilt made from thousands upon thousands of silken sections stitched painfully to one another. With each step, he could hear the quilt moan and sigh. And Mr. Perkins thought sadly about the stories his grandmother told him.

She told him *what happened* to the souls stolen by the Lady.

She told him to stay away from the old schoolhouse.

She told him that without a soul there is nothing—no memory, no mourning, no mark upon the green earth to show that you had once been alive. Just a gap. Mr. Perkins shuddered.

The quilt under his employer's feet shone and glimmered like tears.

Remember us, moaned each section.

Save us, cried the stitches.

Mr. Perkins reached into his pocket, grabbed onto his section of rawhide and held on tight.

The sun was high now, and the day was hot—hotter still inside the tight cab, with its barely functioning air conditioner breathing out a meager amount of cool air. If Mr. Perkins held his hand right up to the vent, it would mostly dry the sweat on his palm—mostly. His left hand gripped harder on the rawhide, though it was sweaty and slicked, and his hand, he knew, would smell of leather for days to come. *No matter*, he thought. *Better to stink than lose a soul.*

Tim leaned forward, and rested his fleshy chin against the dashboard, squinting into the sunlight. "Now who in tarnation is standing all over the yard? Are those balloons?"

"No, I'm sure it's just the foreman and his crew," Mr. Perkins began, but he did not finish. It wasn't the foreman on the Fitzpatricks' lawn, or any kind of crew, either.

Neighbors lounged on blankets and chatted on the porch. Mr. Fitzpatrick filled brightly colored balloons and tied them to the extended wrists of children, who shrieked as their balloon shuddered and bobbed while they ran across the yard. Mrs. Fitzpatrick moved through the growing crowd with a stack of clear plastic cups and a very large pitcher of lemonade. She poured cup after cup but didn't seem to run out.

This may have struck Mr. Perkins as odd, but he was too busy noticing something else.

"Are they coming from"—his voice was fragile and dry—"they *couldn't* be coming from the field."

But they were. The corn opened like curtains and

people poured out. They looked around, blinking, as though astonished to be where they were. They looked in surprise at the red and white checked blankets draped over their right arms and the picnic baskets in their left hands.

One by one, they shrugged, snapped their blankets open, and sat down. They opened their baskets and pulled out large ceramic bowls of potato salad, and Jell-O molds, and green bean casseroles. Dishes passed from blanket to blanket, and people scooped large, glistening mounds onto white paper plates.

Tim turned to Mr. Perkins. "Someone has to call the sheriff. Demolition properties are supposed to be cleared out and vacant. You can't go around demolishing a town picnic."

"Indeed," Mr. Perkins said, and nervously looked behind him. Where his boss had stood just a moment before was now obscured by a large black cloud rising in a large plume over the street. From inside the cloud, a woman's voice raised itself into a scream.

"Get these people out of here," roared Mr. Avery. "They're ruining *everything*."

Chapter Forty
Eruption Points

JACK AND ANDERS POUNDED DOWN THE BEATEN TRAIL through the cornfield. As they ran, Anders noticed that the corn looked worse and worse the closer they got to the schoolhouse. With each step, the green corn paled, browned, and shriveled. The ears went from swollen and ripening to underdeveloped to drooping, sick, and moldy. Anders, like his brothers, his mother and father, and his grandparents going back a thousand years, had a farmer's heart, and his farmer's heart broke at the sight of that dying corn. He didn't stop, however, and ran alongside

Jack until they reached the bright green rectangle of grass where the schoolhouse once stood.

Jack stopped.

Slowly, an outline of the old building began to emerge in the air—just the steps at first, then the sagging roof, then the boarded windows, then the outline of the door.

"Do you see that?" Jack said, pointing.

"Right," Anders explained. "You see, it's grass, but it's not regular grass, if you understand me." Anders spoke slowly and patiently, as though explaining something complicated to a very young child.

"No, no," Jack said. "I get it about the grass. It's not… *regular*. I don't even know what that word means anymore. But I'm talking about the *air*. That *outline*. Don't you see it?"

But Anders didn't see it. "An outline of what?"

"The school. Or the husk of the school. See? There's the stairs. There's the roof." Jack put his hands in his pockets and looked at the ground. "You don't see it, do you?"

"No, but that doesn't mean it isn't there." Anders took a deep breath and rubbed the top of his yellow head. "Things get wobbly on an eruption point. This place is one. Your aunt and uncle's house sits on another. And down in Henderson's Gully too. That's where they pulled out Frankie. I was little, so I don't remember much of it, but he was fine before it happened, and then he was gone. And he was, you know…*wrecked*."

"Yeah." Jack was silent. He thought about Wendy.

When he first saw her, she blocked out the sun and stood over him like some kind of angel. His first friend. "We have to get her out of there."

At that moment, from the direction of the town, came a high-pitched scream that seemed to hang in the air for a moment before blowing out across the land like wind. A thick black cloud rose over the broad trees and grew. Jack shivered. The back of his neck sweated and itched. *She's looking for me*, he thought over and over again. He reached into his pocket and pulled out the Portsmouth.

"You do know where you're going," Anders said. "Even if you don't think you do."

He took Anders's hand and slammed the Portsmouth onto the ground. Without knowing he would, he opened his mouth and called out to the land, the sky, the darkening, growing cloud. "Wendy!" he shouted.

The ground split, yawned, and pulled them inside.

Chapter Forty-one
Buried Alive

DESPITE THE FACT THAT CLAYTON AND FRANKIE WERE DEEP underground, both boys had light enough to see. One wall was made of some sort of flexible resin—and it had light on the other side. Not much, but enough to cast a weak glow into the underground space. And moving around on the other side of the wall was the shadow of a girl.

"Wendy," Frankie yelled at the wall, hitting at its surface with his fists. The wall vibrated and thrummed like the skin of a drum, but it wouldn't break. And the silhouette of Wendy didn't seem to notice.

Frankie stepped back, rubbing his hands against his face and grunting in frustration.

The walls of the hole were damp. They smelled. Every once in a while the ground around them rumbled and shook, and large hunks of damp soil fell from what served as the ceiling onto what he supposed was the floor. Clayton put his head between his knees and tried to shield his hair with his hands.

"I don't know why you're bothering," the sneak Frankie Schumacher said. "You're already filthy."

"We're going to be buried alive and it's all your fault," Clayton moaned. The dirt was dark and alive. It wormed into Clayton's eyes, itched at his ears, and filtered into his nose. He sneezed.

"We're not going to be buried alive," Frankie said. His hands pressed against the membrane wall. Each time he did so, a sharp, bright smell attacked their noses and retreated. It smelled, Clayton thought, like sap. He hated sap. It stuck to your hands, collected dirt, and wouldn't wash off.

Frankie shook his head. "There's a story that's kind of like this," he said. "Did you know?"

Clayton decided not to answer. If Frankie could pretend to be a stupid mute, then Clayton, for one, could do it too. He wasn't going to be shown up by a kid who looked like a circus freak.

"The heroes were sent to rescue the maiden who had been captured by a wicked creature. They wanted to know how to reach the maiden, as she was nowhere to be seen. They learned that in order to find the lair of the creature, they had to go down. They had to go inside and between. But we're in a different kind of a story. I don't even think we're the heroes."

"What are we if we aren't the heroes?" Clayton sniffed.

Frankie shrugged. "We could be innocent bystanders," he said. "Or roadkill."

Clayton pursed his lips together.

"That's not even a real story," he said.

"Of course it is. And anyway, how would you know? You don't even read."

"I can *read*," Clayton said.

Frankie shook his head and turned back to the membrane wall. "And you don't listen properly either."

Frankie put his face right on the skin of the membrane. It was springy and tough. It yielded to the slightest touch but sprang back instantly. It wouldn't break. He peered through. The light behind Wendy was brighter than before, sharpening the shadowed edges of her body as she bent and reached, bent and reached.

"What are you doing?" Frankie whispered, shaking his head. "Why can't you hear me?"

"What is that thing, anyway?" Clayton asked, pointing to the resin wall.

"It's a membrane, I think. The whole thing is something like a seed," Frankie said, tapping on the wall.

Clayton snorted. "That's the dumbest thing I've ever heard. A seed is small. Plus seeds aren't even *alive*."

"You should pay more attention in school. A seed *is* alive. There's a whole universe inside of it. A limitless world curled around and around itself like a spring. A seed is powerful and infinite. And by the way, you're an idiot." Frankie gasped. After all these years listening and reading and *thinking*, it felt incredibly good to finally speak. And what's more, he realized with a jolt that he had quite a bit to say. And even though he knew it wasn't very nice, it felt even *better* to insult Clayton Avery. He smiled.

"I hate you." Clayton folded his arms and looked away and Frankie turned back to the membrane wall.

"Look over here, Wendy," Frankie whispered urgently. "Look this way. I'm *right here*."

Clayton started to cry. Frankie groaned in frustration.

"Listen," Frankie said savagely, "we're *not* going to get buried alive. We are going to get out of here, okay? Just pretend you're in a story. Pretend none of this is real. It's easier to be brave if you think there are no consequences, know what I mean?"

"No," Clayton said, wiping his nose with the back of his hand, which left a dark, muddy streak that swooshed across his face.

"Listen, the story goes like this: the heroes go on a quest. They go down, inside and between, and still they can't reach the maiden. But what they don't know is that two other heroes are on the same quest. They're coming from the other direction. You see? Help is on the way."

"What story is that?"

"Our story. It's happening right now."

"You're crazy," Clayton said, hyperventilating. "You're absolutely nuts."

He stood up and smacked the membrane wall as hard as he could. The smell of sap nearly brought him to his knees. "We're miles and miles underground and all you can do is quote some stupid fairy tale? Listen, Freak Show, *no one else is coming*. We're *by ourselves* and we're *trapped*. We have no food and no water and I don't know who you think is on the other side of this" — he pointed weakly at the membrane — "whatever it is, but no one is crossing it any time soon. The walls are going to come down, we'll run out of air, and we'll die. The—"

He was about to say *end*, but he was interrupted by a sudden rupture in the earth wall, and two boys tumbling in, right on top of him.

"Uff!" Clayton grunted.

"Frankie!" Jack said.

"Ha!" Frankie said. "You see? I told you!"

Chapter Forty-two
The Repair

I t didn't take long for Wendy to come to a decision: if the Lady — or whatever She was — once used the mirror to see what was going on above the ground, then Wendy was going to do the same. Wendy was not the sort of girl to be shown up by anyone, least of all a soul-stealing bully like the Lady.

After years of meeting that creep Clayton Avery with her fists, she had learned one important thing: bullies fall to pieces when someone fights back. None of these poor souls had the strength to fight back, but Wendy knew *she* did. No one was going to take *her* soul, she decided. And no one was keeping *her* underground forever. She was getting out.

She'd use the mirror. If for no other reason than for the light, since she couldn't do a darn thing in the dark. And if it happened to be magical...well, all the better, she figured. She started piecing the mirror together, watching it grow and grow.

What's she doing?

What does it matter? She'll leave us too.

She'd never!

Look at the mirror! I know that house. I've been in that house.

No you haven't. We've only ever been here.

Liar.

Wendy did her best to ignore the voices in the dark. Her hands were cut and raw, but she didn't slow down. The mirror—or at least *part* of the mirror—hung in mid-air, as stable and immobile as if it had been hanging on a wall. But there was no wall. The edges were sharp and ragged and *painful*. Wendy chose another shard from the scattering of pieces littering the ground. Each shard of the mirror glowed more brightly as it neared its interlocking piece, and once connected, it flashed briefly, knitting so seamlessly together that even she couldn't tell where the break had been. Shard after shard glowed, then flashed, then healed, and Wendy kept working. After a while, she didn't notice the pain in her hands. She didn't mind the deep slashes in her skin, nor the way her blood ran down her fingers to her palms and dripped off her wrists to the ground. Meanwhile, the mirror grew and grew.

In the mirror, a field of corn transformed from lush and supple green to yellow to brown. A green woman and a small boy hid behind a house—and then the woman *was* the house. Or the house was the woman. It didn't matter in any case, because the house was falling apart, shedding pieces of itself the way a bird sheds feathers. In another part of the mirror, another woman drove a car around and around in a circle, and a boy tumbled down a wooded hill-side and fell into a hole. These images slid and flickered at the edges of her vision, and she paid them little mind.

You need to hurry, the older voice hissed in her ear. *She'll be back soon. She'll be coming for you.*

"She'll be sorry if She does," Wendy murmured as she fitted another shard into place. "I don't truck with bullies."

The mirror shivered and hummed, its images sharpening. Wendy could see that they told a story. She could see a lovely woman making a terrible and rash decision. How She, in Her grief and shame and triumph, had split into two halves, one good and one bad.

"Is this a true story?" Wendy asked.

Of course. All stories are true. Or mostly *true anyway.*

"It's terrible."

Terrible, one voice agreed. *And I think it might be my fault ... but I ... I can't seem to remember.*

Wendy kept staring, but her own reflection never appeared. She waved at the mirror, but still nothing. *Well, that can't be good*, she fussed.

"Have I died?" she asked. Wendy looked at her hands. They still bled, though they did not hurt. *Of course not*, the same male voice said. *Dead people don't bleed. They rot.*

Good point, Wendy thought. "Are you dead?"

You mean my body? Oh, certainly. She took my life force and I died, all right. Just as you will. But my soul...Souls go on, you see. They go...elsewhere. Or they're supposed *to anyway. But not us. We're stuck here.*

"Can I save you?"

I don't know. Once, a soul grabbed on to Her skirt when She went through the mirror. We never saw him again, and the Lady wept for days and days. I didn't know wickedness could feel grief, but She certainly seemed to. Or perhaps it's just the memory of grief—a gap where the feeling used to be.

Wendy continued to piece the mirror back together. "I'm getting out," she said to no one in particular. "I'm getting out of here." She could feel the souls gathering behind her, pressing their papery hands and faces to her back. She didn't shrug them off. She didn't turn around.

"We're *all* getting out of here."

Chapter Forty-three
Ripped

VINES ERUPTED FROM THE WALLS OF THE UNDERGROUND space.

"Poison ivy!" Clayton screamed.

"It's not *poison ivy*," Anders said scornfully. "Jeez, toughen up, will you?" Despite the calm in his voice, the vines lashed quickly around his legs and waist and wound around his throat.

"It's Her," Frankie said through a mouthful of leaves. "She knows we're down here."

Jack looked down. There were so many vines binding

his legs that he looked like the trunk of a tree, woody and leafy, brown and green.

Although he was scared, there was something to this greenery.

It looked *right*, somehow.

"No," Jack said. "It's not Her at all. I think it's *me*."

From somewhere—whether it was a dream or a memory, or a dream of a memory of a dream, he did not know—Jack could recall looking down once on his hands and legs and torso, and he did not see skin, nor T-shirt, nor khaki shorts. Instead: leaf, bark, and wood.

"I used to look like this," Jack said—more to himself than anyone else. "Leaf and wood."

He squirmed under the vines. He could feel the runners moving over his body—poking through his clothes, curving around his knees, pushing their way past his skin, as though it were nothing more than tissue paper. Piece by piece, he could feel his skin pull up and flake away. To Jack's surprise, it did not hurt. Instead, he only felt relief—as though he were finally shrugging out of an extremely uncomfortable suit or a shirt that itched.

Clayton started to cry. "The plants are killing the new kid!"

"No, they're not—" Jack began. He flexed and extended his woody fingers. "They're *fixing* me, I think."

"I want to go home," Clayton sniffed.

Anders, pinned to the wall, was not uncomfortable. On the contrary, the vines seemed to wrap him cautiously, almost tenderly. And while the magic in the vines buzzed against his skin and sometimes pricked unpleasantly, on the whole, he found the experience more *interesting* than frightening. He watched the snaking vines with fascination. The vines, he noticed, were intelligent. They operated with forethought and intention. Then, very gently, the vines began to wrap around him more tightly than they ought, and Anders began to choke.

"It's too tight around your neck," Jack said, suddenly alarmed. "Let go," he pleaded. To his shock, the vines around Anders's neck loosened and drooped.

"Jack!" Anders said. "They listen to you! Don't you see? Try it again."

Jack didn't have time to disbelieve—he just *knew* it, just as he knew that the woody skin was his *real* skin, and the leafy hair was his *real* hair. "Back off," he said loudly, and the vines peeled away and slithered on the floor. "No," Jack said, more loudly this time, "I said *back off*!" His voice echoed and boomed. All at once, the vines shot at the side of the small cavern. The wall broke open with a loud, painful ripping sound, unleashing a riot of dust and gravel and rock. Jack, Frankie, Anders, and Clayton covered their faces with their hands, and waited for the ceiling to fall.

But nothing did. The vines covered the ceiling and the walls. They crisscrossed, and wove a tight scaffolding, holding the dirt at bay. Meanwhile, more vines twisted and burrowed into the far wall, widening the opening until the boys could see a leafy tunnel stretching straight up toward daylight.

Anders whistled. "Nice work, Jack," he said.

Clayton, certain that he had already suffered suffocation, contusion, and death, was surprised to hear a voice calling his name. It sounded suspiciously like his mother, who he knew—or at least felt pretty sure—was not dead, which provided a compelling argument that Clayton was not dead either. He sniffed hard.

Frankie turned away from the tunnel and went back to the strange membrane separating them from the place where Wendy was. He shivered. It had been four years since he was last inside the house of the Lady, the World-Under-the-World, but it terrified him to be this close nonetheless. He could see Wendy, who was kneeling next to a very large mirror.

"Wendy," he yelled. "Wendy, we're here!"

The vines wrapping around Jack's body did not fall away, nor could he rip them. Instead, they withdrew into his skin, absorbing quickly like lotion. Most of the skin on his legs was gone now. He stared down at himself. He was supple and strong as a sapling. He knew that he shouldn't believe it, or if he did, he should be frightened.

But he *did* believe, and he wasn't scared.

His legs looked *right*—righter than they had ever looked for as long as he could remember. On the other side of the membrane wall, Wendy approached. She knelt down by the rip and laid her hand in the space. She couldn't push through either.

Jack stood up and stretched his arms. His old skin fell off like old, dry leaves, and the new skin on his arms was green and alive. Each time he moved, he released the strong scent of sap.

"Ugh!" Clayton said. "What's that smell? And shouldn't we be going *that* way?"

No one answered him. Clayton looked suspiciously at the thick vines lining the new tunnel. It *looked* strong enough to climb, but he figured he'd wait for someone else to go first.

Jack knelt next to Frankie. Frankie glanced up and down at Jack's body, more brown and green now than pale and pasty, but said nothing. Really, what was there to say?

"So She took me out and pulled you in?" Jack said.

Frankie nodded, swallowed. "But it was wrong, you see? Mr. Avery was supposed to say 'my son for your son'—and he *did*. It's just that he hid Clayton and used me instead. So it was a lie and the Magic backfired."

"Yeah…" Jack struggled with a memory that flashed deep in the back of his mind. "They were supposed to say *yours* and *mine*. Is that right?"

"The Magic didn't know which way to go. It scattered. I woke up in there"—he pointed to the membrane wall—"but She was too weak to take my soul away from my body. It was like She was slowly going dormant, or something. Or maybe I held on to it too tight. And then Clive got me out and She went completely dead. But, She wasn't dead at all. Just sleeping."

Jack held his breath and let it out in a long, slow hiss. He ran his hand through his leafy hair. "Clive said I have to even the score. Wendy's taken *your* place, so I have to change places with her, don't I?"

Frankie laid his hand on the nest of scars on the side of his face and Jack wondered if they hurt. He wondered, too, if he should feel guilty for Frankie's pain. Most likely, he decided. Guilt, then.

"Someone has to," Frankie said, closing his eyes. "That's why I came down here. To get her out."

Jack shook his head. "No, Frankie. It can't be you. She'll take your soul and get stronger. Then She'll take more. If I'm in there... I don't know. Maybe I can fix Her. Someone needs to fix Her. Right?"

"You have to choose it," Frankie said. "I'm pretty sure that I can't make you, if that's what you're asking."

"But if I don't choose it, then either you or Wendy can't get out."

"True," he said, "but if you *do*, then I don't think you can get out *either*. You'll belong to the underground place. Or it will belong to you. Whichever."

Jack looked back at Anders, who removed his cap and scratched the back of his head thoughtfully. Jack thought about his mother and father, how they seemed constantly surprised to see him in the room, how they were hardly ever aware that there was another kid in the family besides Baxter, which, in retrospect, was actually true. There wasn't another kid in the family. There was only Jack, who was, well, something *else*.

Jack nodded. "Once Wendy's out, go back to my aunt and uncle's. I don't know how to put things back together, and I might screw it up. I just know that while She's broken, the Lady makes things go wrong. If everything was okay before She was split apart, then maybe they'll go back to being okay if I can put Her back together again." He swallowed. "I mean, in the end, they are *both* my mother, right? They're *mine.*" That word sent a shiver through his body. *Why?* he wondered. "Obviously, *they* can't put them*selves* back together." Jack paused. "Or they would've done it by now."

"Use the mirror," Frankie said. "That's what She did anyway. A long time ago. She would reach through it and pull people's souls into the underground, leaving their bodies behind. If you could pull Her back inside — both halves of Her. I don't know. It worked in a story once anyway."

Jack nodded. "My mom and dad. And my brother. Well, they were pretend, I know, and they probably don't remember me. But I remember them. I loved them, you know? Tell them that for me, okay? Tell them again and again so that they remember."

He didn't wait for an answer, and, wiping his eyes

with the back of his brown and green hand, he climbed into the gap. He pressed his hand just opposite of Wendy's on the other side of the membrane wall. Laying the Portsmouth on the membrane, he said, "I need a place for swapping places. I need a place *between*."

The membrane rippled, and Jack slipped inside.

Chapter Forty-four
Even the Score

THE INTERIOR OF THE MEMBRANE WALL WAS LARGER AND wider than Jack would have believed. Indeed, looking over his shoulder, he saw the muted images of Frankie and Clayton, their eyes aghast, hands flat against the resin surface. They mouthed his name, though he couldn't hear their voices. Jack looked around. Though he knew—he *knew*—he was *inside* the wall, it appeared as though he stood in the center of a long, straight hallway—dark walls, dark ceiling, and a packed earth floor. Jack turned to Wendy and waved.

Wendy, peering curiously at the two-dimensional image of Jack in the wall, pressed her forehead to the surface. To her astonishment, the membrane wall broke around her face like water. She stared into the *in-between* space in wonder.

"Jack," she called. "Jack, is that really you in here?" *And where is here?* she wondered.

"Yeah, it's me. Come all the way in. I'll show you how to get to the other side."

"But I can't. I don't think anyone can." She pushed her hands into the surface, felt the edge of the wall ripple across her arms in waves.

"You can now. Come here. I've got to explain something to you."

She ducked in, yelped a bit, and hit the cold stone floor with her worn-out sneakers. Jack watched her run toward him and he realized that there was nothing he could explain. He couldn't explain the alterations in himself, nor the fact that his aunt and uncle were actually no relation, nor were his mother and father and brother. He couldn't explain the split mother, or the imprisonment, or the talking house, or the sneaky interventions of Gog and Magog. All he knew was that she was running toward him, that she would be free and he would not, but that he did not resent her for it.

He *wanted* her freedom.

It felt right, just as his new body felt right, and the truth about himself felt right too.

She ran to him, and threw her arms around him. She smelled like green grass and summer dust and too much sun. He inhaled and felt a dense, green knot form around his heart. "Jack," she said, "you'll never believe—"

"Yeah," he said, "you'd be surprised. Listen, run to the other end of the hall, and head toward daylight. I'm not sure where you'll come out, but just get yourself to my aunt and uncle's house quickly."

"What are you talking about? You're coming too." But even as she said the words, Jack could hear in her voice that she knew they weren't true. "Oh, *Jack*—" she began. She looked at him and gasped. Her voice seemed to shatter in her throat. "But I can't leave! I have to help. I promised. There are people in there—or not people anymore, just souls. The—whatever you call Her—the Lady, She's got them trapped in there and—"

"It's okay, I'll figure it out. Things seem to...*listen* to me down here. I can't explain it. I just know that I'm supposed to be *here*. And I think I'm *supposed* to fix things."

"I can't just leave you behind. I can't leave them either. Grab my hand and we'll run for it. If there're two of us, we could probably force the thing open. Maybe leave a space for the souls to get out."

Jack shook his head. "That's not how it works."

Wendy stamped her foot and grunted in frustration. She turned away and hastily wiped both eyes with the backs of her hands.

"Wendy," Jack said, putting his hand (or what *had been* his hand but was now a complicated network of roots and stems in the shape of a hand) on her shoulder. "I need to stay. I need to fix —"

"So you're just giving up?" she asked, rounding on him savagely. Her eyes were red. Her breath came in tiny gulps. "Just like that? You're not even going to try to get out?"

Jack shook his head. "Listen, Wendy, you were my first friend. I never knew I was lonely before, but I *was*, and now I'm not. This was the first time I got to feel like a person—a real person, like you and Anders and Frankie. I know I'm not—not *really*—and I know it wasn't for very long, but it meant something to me. I'll never forget it, Wendy. *Never.*" And without meaning to, he stood on tiptoe and kissed her once, briefly, on the mouth.

Embarrassed, he turned and ran into the darkness.

He didn't look back.

Chapter Forty-five
Emergences

WENDY LED THE WAY.

She pushed off the advancing hugs from her brother and Anders, and while the sound of her brother's voice calling her name nearly broke her in half, she couldn't stop and think about it just yet. She had to *move*, despite the tiny cracks that were, even now, cutting across her heart.

"We have to get to Mr. Fitzpatrick. Jack's trapped inside that…whatever that place is. Mr. Fitzpatrick will know how to get him out."

"But, Wendy," Anders began, "I'm not sure that's what we're supposed to—"

"*Climb*," Wendy commanded savagely, reaching up to the thick-limbed ivy and swinging her legs to the wall of the vertical tunnel. "It's only—what—twenty-five feet *maybe* to the top. We've all climbed that high before."

"I haven't," Clayton said.

"Well, then, you're going to get left behind." And without looking back, Wendy climbed, Clayton scurrying behind her.

Frankie and Anders watched them ascend, waiting to make sure no one fell.

"After you, Frankie," Anders said, with a flourish and a bow.

Frankie climbed, though much more slowly than his sister, his movements careful and deliberate.

Anders looked closely at the structured vines. They rustled pleasantly, though there was no wind this far underground. "You are a curious little thing, aren't you?" Anders murmured to the plant. "Are you part of Jack, or is Jack part of you? I can't decide whether you took him away, or if you were inside him the whole time. In either case, I hope you don't mind if I just do this." Very gently, he brought his fingers to the base of a small branch of the vine and pulled it free. He inspected the larger plant to see if it minded, but the leaves continued to rustle in the nonexistent wind. Anders nodded, satisfied.

It could be useful, Anders reasoned, to have a magic

plant on the farm. *If* he could get it to grow. "Besides," he said to the plant as it wound itself—quite on its own—around his arm three times before twining a tendril around its beginning, latching on securely, "If you really are a part of Jack, I think I like the idea of keeping a bit of you rooted to the surface. Just in case." And with that, Anders hoisted himself up and climbed to the gap of open blue.

The cats were waiting at the mouth of the hole. So was Lancelot. Wendy scrambled out of the tunnel, though she had a sneaking suspicion that the vines were helping her along. The whole way up she felt them shift when she needed them to shift and tighten when she needed them tightened. It was as though the vines *wanted* her to make it to the top in one piece.

"Pfft," one of the cats said—Gog, or Magog, she couldn't tell them apart.

"How did you three know to wait for me here?" she asked, and then she shook her head. "Actually, never mind. I don't want to know." She didn't wait for the others, but took off out of the gully at a run, with the cats bounding just ahead and the bird soaring just above the limit of the trees.

Clayton emerged out of the green, scraped and slapped by thorns and stray branches. He heard his mother's voice from...somewhere. He crawled away from the hole on his hands and knees and flopped onto his back, looking up at the sky. He had never noticed it before, but the sky was amazingly beautiful. And the trees were beautiful. And the rocks and the masses of birds flying overhead. Even that Schumacher girl was beautiful, if she wasn't punching you in the face. He had never much cared for Wendy, so his surge of happiness when she emerged through the membrane wall mostly unharmed surprised him. Clayton was not normally one to spend much time thinking about the welfare of others.

"*Clayton!*" he heard his mother scream. "*Oh, please, no!*"

He tried to sit up, but his mother came hurtling out of nowhere and pinned him to the ground. She sobbed and smiled and squeezed her eyes tight. "You're alive," she gasped. "You're whole and you're alive."

"Of course I'm *alive*. What else would I be? Jeez, Mom, toughen up, will you?"

By the time Wendy made it to the road, Frankie and Anders had caught up with her. The three sprinted toward the Fitzpatrick house.

"Who brought the cats?" Anders panted.

Wendy ignored this. "Anders, do Mr. and Mrs. Fitzpatrick know I went underground?"

Anders nodded. "And Avery has every construction crew in Iowa poised in front of their house. We heard him say that if he could kill Jack and destroy the house at the

298

same time, the Lady's good half would be so weak that She'd break apart and scatter. But they don't have Jack."

Wendy nodded. "So we'll just do the first part."

"What?"

"I saw it in the mirror. The house needs to break apart. It has to happen while She's strong. The *good* part of Her, I mean." Wendy sped up without explaining, leaving the boys behind to wonder what exactly she had seen underground.

Chapter Forty-six
The Gap Between Good and Evil

JACK LOOKED AROUND THE DARK, TIGHT SPACE. HE LOOKED up and loose dirt sprinkled into his eyes. He was utterly, utterly alone. "Oh no," Jack said. "This won't do at all."

And, without even trying to, Jack made the world.

Grass, green and thick as moss, unrolled like carpeting under his feet while the walls became horizons that broadened with each coming breath. As he walked, hills erupted from the ground, forests sprouted like weeds, and abundant farms spilled across the land. Above his head, the hard-packed dirt of the ceiling lifted, brightened, and widened out into a sky. "I know this place," he said. Birds flew in great masses over broad fields and rested next to newly formed lakes, already crowded with silvery fish.

"Of course you do, my boy, of course you do," an old man's voice said just behind him. Jack jumped, and when he saw the figure in front of him, he screamed. "Oh, come now," the old man's voice chided. "Your friend was far more civil."

"Well, now I know you're lying," Jack said, his voice trembling. "Wendy's hardly ever civil."

A crowd gathered in front of him—each of them shaped like a human being, but see-through and hollow, as though made from tracing paper. Most were children, but there were a couple of adults, including the first person who spoke, an ancient-looking man wearing the reversed collar of a minister. Each figure reached over to touch Jack on his arms or his face or his leafy hair. Jack gritted his teeth to keep from shuddering. Their touch was as light as dandelion seed; their skins rustled and whispered as they moved.

"You're souls, aren't you?"

"Oh, come on now," the minister-soul said, his voice both pompous and impatient. "No time for chitchat. Come and see what your friend was able to accomplish." He floated away, feet hovering just above the ground, and Jack followed at a run, stopping in front of the mirror. It was tall and narrow, with ragged edges, and was hanging in the air without holding on to anything. As

Jack drew nearer, the extra shards on the ground started lifting up of their own accord, attaching themselves onto the mirror with a patter of flashes.

"There, you see?" the minister-soul said. "Your home is responding to you already. Oh, I did so hope this would happen!"

"I need to get you out of here," Jack said, though in truth it was not so much for the souls' benefit as for Jack's own. He turned away from the soul and faced the mirror.

He did not see his own reflection, but instead, the image of a purple house with missing windows and doors quivered in front of him. Shingles flew from the wobbly roof and the rafters buckled and swayed, as though the house itself was gasping for breath.

"It's Clive and Mabel's house," Jack said. "What's happened to it?"

"It won't last long. Your mother—well, half of Her anyway, the good half, is gaining in strength. She's been stuck in there, but She's ready to come out. Someone has gathered happy people all in one spot, you see? All that joy causes a sort of soul-heat. Creatures like your mother feed off it. See how the house trembles? If She can get enough power, She'll be able to step free. And you see that bulge on the ground? That's the wicked half. The Lady." The soul shuddered.

"What happens if they both come out at the same time?" Jack pressed his hands to the mirror. It was cold, but his breath didn't cloud the glass. And the sap from his hands didn't leave a mark. He did notice, though, that it wasn't rigid like regular glass. He pressed in, and it bounced back like a trampoline.

"It's tough to say. For as long as I've been here, they've avoided each other. But now that you've arrived, I can only see their dual emergence as one thing." The soul cleared his throat importantly.

"What?" Jack said, rolling his eyes.

"An opportunity."

Outside the Fitzpatrick house, a storm twisted and raged, the Lady in the bulging ground howled, and the Other in the house sang and sang. The people on the lawn assembled themselves into a tight mob and opened umbrellas for shelter. They still passed plates with lemon meringue pie and Jell-O salad and butter cookies with pink frosting. They still smiled and laughed and told jokes. It was as though they noticed the rain but not the storm.

Wendy, Anders, and Frankie could hardly see the house through the flying dust and debris. Storm clouds flew at the house. Then lightning and rain, hail the size of softballs. Even snow.

"We need to do something," Wendy said.

"I didn't think…" Frankie began, the unscarred portion of his face gray with fear. "I didn't think She would be this strong already. I don't know what...I mean I don't think we can..." He choked back a sob. His face was a mask of terror.

"*Give me the boy*," a voice sounded. It rumbled through the ground and cracked across the sky. "*Give me the boy and you can have the girl.*"

"She doesn't know I'm out," Wendy whispered. "So She doesn't know that Jack's in there either. That's good, I think." Wendy reached for her brother's hand and squeezed. She held on for dear life.

Jack stood next to the mirror, pressing his hands against the surface. It wasn't glass, he knew, though its edges were sharp like glass. But there was one thing that Jack was absolutely sure about: the mirror was *alive*.

The pompous soul cleared its voice. "Your mother— both halves of Her are in the same place. If you reach into the mirror, you might be able to snatch the pair of them. Serves Her right, really," he added bitterly. "She's snatched half the souls here through that mirror."

"But how can you go free?"

"I don't think we can, my boy. You see, we're trapped here."

"Maybe. But if She could reach through and pull people *in*, surely I can push you *out*. If you get to the other side, where do you think you'll go?"

"I don't rightly know, son. I suspect we'll do as souls

normally do when their bodies fall away. We'll go on."
The soul's face took on a sudden, wistful expression.
"Oh! To go *on*!"

Gog and Magog leaped to the roof of a car and stared
down at Frankie and Wendy with an unmistakably
annoyed expression.

"*What?*" Wendy asked, exasperated.

"*Pfft,*" hissed the cats. They turned and bounded to
the ground, before leaping upward again into the cab of
an idling bulldozer.

"Bad kitties!" Anders whispered as the cats batted
their paws at the controls. "They're going to get hurt if
they—oh! I get it." He turned to his friends. "I know
how we can help Jack." He ran into the idling bulldozer
and, after a few false starts, knocked it into gear.

"What are you *doing?*" Wendy shouted. Anders drove
the bulldozer directly to the house. She nodded. *Good
plan*, she thought.

"Hey! *Hey, kid!*" One of the drivers took off after the
runaway bulldozer while three others ran hard at his
heels, leaving their trucks idling in place. Wendy shook
her head. *Adults are so stupid sometimes*, she thought as
she slipped into an unlocked truck and put it in gear.
Frankie jumped in next to her, and she fed the engine to

a roar. They sped toward the house. They shut their eyes tight and gripped their seats, and their trucks ripped into the western wall with a crash.

The World-Under-the-World wobbled, buckled, and thrashed. The sky darkened; the land erupted in waves, knocking Jack to his knees.

"What's going on?" Jack shouted over the wind, but he didn't wonder for long. Two voices rang through the rocking world. "*I'm free!*" they shouted as one—a voice filled with rage and triumph harmonizing strangely with a voice filled with joy and love. Jack looked at the mirror. It flashed to an image of a house—or what used to be a house. It was now just a pile of rubble covered over by thick ivy and heavy blossoms, with heavy machinery shoved against the side. Two women stood next to the rubble, rubbing their eyes. They were both impossibly tall, with hair made of grass and skin made of supple new leaves. They looked at each other with the utmost revulsion.

"Look at them," Jack gasped. "They're *broken*." Pity stabbed painfully at his heart.

"Now, boy," the soul said. "Reach in now."

Jack pressed the Portsmouth against the mirror. "After you," Jack said, and he pushed the souls through.

The house was a tangle of wood and stone and furniture scattered on the ground. Two—*whatever* they were. Women, mostly, though they didn't look like any women that Wendy had ever seen, all leaf and bark and corn silk and earth, stood in the yard at the side of the house. They could hardly stand to look at each other. Indeed, they looked like they were about to be sick.

Wendy ran through the wreckage that once was the house to see if Anders was all right, but she stopped in her tracks the moment the mirror appeared. Her mirror, hovering just over the ground. She stared at it. *Was it real?* she wondered. The events of the last twenty-four hours jumbled and swam in her head, and she could hardly separate dream from reality. A figure shot out of the mirror. Then another, then another. They looked like human beings, *mostly*, though they were hollow and papery like dried-out husks. They held their shape for only a moment before transforming into tight balls of light.

"Souls," Wendy whispered.

"*No!*" the Lady cried, trying to catch the balls of light as they spun faster and faster around Herself and the Other. "*Don't leave me!*" But no matter how She tried, the balls of light quivered and spun, staying just out of reach. The Other smiled, blowing kisses at each one, and called them out by name.

"Marcus," the Other crooned. "Timothy, Delilah, Iris. Ichabod, Sylas, June, Eva."

"Thank you," buzzed the balls of light as they increased in brightness and speed. "Thank you."

The souls spun so fast, they appeared at first like a halo around the bodies of the women, then a bright cloud. And then, with a blinding flash, they shot upward and disappeared into the sky. The Lady fell to Her knees, buried Her face in Her hands. Her Other, moved to pity, knelt down next to Her, their shoulders touching.

It was at this moment that a figure appeared in the mirror. A boy like a tree, standing rooted and tall.

"Jack!" Wendy shouted, but he didn't seem to hear her.

He cleared his throat, but the sound didn't come from the mirror. It came from the ground, from the breeze, from the blades of grass underfoot. It was everywhere.

"*You!*" Jack's voice thrummed through the air. It was as though each leaf, each flower, each blade of grass was yelling with one voice. "You left me alone!" The women stared at the boy in the mirror. Their mouths hung open. The edges of their bodies grew bright and blurry.

"*Get me the Avery boy!*" the Lady shouted, but Jack shook his head.

"No, Mom. You can't give me away again. You already said *yours*, remember? What's done is done. The Magic won't give You a second chance. Only *I* can do that." Two hands—both brown and woody, like the branches of a young tree, reached out of the mirror, grabbing both

Lady and Other by their arms. The Lady struggled and tried to pull away, but Jack held on tight.

"But it doesn't matter *what* You did, because now *I* get to choose, and I'm taking back what belongs to me. I choose You, Mom. Both halves of You. You're supposed to be whole, and You're supposed to love me. And I'm supposed to be Your son. And You're mine, do You hear me? Mine!" Jack shouted, his voice raw and ragged around the edges. "*You are mine!*"

The Lady screamed. The Other sighed. And, with a grunt and a terrific tug, Jack pulled the two of them inside.

The mirror rippled and flowed like water around their bodies, and both Lady and Other merged into one. It began with their torsos, then their waving arms, then their legs. Their heads remained separate until the last possible moment, as the Lady screamed and bit, and the Other began to sing, until finally they melded together in a bright flash. A column of light burst from the ground and shot up to the sky. Jack's mother—his true mother, his *whole* mother—blinked. She stopped screaming, stopped singing, and stood perfectly still. Silence spread across the ruined yard and rested heavily on the debris-strewn street. She brought Her hands to Her mouth, then Her cheeks, then Her eyes.

"*At last!*" Her voice rumbled across the ground. It blew across the prairie and echoed against the sky. "*AT LAST!*" she shouted. Her voice was explosive and joyful. And then it was gone.

Wendy, Anders, and Frankie ran to the floating mirror. They glanced quickly at one another, and Wendy laid her hand on its surface.

The mirror brightened, shuddered, and shone. It flashed images of green hillsides and multicolored quilts and swelling corn. Standing in the mirror's image was Jack—mostly. Wendy pressed her hand against the mirror's surface.

It was Jack as she had never seen him, but Jack as he *was*.

She *knew* it.

Just as she knew that the face in the corn all those years ago meant no harm. Just as she knew that the face in the corn—the one that only she could see—was Jack. His face was the color of bark, and each strand of his hair had flattened and greened, like leaves. Around his head, he wore a crown of acorns. He grinned at them and waved.

"*Don't go,*" Wendy whispered.

Jack shrugged and grinned again. There was no sound, but the words his mouth formed were unmistakable.

Thank you, his mouth said.

Just as the picture faded—in the moment before the mirror vanished from sight—they saw a woman appear behind him. She wrapped her green arms around his brown and green shoulders and spun him around and around.

The image flickered, once, twice. And both Jack and mirror vanished from sight.

Coda

"AH," SAID MABEL, LOOKING UP FROM A STACK OF BOXES and a pile of wires, cables, and modems. "Reinforcements. Anders, dear, will you please run around to the loading dock and see whether there are any more boxes? Frankie, why don't you help your mother assemble those units over there?"

Frankie smiled shyly and sat next to his mother, pouring over the manual and connecting towers and drives and shiny new monitors. Silently, he laid the instructions out over the table, and began connecting wires. Though he had never done such a thing before, Frankie discovered that the quiet language of circuits and electricity was one that he could understand and manipulate. He liked the idea of a language made of light, whirring messages under his fingers, communicating poetry and mathematics and philosophical discourse in the blink of an eye.

It was four weeks ago that Clive and Mabel's house was nearly destroyed and Frankie started speaking again. During that time, his scars began to smooth, to lose their redness, and to heal. They would never disappear completely, and would remain, for the rest of his life, as a complicated seal on his cheek, a physical reminder of his brush with death—and worse than death.

They would remind him of Jack too. His friend. Brave and kind, and lost forever as far as Frankie could tell. He shook the thought away and returned to the instructions in the computer manual.

The library hummed with activity and conversation. On one end was the technology team, hastily assembling computers. On another end, people from the town crowded in the local interest section, paging through local history books that had altered of their own accord. Mysterious blank sections suddenly rewrote themselves. Photographs that had once been curiously empty now showed schoolchildren, or mothers holding infants, or an old man standing in front of a freshly built church. And the librarian in charge of records and documents finally decided to require a numbering system to deal with the crush of people bringing in birth certificates and baptismal records and marriage licenses, all of which, until very recently, had been unaccountably blank.

Frankie smiled at the activity and commotion but said little as he completed the steps laid out in the computer manual. Though it was now common knowledge that he could and should speak, he still found himself shy in large groups. With familiar people, he spoke all the time—to Mabel in the shop, to his sister or Anders on their walks, and curled up with his mother and father, reciting story after story until they drifted asleep and Frankie kissed them both good night.

Anders wheeled in a cart full of boxes and went back for more. Mabel shook her head.

"I believe our dear Mr. Avery has rather overdone it, don't you agree, Frankie?"

Frankie shrugged, though, in truth, he did agree. Mr. Avery, upon the reunion of his little family, decided to break up the Grain Exchange and Trust into separate entities and sell each one—along with the Avery house—to the highest bidder. That done, he used the proceeds to rebuild Clive and Mabel's house, to broker a deal for his family's relocation to the mountains of Colorado, and to purchase an army of computers for the library, the school, and the college, none of which had thought to purchase them before.

In those last days before he moved to the mountains,

Mr. Avery became wildly generous: books for every child, a scholarship fund, a playground, a new nursery school, and an updated clinic. He gave a substantial donation to the Schumachers' bank account—anonymously, of course, but they knew. Who else had that kind of money? People joked that he just wanted the council not to take down his portrait from the town hall. There were rumors of a commemorative statue.

Clayton hadn't wanted to leave Hazelwood, and he protested the move until the bitter end. Finally, his mother and Mrs. Fitzpatrick—who had become quite close—agreed that it would be a good idea if Clayton was to spend the following summer with Clive and Mabel, working at the gallery and receiving a tutorial from the old professor. "It's always best to keep a child connected to his *roots*, don't you think?" Mrs. Avery said on their final day in town. No one disagreed with her.

Mabel sat down next to Frankie to inspect his work. She laid her hand across Frankie's knuckles. "And Wendy, dear," she said. "How is she doing?"

He shrugged. "Okay, I suppose," he said very quietly. This, of course, was a lie, and Frankie suspected that Mabel knew as much. Still, it felt good to say, and who knew? Perhaps all a person had to do was to say a thing enough times until it became true on its own. Perhaps, if he said that Wendy was okay every day, eventually she actually would *be* okay. Perhaps wishing could make it so.

Despite the loud arguments at home, where Wendy was apt to shout and throw things and her mother was bound to crumple up and weep, things were close to normal at the Schumacher house. Wendy often bristled at the hovering attentions of her parents, but after three weeks of it, Clive and Mabel were able to convince them that Frankie's reintegration as a normalized child was more important. Nothing could hurt Wendy anymore.

Nothing, of course, except the impending start of school.

Nothing except the niggling sense of loss for a friend she barely knew.

Nothing except the constant flashes of Jack's face that appeared in rain-soaked window panes or the surface of puddles or in the face of the pond before it was rippled by a breeze.

He looked happy. Mostly. And it was the *mostly* that bothered Wendy and kept her up at night.

The day before school was set to start, Wendy woke just as the sun rose. The house was quiet and soft with the sounds of openmouthed breathing and the rustle of dreams. Wendy slipped on her sundress and sandals and peeked into Frankie's room. He was asleep on his back, his head cradled in his hands. Talking in his sleep. He did it all the time now.

Wendy closed her eyes and smiled. Despite everything—the sadness, the loss, the guilt—she thought she could listen to her brother all day long. And though she had half a mind to wake him up and bring him with her, there were some things that are better done alone. She grabbed the skateboard that had once belonged to Jack—the one that Clive and Mabel gave to her after they retrieved it from the wreckage of their house. They said he would have wanted her to have it. She couldn't look them in the face, couldn't even say *thank you*, but she knew they felt her thanks all the same. She rode it every day now, and kept it in her room. It was one of the few things she had to hang on to.

She tiptoed down the stairs, across the kitchen, closed the door behind her with a quiet click, set Jack's skateboard on the pavement, and skimmed down the road. It never came close to nearly flying for her the way it did for Jack, but still. There was something special about that board.

Across the field, crows gathered in great, black clouds. They rose and swelled against the sky. The gatherings were large already, but by autumn they would enlarge to thousands upon thousands calling to one another, their voices shrill and echoing across the wide, flat land. Wendy passed the elementary school and the college, saw that the vans full of fiber optic technicians had already arrived and started to work. Her school would now have a computer lab and work stations in each classroom, thanks to Mr. Avery's parting gift. People called it generosity, but Wendy knew better. If guilt was the reason behind a good deed, was it *still* a good deed? She doubted it.

The gully was chilly and damp, and Wendy wished she had brought a sweatshirt. She considered taking her shoes off, as Anders would have, to see whether she could feel, as he did, the energy and life of the world under the bluff. To see whether—just maybe—she could catch a snippet of Jack's new life, and perhaps ask him whether it was really—really and truly—the life he would have chosen. But she didn't have that particular talent, and there was no way for her to know.

At the bottom of the gully, a stream widened into a small, deep pool. She crouched down and peered at the smooth water. Again Jack's face looked back. She had seen his image, again and again, always in water, always looking up at the sky. His eyes were wide and calm, and while they didn't seem to see her at all, she could see in his dark pupils a reflection of the clouds slipping away in a limitless sky.

"Jack?" she said tentatively. "Can you hear me?"

"I'm afraid he cannot," Clive Fitzpatrick said, coming up from behind and, his knees creaking and snapping prodigiously, crouching next to her at the edge of the water.

"But he's looking at—"

"The sky, yes. I daresay it's the thing he misses most."

Wendy felt a sharp stab at her heart. She wiped her leaking eyes with the back of her hand and sniffed deeply. "It's my fault," she said. "It's all my fault."

"Not at all, my dear," Clive said, giving her a stiff pat on the shoulder before folding his hands at his knees. "He did what he had to do to undo a terrible wrong. That he was particularly motivated to do so for *your* welfare, well, all the better. Jack has his early memory restored to him, and, more important, his true mother restored to him. Not *just* Her good half or *just* Her bad half either. Instead, She is whole, complicated, and real. She has the same struggles of right and wrong, just like you and me, and what's more, when She chooses good, for the first time in over a century, it *matters*.

"It's a great gift to Her, and you helped make that happen. You should be proud."

Wendy did not feel proud at all. She only felt sick.

"What about Jack," she said. "What about his choice?" Clive stood, offered his hand to Wendy, who took it. He hooked his arm in hers and they began walking up the slope. "It's true, he's dependent on his mother's wishes and choices, as are all children until they grow. But don't forget, he chose to take your place. And what's more, he chose to finally experience the love of his mother. That's no small thing, after all. But don't worry. You haven't seen the last of him. The only question is, *How long?* It is my greatest hope that I may see that boy again before I die." His voice caught in his throat and he nearly choked. He tightened his hold on Wendy's arm and began walking again.

Wendy felt his hand tremble and shake. She wanted to say *something*. Anything, really. But her thoughts jumbled together and her heart felt cold and heavy, and really, there was nothing more to say. She made a friend; she lost a friend; and that was that.

So, instead, she listened to the gentle rhythm of their footfalls on the mossy undergrowth. She listened to the papery rustle of the leaves and the sigh of the swaying tree trunks. She listened as the sounds vibrated and hummed and organized themselves into words. Wendy closed her eyes.

Don't worry about me, Wendy, sighed the trees.

I'll be back, whispered the leaves.

I believe you, Wendy whispered in return. A memory, she knew, is like a soul — slippery, fragile, and easily lost. She felt her heart send out tendrils, grasping onto Jack's memory, gently winding around it, holding it fast.

I won't forget you.

She held on tight.

In Gratitude

No one should have to write a book alone. The people who guided and supported me on my journey from wobbly beginnings, through shadowed middles, toward a fragile and delicate endpoint—well, they are *many*. Too numerous to count. Those named below are merely a fraction of the multitudes of terribly kind individuals who cleared away the stones, who whispered hints and wisdom in the dark. Thank you to everyone both named and unnamed.

I'd like to thank the Loft and Intermedia Arts for

their tireless support of writers, for their programs of mentorship and guidance that built me into the writer I am today, and for the teachers I had during that period: Lyda Morehouse, Pete Hautman, Shay Youngblood, Mary Rose O'Rielley, Thomas Glave, Arthur Sze, and Jim Moore, and to Jerod Santek, who ran everything. Thanks, too, to the writers who slogged through the trenches with me: Rosanne Bane, April Lott, Britt Aamodt, Rob Tregay, Laura Flynn, Vina Kay, Francine Marie Tolf, Lisa Higgs, Nena Johansen, Michele Heather Pollock, Matt Rasmussen, Swati Avasthi, Heather Bouwman, Heather Goodman, and Scott Wrobel.

I'd like to thank the Jerome Foundation for its generous financial support of my work at a time when such support was critical.

I'd like to thank my two wonderful agents: Lindsay Davis—clear-eyed and thoughtful agent extraordinaire, able to leap tall buildings in a single bound, who first said *yes*; and Steven Malk—heroic über-agent (white steed, drawn sword, cape flapping dramatically in the wind), who has rescued me more times than I can count. Thanks to the two of you for your patience, guidance, and care.

I'd like to thank Nancy Conescu, first for believing in my book and second for keeping my feet to the fire, bringing me back to the text again and again to rethink, reimagine, re-create, and make it new again. I'm a better writer now than I was before, and I will appreciate that forever.

I'd like to thank James Regan, who first gave me the notion of slippery invisibility. You were only twelve, and you likely don't even remember. But I do. So thank you.

I'd like to thank Jennifer Regan, Sheila Regan, and Lucille (Regan) Decoux, for your willingness to look at my earlier drafts and provide kind feedback and support (and never once, though I'm sure it occurred to you, pointing and laughing). I'd like to thank Katie and Rob Cullen and Leah Drury and Dave Dobish, who kept me from going mad when madness seemed imminent. And I'd like to thank my dad, Tim Regan, for forcing me to read "On Fairy-stories" by J. R. R. Tolkien, without which this book would have never existed. Thank you.

And, most important, I'd like to thank Ted, who read more versions of this text than anyone should ever have to, and who is as flinty-eyed and clearheaded a reader as any writer could ever hope for. Since you wouldn't allow me to dedicate the book to you, I must instead dedicate the following: these hands; this heart; this mind; this life.

Estacada Public Library
825 NW Wade St.
Estacada, OR 97023